MW00639137

DANGEROUS LOVE

ANTHOLOGY

JAMIE BEGLEY

Young Ink Press Publication
YoungInkPress.com

Copyright © 2019 by Jamie Begley

Edited by C&D Editing & Hot Tree Editing
Cover Art by Cover Couture

All rights reserved.

No part of this book may be reproduced in any form or by any electronic or
mechanical means including information storage and retrieval systems,
without permission in writing from the author. The only exception is by a
reviewer, who may quote short excerpts in a review.

This book is a work of fiction. Names, characters, places, and incidents either
are products of the author's imagination or are used fictitiously. Any
resemblance to actual persons, living or dead, events, or locales is entirely
coincidental.

Connect with Jamie,
facebook.com/AuthorJamieBegley
JamieBegley.net

HEAVEN SENT

CHAPTER 1

"What are you giving Razer for Valentine's Day?" Lily questioned her sister Beth who was rummaging through another stack of clothes that she had stored in her twins' bedroom closet.

"I haven't decided yet. What are you giving Shade?"

"I was hoping to get some ideas from you," Lily confessed.

Buying anything for her husband Shade was difficult. He preferred buying his own clothes, hated sweets and, other than his wedding ring, wore no jewelry.

"We could ask Razer," Beth suggested. "It could also get me some ideas for him."

"That's what we did for Christmas. He liked the coat I got him, but I wanted to do something special for Valentine's Day."

"Buy a sexy nightie for yourself; that'll make his day," Beth joked, placing a stack of the boys' jeans in a box.

Lily flushed, her eyes shying away from her sister's. She never felt comfortable discussing any part of her and Shade's intimate life with Beth or any of her friends. She had always been reserved, and despite her marriage and children, it hadn't changed that aspect of her personality.

Reaching for a T-shirt that fell from the bed, she placed it back on the stack of clothes. "I was thinking about giving him a new watch."

Beth stared down at her, as if mulling over the idea, before saying, "That might be a good choice. If you change your mind, let me know. Razer could use a new one, too."

"I will." Lily reached out for the T-shirt that was about to fall again. "I can't believe how fast Noah and Chance are growing."

"I can't either. It seems like I just bought these clothes." Taking some shirts, she laid them onto the jeans. "That's the last of them. What you can't use, you can take to the thrift store."

"Are you sure? They still look new."

"I'm sure. The boys have outgrown them, so there's no need to keep them stored, collecting dust."

"What if you decide to have more kids?"

Lily glanced up from the clothes to see a strange expression cross her sister's face.

"Two boys are enough for Razer and me. The boys are still a handful. We don't have enough energy to have another child."

"I don't believe that. Razer and you are wonderful parents. Beth, I know when you had the twins, it was a traumatic experience—"

"It was a nightmare," her sister cut her off. "Which I don't want to talk about."

Lily didn't blame her. The night Beth had the twins had been traumatic. She and Beth had spent the night at Evie's home. Evie had thrown Beth a baby shower while the men had gone to spend the night at Cash's cabin.

Thank God Beth had slept downstairs on the couch and

heard someone trying to get through the front and back doors. It saved their lives. Going upstairs, she had given them precious seconds to get in the bedroom Lily had been sleeping in. Their luck ran out, though, when Beth went into labor. If Shade hadn't known how frightened Lily was of storms and decided to come back to check on her, the night would have ended far differently. Neither she nor Beth would be sitting in her bedroom now, sorting Noah's and Chance's clothes, so yes, Lily could understand why Beth never talked about the nightmarish ordeal she had suffered through that night.

"Who's going to keep the boys for you? Evie offered to keep John and Clint, but if you can't find someone, I could keep Noah and Chance," Lily offered.

"Razer and I decided to spend the night home with the boys. They'll be so wired after the wedding and playing with Rocky that I'd feel bad about leaving them with anyone."

"Are you sure? We wouldn't mind." Lily grinned. "Shade does a pretty good job at keeping them in control."

"No, you and Shade enjoy Valentine's Day. Razer and I don't have anything special planned for it anyway." She shrugged.

"Shade and I don't either. He usually takes me to Cracker Barrel, but because we'll be eating at T.A.'s reception, we won't be going."

Beth lifted an eyebrow at her. "Then, why did you plan to have a babysitter?"

Lily grinned back at her. "Shade was keeping our options open."

Closing the box after she finished sorting the clothes, Beth looked at the clock beside Noah's bed. "Shouldn't you be going back to the thrift store? It's nearly one."

Lily's grin faded. "I asked Pastor Dean to take over the store until two."

"Why? You never ask him to watch the store."

She shrugged. "I had planned to have lunch with Shade, but he was in a meeting with Viper."

Feeling her sister's gaze on her, she rose from the bed. "If you're sure you don't want the clothes, they'll come in handy for John. I appreciate them."

"You're welcome."

Lifting the box into her arms, she carried them down the steps with Beth following behind her, feeling Beth's curious gaze on her as she went to the door.

"Lily... are you sure nothing is wrong? Are you upset Shade wasn't able to have lunch with you?"

"Of course not. Everything's fine." Seeing the disbelief in her sister's expression, Lily put an arm out to hug her. "Really, nothing is wrong. I better go; I want to have dinner started before heading back to work."

"Bye."

Lily left for home. Once inside, she set the box down beside the door before going to the kitchen. She had a new recipe she wanted to start in the slow cooker before heading back to work.

She was putting the last of the ingredients inside when she heard the front door open, then close. Glancing up, she saw her husband taking off his jacket.

"How did your meeting with Viper go?" she asked.

"Good."

Feeling him slide his strong arms around her waist, she leaned back against him as she put the top on the crockpot.

"I would've rather had lunch with you."

Turning around in his arms, she twined her arms around his neck. "I just made sandwiches, so you didn't miss much."

"I missed spending the time alone with you."

She shuddered as Shade ran his lips along the side of her neck to her ear. "Me, too. I miss having some of the lunches we used to share when I was working at the factory."

Shade raised his head to stare down at her. "That's not the way I remember it. You tried to get out of them."

"That was when I wasn't in love with you."

"You were in love with me; you just didn't know it then."

"I wouldn't go that far." She laughed at her husband's arrogant boast, loving the man smiling down at her so much that she wanted to pinch herself to make sure she was really standing within his arms.

His expression suddenly turned into the watchful one she was used to the most. "What's wrong?"

"Nothing. I made you a sandwich; it's in the fridge."

"I'll eat after you tell me what's wrong."

"Nothing is wrong, other than I need to get back to the thrift store. I'll be back in a few hours." Slipping out of Shade's arms, she went to put her coat on.

"Funny, I can't remember the last time you took off in the middle of the day to eat lunch with me."

Feeling nervous, she started buttoning her coat. "Me neither. That's why I asked Pastor Dean to watch the store so we could."

Shade narrowed his eyes at her. "Why didn't you ask Willa or Rachel?"

"I didn't want to bother Willa; she's been so busy lately with T.A.'s wedding. And I didn't want to ask Rachel to drive into town with Ema and Jaxon. Jax is running a fever, and she already asked to switch tomorrow out for my day off."

Lily swallowed hard when Shade crossed his arms over his chest and leaned against the counter to study her.

"With everybody being so busy, you still wanted to have lunch?"

Placing a cheerful smile on her lips, she walked back to him. "You've been gone so much lately, watching over Ginny,

I just wanted to spend extra time with you before you have to leave again." Lily tried desperately to shield her emotions behind her lashes, fearing that Shade would see the fear that she was hiding from him. Then, brushing a quick kiss on his lips, she gave a half-laugh. "I better be going. I'll see you this evening."

Slipping out of Shade's arms, she went to open the door.

"Lily."

From over her shoulder, she saw that Shade hadn't moved from the counter.

"Take care."

Nodding, she went out the door, closing it behind her. She hadn't missed his subtle warning. Shade was always able to sense when something was bothering her. For now, though, he was giving her the opportunity to tell him what it was. If she didn't get her act together, the next time he asked, Shade wouldn't stop until he found out the reason.

Putting on her gloves, she had to stop in the middle of the path that led to the parking lot when one dropped to the ground. Picking it up with a shaking hand, she was finally able to put it on before fumbling in her coat pocket for her car keys. Her thoughts scattered, she didn't notice there were two pairs of eyes watching her leave.

The air was chilly, making her wish spring would arrive, looking forward to the morning that she would walk out her front door and hear the birds chirping again. Usually, she loved winter for the snow, but for some reason, this year, the bleak sight of trees without their leaves brought a sadness that was unexplainable to her.

Valentine's Day was just two days away. She wished she could come up with a better idea for Shade's present, other than a watch. She had been married to him long enough that she should be able to come up with something that would knock his socks off.

She was getting in her car when a SUV pulled into the parking lot. About to wave at the driver before leaving, a sudden thought occurred to her. Without giving herself time to change her mind, she closed her car door and walked over to Killyama as she got out of the vehicle.

"Hey, girl, what's up?" Killyama greeted her, moving to the back seat to take her daughter out of the car seat.

"I was wondering if you could help me with a problem I'm having?"

"You're asking me for help instead of Shade or Beth?"

Lily nodded. "If you wouldn't mind?"

"Bitch, who you think you're talking to? I love to give advice."

CHAPTER 2

Lily looked toward the door when the bell rang as it was pushed open, alerting her that a customer was entering. Placing the folded man's sweater on the shelf she had been straightening, she walked toward the counter in the middle of the thrift store.

She didn't give the man approaching the counter a welcoming smile, regretting that she hadn't kept Pastor Dean talking longer before he left to go back upstairs to the church.

Her flesh crawled at the smirk that was on Harvey Green's face as he came to a stop.

"I missed you when I stopped by this morning."

"I had lunch with Shade." Lily kept her eyes on him, refusing to be afraid of the man who was making the job she had always loved into one she dreaded from the moment she walked inside until she was able to close for the day. "Why are you here? I left the cans of baby formula and diapers for Lucky to give you."

"I got them, but I wanted to ask if it would be possible to get a few things for Nicole?"

"Why didn't you ask when you were in earlier?"

"It's hard for a man to admit he needs to ask for help to get his woman something for Valentine's Day."

The friendliness she made a point of showing each person in need who walked through the door was absent as she deliberately remained aloof under Harvey's assessing gaze. Lily knew he was waiting to see how far he could push her before she demanded he left the store. It was a cat and mouse game she refused to play with him.

"Then you should have swallowed your pride. I told you not to come back in here anymore. I don't mind giving Nicole formula, diapers, or anything else she needs for herself and the baby... as long as she picks it up herself."

Lily tensed as Harvey came around the counter to lean back against it and look down at her. The way he was focused on her gave her the creeps.

"Why? Does it get you hot when I come in the store?"

She wanted to gag at the come-on. "No, it doesn't get me hot. It disgusts me."

When he straightened off the counter, she grabbed the large stapler that was sitting beside the cash register. His eyes followed the movement, his smirk becoming one that had fear curling in her stomach.

"You fucking bitch, you know you want me. I don't know why you're pretending."

She glared at him furiously, tightening her hand on the stapler. "I'm not pretending. I'm married. And even if I weren't, I wouldn't want you. Nicole loves you. It would break her heart to know how you're acting."

"Why don't you tell her?" Amusement curled at his lips. "I'll tell you why. You want me as much as I want you."

"That's not why I don't tell her. If Nicole knew how you were treating me, she wouldn't come back to the store, and she needs the diapers and formula."

"That's not why, and you know it."

Lily could only stare at the man, dumbfounded by his arrogance. "Are you seriously this stupid? I haven't said anything to Pastor Dean, but I will if you don't stop."

"If you were going to say anything to the pastor, you would have already. He was right friendly to me this morning, so you haven't opened that sexy mouth of yours to say a word about me." With a lone finger, he touched her cheek.

Jerking her face away, she took a step back and lifted the stapler threateningly. "Don't you dare touch me."

Laughter wasn't the reaction she was hoping for.

Her anger nearly had her wanting to take a swing at his lust-filled expression, while she felt the effects within her body heralding the start of a panic attack. It had been years since she had one, but like an unwelcomed friend, she felt the signs approaching, with her skin growing clammy and her breathing escalating.

"Leave, Harvey. Now. If you try to come back in the store, I'll call Knox."

"Calling Knox is the last thing you'll do. You don't want that husband of yours to find out what's going on between us."

The man was certifiable.

"There's nothing going on between us!" she yelled.

She had made a terrible mistake. She should have talked to Pastor Dean before it reached the point she was facing now.

"Harvey, I seriously only wanted to help Nicole. If you misinterpreted my intentions, then that's not on me; it's on you. I have never, at any time, given you any sign that I was interested in you, other than to help Nicole and your son. I'm giving you one last chance. Use it wisely. If Shade finds out that you have been bothering me…." Lily took a deep breath to calm herself down, afraid she would pass out if she couldn't get ahold of herself. The last thing she wanted to do was to appear weak in front of the unstable man.

She still couldn't understand how the man that she had gone to high school with had changed so drastically. When he had come into the thrift store with Nicole, she wouldn't have remembered him if Nicole hadn't reminded her that they'd gone to school together. Other than a courteous "hello" to him, she'd directed her attention to Nicole, who filled out the paperwork as Lily held the baby.

Harvey hadn't even spoken to her that day, leaving with a quiet *goodbye*, his only words to her. After she approved Nicole for assistance, the problem with Harvey started. For the first two weeks, Nicole and Harvey had both come to receive their aid, but by the third week he had started showing up alone.

At first Lily had been friendly, sure she was wrong that the new father was actually making passes at her. Most of the town's population were wary of Shade, so she truly thought she was mistaken by Harvey's overtly friendly behavior. When he started trying to touch her arm, though, she had quickly and firmly pulled hers away, her own friendliness disappearing.

From there it went downhill.

She knew she should have talked to Pastor Dean, but she also knew how protective he was, and any aid to Nicole would have been cut off. More importantly, he would have told Shade. She really didn't want Harvey hurt; she just wanted him to stop flirting with her. Clearly, she had made a terrible mistake by not calling Nicole and, regardless of her feelings, made it known that, unless she was the one who came into the store, no further aid would be given.

The problem was that she couldn't bring herself to hurt the woman. Lily remembered her from high school. She was sweet and kind and certainly didn't deserve the father of her child coming on to someone who was only trying to help their small family.

"You know what I think, Lily? I think you're so afraid of your husband that you don't want to admit how much you're attracted to me."

Any feeling she'd had that she was going to faint vanished in a heartbeat.

"I'm not afraid of my husband. You're the one who should be afraid. Leave, Harvey. Now."

Lily straightened her body, prepared to strike out at him. She could tell from the determined gleam in his eyes he was going to make a move. She promised herself that if he took one step toward her, she would hit him with the stapler.

Harvey must have been irritated that she hadn't been there when he showed up this morning, losing what sense of caution that had previously held him back. Lily was poised, though, ready to respond to any movement from Harvey, when the sound of the bell over the door had them both turning at the jangling peal.

She went pale at the sight of the man who was striding toward the counter, Shade's inscrutable expression targeted on her.

Though startled at her husband's unexpected appearance, the fear inside of her evaporated. Shade had always been able to calm her frayed nerves, making her feel safe and loved.

Harvey might be twice Shade's weight and ten years younger, but if he thought that gave him one over on her husband, then he was making a mistake.

A fatal one.

CHAPTER 3

She set the stapler down on the counter as he came to stand next to her, feeling the tension within her ease now that he was a barrier between her and Harvey.

"I needed to file some paperwork at the courthouse for Viper and thought I'd stop here and see you before going home."

Lily saw that Shade's attention was no longer on her once he was by her side but fixated on Harvey.

"I'm glad. I could use some help moving some boxes from the donation bin."

The two men staring each other down had her trying to break the tension that was practically crackling between them.

"Shade, this is Harvey—"

"We're acquainted. Aren't we, Harvey?" her husband cut the introduction short. "He worked at the factory for a couple of months before Jewell fired him."

The revelation that Harvey had worked at the factory was unexpected. Neither Nicole nor Harvey had mentioned that fact. It wouldn't have made a difference to the aid they received from the church, so it made no sense why they hadn't mentioned it, especially when Lily suggested they apply for jobs at the church.

Harvey glowered at Shade. "Jewell doesn't wipe her ass unless you tell her to."

Lily tensed at the harsh words coming from the man standing in front of them. Sickeningly, she was beginning to realize that Harvey held a grudge against her husband and had been using her as payback. Her Christianity was the only thing keeping her mouth shut at the hatred that Harvey wasn't making any attempt to hide.

Shade, on the other hand, was coldly examining Harvey as if he were an irritating fly that he wasn't going to be bothered to swat away. She was used to her enigmatic husband's ability to hide his reactions.

As a cold chill ran up her back, she instinctively reached out, placing a calming hand on Shade's arm. "Harvey was just leaving."

"That would be a smart move."

She tightened her hand on Shade's arm when Harvey made no move to leave. Holding her breath, she could feel the escalating tension between the two men.

Just when she was about to reach for her cell phone to call Knox, Harvey's hate-filled expression switched to one more amiable.

"It was good seeing you again, Shade. Lily, I'll see you next week."

Lily didn't miss the underlying provocativeness that Harvey made no attempt to hide from his voice. She swallowed hard, knowing that if she had heard it, then Shade had, too.

Lily stared at Harvey's back as he moved from the

counter and made his way out of the store, waiting until the door closed behind him before taking her hand off Shade's arm. She regretted it as soon as she did, finding herself having to face him.

"What was Harvey doing here?"

"He comes to the store once a week for formula for his baby," she answered immediately.

Her mentioning that Harvey had a small child didn't soften Shade's features.

"He wasn't carrying any when he left."

"He came by when I was gone earlier and Pastor Dean was here."

"That doesn't explain why he was here now."

"He was asking me for help to find Nicole a Valentine's Day present."

"You're afraid of him."

"He frightens me. I was asking him to leave and to send Nicole from now on." Lily was incapable of lying to her husband.

The look on her husband's face frightened her. The sudden movement of him turning toward the door had her rushing to block him.

"I handled it, Shade. He won't be coming back."

"No, he won't."

The deadly finality in his voice had her reaching out to cup his face, drawing his gaze down to hers. "You know what I want for Valentine's Day?"

His jaw clenched in a hard line. She hastened to tell him as he tried to sidestep her.

"I don't want you to hurt him."

"That's one present you won't be getting."

"Please… Shade," she begged. "Harvey isn't worth the trouble he would cause our family."

"Taking care of him won't cause it any trouble," he said grimly.

"What if it does? John is in school now. What if you're arrested and John finds out? Do you really want our son to find out that he can solve his problem by using his fists?"

"It's not my fists I plan to use on Harvey."

His bone-chilling reply had her shaking.

"He's not worth it. He's obviously trying to get at you through me. Don't let him succeed."

He narrowed his eyes down on hers. "How long has he been bothering you?"

She wasn't afraid her husband would hurt her, but she knew the answer she was about to give would inflate his anger.

"For about three weeks, but it's never been as bad as today or I would have said something to you. He just made me uncomfortable. I told him that unless it was Nicole who came inside, I would no longer be able to provide any services. I didn't trust him that Nicole would be the one to come today and asked Pastor Dean to watch the store."

"Did you tell Lucky why you wanted him to watch the store?"

"No," she admitted.

"Why not?" Shade didn't raise his voice to her, but she could tell he wasn't happy with her admission.

"I knew he would tell you. I had hoped that I had put a stop to Harvey's behavior. I was mistaken."

"What did he do?"

"He thinks I'm attracted to him. He knows I'm not. Clearly, he was just getting back at you because he feels you were responsible for getting him fired."

"I was. Jewell didn't want to fire him because she knew he was expecting a child. I told her to fire him or his salary would be taken out of her paycheck."

Lily's gentle soul was distressed at the cold-hearted reaction of forcing Jewell to fire Harvey.

"He was given several chances. All he had to do was make an effort to do his job. He came in late, he was missing items from several of the orders that customers were billed for, and he had his buddies clocking out for him when he decided to leave early, which was a regular occurrence with him. The Last Riders give to charity, but they don't run one."

Lily nodded. "What are you going to do?"

"Do you really want to know?"

She did, and she didn't.

"Nicole is really sweet."

"I'm sure she is. Harvey makes a habit of picking sweet women to keep himself out of trouble. This time he picked the wrong woman. He took a chance that she wouldn't say anything to me, and when he came in earlier today with Lucky, he knew he had you running scared but that you hadn't alerted Lucky to how he was acting toward you. Harvey took a chance that, sadly for him…" Steel laced his expression when she couldn't contain her troubled fear about what Shade would do. "He miscalculated. While he doesn't give a fuck about his woman, I do."

"Shade, please don't."

"Where are the boxes you needed my help with?"

With the change of subject, Shade was done discussing Harvey.

Showing him the overfilled boxes, she mutely pointed where she wanted them stacked beside the counter.

Waiting tensely for Shade to lecture her about how she handled Harvey coming on to her, she unconsciously began twisting her hands together. Tears brimming her eyes, she then started to go in search of hangers when a tug on her long hair had her turning to see him casually holding a long strand gripped in his hand.

"Come here."

Walking back to him, she stopped in front of him.

"Are you okay?"

"I don't want you angry at me."

"I'm not angry with you. I'm angry at Harvey."

Her eyes widened. "You're not?"

"No, I'm not."

Lily breathed a sigh of relief. "Thank you."

"For what?"

"For being so understanding."

"Harvey is the one at fault, not you. He realized you're soft-hearted and tried to take advantage. Unluckily for him, I'm not soft-hearted. I knew when you came home something was wrong. It's been a long time since I've seen fear in your eyes." Shade reached out and gently laid a possessive hand on her cheek, his lips curled in a half-smile. "I don't plan to kill him, if that's what has you worried."

"I didn't think you'd actually kill him."

"Just fuck him up?"

She flushed guiltily.

"I won't. I won't lay a hand on him. Does that make you feel better?"

Happily, she smiled up at him. "Yes."

"Good. Now, do you need any more help before I leave?"

Her smile dropped. "Where are you going?"

"I have a few errands to take care of for Viper. Why?"

"I thought you would keep me company until it was closing time." She didn't try to hide her disappointment that he was leaving her alone.

"Are you afraid to stay here alone?"

"Of course not."

"Good." Shade dropped his hand from her cheek. "Because Harvey won't be bothering you anymore. Whether

I'm here or not in person, you will be under my protection and I won't let anyone hurt you. Do you believe me?"

"Yes. But what are you planning to do?" There wasn't a doubt in her mind that Shade had a plan in mind.

"Don't worry about it. I've got that."

CHAPTER 4

Shade entered the dim interior of the bar, nodding toward Mick as he came through the door. He hadn't expected the bar to be busy at this time of the day, and it wasn't. Mick's customers wouldn't fill the local watering hole for at least another hour, making a pit stop before heading home.

With his eyes, he searched the dark room for the man whose car was parked outside. Seeing Harvey sitting at a small table against the wall, he soundlessly made his way through the bar.

Without asking, Shade sat down across from Harvey, enjoying the satisfaction on Harvey's face that he had angered him enough that Shade had sought him out.

As soon as he sat his ass down, Mick came over.

"Can I get you a drink, Shade?"

"No."

The owner of the bar turned on his heel, leaving the two men alone.

"If you came here to threaten me about Lily, you can go fuck yourself. I'm not afraid of you."

"I didn't come here to threaten you." Shade leaned back in the chair, carefully laying his hands on his waist when all he wanted to do was tear the slimy fucker into a million pieces. "I came here to save you the trouble of planning to make any further attempts of getting within a five-mile radius of my wife."

"Whatcha going to do if I do? You can't do jack shit about it."

Shade narrowed his eyes on the man sitting across from him, continuing to speak as if Harvey had never spoken. "Do you care about Nicole and your kid?"

"If you're going to threaten me with them, that won't work either." Harvey smiled smugly, showing rotting teeth.

"No. I don't use women and children as ammunition when I want to get back at someone."

Shade knew the barb had hit home when Harvey gripped his beer mug as if he wanted to throw it at him.

"The only reason I mentioned them is so that, if you do, then you should be making some plans for them when you're gone."

"You hear that, Mick? He just threatened me!"

"I didn't hear shit."

Out of the corner of his eye, Shade saw Mick go to the other side of the bar.

"That sweet little cunt is too good for you." With rising resentfulness, Harvey turned red as his anger mounted.

"Better men than you have said that to me before. You want to know how much of a fuck I care about when they do?" His lips twisted in mockery. "The fact is that she is mine. Another one is that you're not man enough to come at me for being fired and thought you'd use Lily to draw me out. What was the plan? Provoke a fight with me over Lily so that you could use that to say why you were fired? Or were you willing to take the beating that you're trying to provoke me into giving you so you can sue? Get a nice fat settlement and sit on your ass for the rest of your life?" Shade gave a shrug when he saw Harvey's eyes widened at the last one.

"It's your fault that no one in town will hire me!"

"You haven't been able to find another job for two reasons. One, you have to actually look for one, and two, when you do get offered one, you have to take it. Knox offered you a job as a janitor at the police station, which you turned down, even though you would have made more money than you made working for The Last Riders."

"I'm not going to mop floors or empty trash cans."

"Why? Because it wouldn't give you the ability to steal from another business like you did from The Last Riders? You think I wouldn't do menial labor if I needed to feed my woman and child? I'd empty bedpans if I had to. But that's the difference between you and me. I don't mind doing a day's work for what I have. Unlike you, who wants to take what's not yours or have it given to you."

"I didn't steal."

"Don't lie. I found the items for sale on eBay that you stole, and I can prove it, so don't sit there and pretend you didn't. It makes you look pathetic—you are—but I wouldn't flaunt it any more than you already have."

His ridiculing got the reaction he was waiting for. Harvey stood up so fast his chair fell backward.

"You're just jealous that Lily wants me!"

Shade's eyebrows rose humorously at Harvey's shout.

"I have pictures of us together!"

He had to use all his military training not to pull out the gun nestled under his jacket and put a bullet between Harvey's eyes. Instead, he gave him a grim smile.

"Prove it."

With a cunning demeanor, Harvey sat back down. "No. I have plans on who I'm going to show them to."

"Let me guess; you want me to pay you for pictures that don't exist?"

"They exist." Harvey lowered his voice deviously, no longer wanting to draw attention to himself. "Even if it's not her, which I ain't saying it's not, if I pass them around town to several of my buddies and say it is Lily, they'll believe me."

"No, they won't."

Harvey's rotted smile turned gloating. "Even if they don't, Lily will think they will, and I'll make sure that Lily knows the pictures are going around town."

"Oh, I'm sure you will," Shade drawled out.

"Of course I like Lily. She's a good lay, but damn, you could spare her a lot of heartache if you see things my way."

"And your way involves money for your silence? Is that what you're saying?"

"I want my job back. Of course I'd need a raise, too."

"I'm sure you'd like that, but it isn't going to happen."

"Then I guess we're done talking, aren't we?"

"Yes, we are." Shade rose, laying his palms down on the table as he stood over the blackmailing shithole. "You should order a hamburger. Mick makes the best one in town." Straightening, Shade took out a hundred-dollar bill and laid it down on the table, enjoying the greedy light that appeared in Harvey's eyes.

"What's that for?"

"For whatever you want to use it for. Let's just say Jewell forgot to give you your severance pay."

"Does that mean you're willing to come to an agreement on the pictures?"

"It means have a beer and burger on me. They'll be your last."

CHAPTER 5

"Is something wrong with the cake?"

At Willa's question, Lily realized she hadn't taken a bite of the cake she was holding in her hand.

"No, I was waiting to see where Shade wanted to sit, but he seems to have disappeared."

"I passed Shade and Rider as they were going into the garage. They want to see the new motorcycle that Colton built."

The dread that filled her when she couldn't find Shade lightened. It didn't disappear completely, though, because of the way her husband had been acting since he came into the thrift store and discovered Harvey harassing her.

He hadn't mentioned it again after leaving her in the store. In fact, when she tried to bring it up that evening, Shade had changed the subject.

Seeing that Willa was still looking at her expectantly, she lifted her fork and took a bite of the cake.

"It's delicious," she told her, forcing herself to give her a carefree smile. "It's almost as good as the one you made for me."

Beaming, Willa started talking about how beautiful the ceremony was.

"She made a beautiful bride," Lily agreed, her thoughts still on Shade.

"Dalton didn't look bad either."

Both women flushed when Dalton flashed them a smile. As if sensing they were talking about him, he came out of the dining room, holding a generous portion of his wedding cake.

Their eyes weren't the only female gazes following him throughout the room. The movie star's charisma was like a magnet for women. That he was nice made him harder to resist.

Shyly glancing away from his smile, Lily found hers caught and held by her husband's. She wasn't the only one caught staring. Willa had been caught, too.

While Lucky's expression was indulgent and speculative at watching his wife ogle another man, Shade's had her body going taut. Lust hit her like a strike of lightning. It always did when he looked at her as if he could read her mind.

Shade was possessive, dominant, and protective of her. They were characteristics that stabilized the panic attacks that had chained her within their grasp until he set her free. He kept all her fears and anxieties at bay by knowing that anything or anyone that could harm her would be dealt with by him.

She had grown older and stronger during their marriage. At one time, a man like Harvey would have sent her into a full-fledged panic attack. Now, she wasn't frightened by him. She just pitied him that he was courting his own death.

Lily was under no illusion about what Shade was capable of. She had had the proof laid before her eyes when a woman who was in love with him had tried to blackmail her into leaving him. She had tried to leave him for his own safety,

27

but Shade had said something then that always stayed with her. *If you leave me, I might as well be dead.* To hear him put into words the same exact feeling she felt, each step away from him tore her soul apart.

John's sudden arrival had put a stop to her leaving, and even knowing what Shade was capable of, she never considered leaving him again. It had taken a lot of soul-searching to come up with the answer. She had found her answer in a passage from the Bible that Pastor Dean had left in her hospital room when he visited her after John's birth.

She had seen the Bible sitting on the table by her bed and opened it to the page with a book mark sticking out.

(Psalm 10:17-18)

O LORD, you hear the desire of the afflicted;
you will strengthen their heart; you will incline your ear
to do justice to the fatherless and the oppressed,
so that man who is of the earth may strike terror no more.

Lily still remembered reading that verse and looking across the room, seeing Shade holding John and the love in his expression. The love he had shown her when he looked up and saw her watching him.

God had gifted her a warrior. A warrior who sometimes did the dirty work that no one else wanted to do because society or their own conscience wouldn't let them. A warrior who believed his deeds were branded on a soul that would never deserve love. From her or God.

She did. God, how she loved him.

Moving to his side, she used her fork to cut him a piece of cake before lifting it to his mouth.

His gaze caught hers as he opened his mouth.

"Do you like it?"

Her husband didn't look toward Willa at the question. "Almost as much as the one you made for me and Lily."

"That's the same thing she said."

Willa's laughter didn't break the spell between them, each lost in the silent duel of desire that was rising between them.

"Do you want some more?"

"Yes."

Lily fed him another bite.

"Willa, I wouldn't mind a bite of yours."

Lily flushed at hearing Lucky's husky request.

"Get your own."

Lily couldn't help laughing, breaking the moment she had been sharing with Shade by switching her focus to Lucky's chagrined expression.

"I would be happy to get you a slice," Lily offered.

"Never mind. If I eat another slice, I won't be able to fit into my *favorite* pair of pants."

"Excuse me. I need to check on something in the kitchen."

Lily watched her friend leave with a flush high on her cheeks.

"Excuse me." Lucky's eyes were following his wife's retreating back. "I have something I need to check."

"I don't think I want to know what Lucky's going to be checking on, do I?" she asked Shade after Lucky was out of hearing range.

"Probably not," Shade agreed, moving his hand to her waist to pull her closer to his side.

Trying hard not to become lost again, she cleared her throat. "What do you want to do for the rest of the day?"

"It's Valentine's Day; it's your pick. You want to hit up your favorite restaurant after we leave here?"

"We already ate," she reminded him. Her nipples tightened in response to the small caresses she could feel through the material of her dress. "Are you still hungry?"

"No."

"Neither am I."

"Do you find Dalton attractive?"

The out of the blue question didn't faze her.

"He's very handsome. But do I find him attractive personally? No. He's not my type."

"He's no cowboy, that's for sure."

"That's not why I'm not attracted to him."

"It's not?"

"No. I'm not attracted to him because he's not you."

She felt his hand tighten on her waist.

"I know how I want to spend the rest of the day."

"Me, too."

Shade took the plate away from her, placing it on the table before guiding her toward the door.

"I need to tell T.A. that we're leaving."

"She's over there. Wave to her. She'll get the message."

"I can't be rude."

"Then let me. I don't have a problem with it."

Lily stopped, giving him a reprimanding smile. "Just let me say goodbye. You can go tell Dalton we're leaving."

"You have three minutes."

"I only need two."

As she started away, he grabbed her hand. Startled, she turned back, her eyes widening at the man.

"Two minutes. I'll meet you at the door."

Lily watched as, releasing her hand, Shade went around the fringe of the crowd, trying to circumvent being drawn into a conversation. She was just as anxious to leave.

Her lips curled in a smile as she approached T.A. Usually, it was T.A.'s friends who stood out when they were together. Today, it was T.A.

The woman was glowing with happiness. Her dress was white and sexy, making Lily wish she had worn something special for Shade.

Coming closer, Lily hugged her. "You look so beautiful. Dalton is lucky he was able to convince you to marry him."

T.A. gave her a surprised glance. "Everyone else has been telling me how lucky I am."

Lily shook her head, releasing her friend. "Dalton is blessed to have you. You're the most open-hearted person I know. You put yourself out there despite knowing Sex Piston, Killyama, or Crazy Bitch would give you grief for trying. You're one in a million, and Dalton recognized how special you are."

"Please don't make me cry. You'll ruin my makeup."

Lily gave her another hug. "Don't cry. You'll make me cry."

The two broke apart, laughing.

"I came over to tell you that Shade and I are leaving...." Lily looked at how stunningly gorgeous T.A. was and came to another decision. She had come up with the perfect Valentine's Day present for her husband... if she was brave enough to see it through. "But I changed my mind."

"You're going to stay a little longer?"

"Would you mind doing me a big favor? I know it's your big day, but it would only take a few minutes." Lily lowered her voice, seeing Sex Piston and Crazy Bitch approaching them.

T.A. conspiratorially lowered her voice. "What do you need me to do?"

"Keep Shade occupied for a few minutes while I slip out."

"Sure thing. No problem."

Smiling, Lily used the opportunity to slip out through the crowd while Shade's attention was focused on Dalton.

"Of course I'm going to want a favor in return."

Lily didn't miss the cunning look in T.A.'s eyes. Greer Porter always had the same expression when he wanted something.

"What do you want?"

"Just how far do Shade's tattoos go down?"

CHAPTER 6

S hade stood at the doorway, sweeping the room with his eyes one more time. Lily was talking with T.A. one second, and the next, she had disappeared when Sex Piston, Crazy Bitch, Killyama, and her mother Peyton circled her within their group. He had lost sight of her when he left Dalton's side to go around the crowd, and when he looked again, the women had dispersed into other small groups.

Had she gone outside to wait for him by their SUV?

Opening the door, he went outside, seeing their car was missing. She left without him.

He took out his phone and texted her, not understanding her reasoning for not to waiting. Not expecting her to reply, though, when she was driving, he went back inside the house. No one seemed ready to leave as the music from a band floated inside from the backyard.

Feeling the vibration of his phone, he saw that Lily answered his text. There was no way she could have reached their home so soon.

Didn't want to wait.

Staring down at the message, his worry switched to irritation.

Not wanting to send another text while she was driving, he texted the only brother who wasn't here and didn't have any plans for the day.

Need a ride.

Ask someone else.

Come and get me from the reception.

I can see where you are. Give me five.

"Shade, would you mind helping Dalton pack my suitcases downstairs?"

About to go outside to wait, Shade gritted his teeth at T.A.'s request.

"He just went upstairs. I can't have him throwing his back out. He's going to need it tonight." She winked.

"Sure."

Impassively masking his irritation, he went up the stairs.

"I told T.A. I didn't need any help," Dalton said, coming out of the bedroom carrying two suitcases and a duffel bag.

Shade took one from him. "She's worried about your back."

At his comment, Dalton handed him the other suitcase, too.

Shade lifted a mocking brow.

"I'm just being cautious. I'm not a young man anymore."

"You look in pretty good shape to me." Shade nodded toward the steps, motioning for him to go first.

"I used to think so. Now I think she's trying to cash in on my insurance policy."

"Both these suitcases hers?"

"Yes. My things are in the duffel bag."

"Could be she's competing."

Dalton came to a stop on the stairs to look back at him. "Competing against who?"

Shade shrugged. "Take your pick. Can't be easy for her having so many women chasing after you. This isn't your first marriage either. Not only does she know that it was very happy, but also that she was a famous model. What would you do if the shoe was on the other foot?"

Dalton paled at the thought that he might be right.

"Jesus," he muttered. "What should I do?"

"You're asking the wrong person. I don't have a bad back."

When Dalton remained unmoving, Shade sighed irritably. He wanted to get home to Lily and see why she had left him behind.

"Do you eat every time you're hungry or do you space it out?"

"What?" Confused, Dalton stared up at him blankly.

"Do you eat pancakes every time someone offers them to you? Even when there're nuts and whipped cream tempting you? Just because she decides those pancakes are too damn good to pass up, it doesn't mean you have to break." Deciding to be even more blunt to save himself further irritation, he explained, "When T.A. wants to fuck, you don't have to give her a full meal every time. There're other ways to keep T.A. satisfied without fucking yourself to death. If that doesn't work, Greer Porter sells a protein drink that will give you the stamina of a rabbit. Knox swears by it."

Doing his one good deed for the day, he gave Dalton a sharp nod of his head. "My ride is waiting."

"Sorry." Dalton finally started moving.

When they reached the bottom of the stairs, Shade paused briefly by Gavin. "I'll be right back."

"I don't have all day."

Shade ignored the rude comment, carrying the suitcases to the garage. Then, leaving Dalton to store the luggage in the trunk of his rental car, he went back inside to find Gavin no longer standing where he had left him.

Thinking that Gavin had gone outside, he was about to go out there when he saw him heading outside the patio door. Turning in his direction, Shade trailed after him, registering that Gavin must have been drawn outside by the music.

"I'm searching for you
Calling for you
Hoping for you
Praying for you
Can you hear me?
Oh, why can't you hear me?"

Stepping outside, Shade saw Mouth2Mouth had set up at the end of the pool and the wedding guests were outside listening.

Spotting Gavin, he made his way to his side.

"I'm ready."

"She's the one you and the brothers have been protecting?" Gavin rasped out without taking his eyes off the woman singing.

"Yes."

If asked, anyone in Treepoint would say Shade was a coldhearted bastard, but even his cold heart felt sympathy for the damaged man by his side.

Gavin had lived through years of hell and humiliation, only to find the freedom he had fought so hard for wasn't a balm for the jagged cuts that had permanently scored his soul.

"I can see why he wants her."

Gavin hadn't shown any interest when The Last Riders had their meeting discussing Ginny's protection. Not that he had attended any of the meetings. Even though he lived in the clubhouse, Gavin either remained reclusive in his room or went on motorcycle rides that would stretch to several days' absences.

The days he was gone were torture for Viper, not

knowing if Gavin would come back or if he had ridden his bike off one of the mountains that surrounded their small town. Each member of the club had unsuccessfully tried to breach the wall Gavin had surrounded himself with.

Shade waited until the song was over before speaking.

"You want me to introduce you?"

Gavin turned his attention to him. "No. You ready?"

Shade raised a mocking brow. "I told you I was."

Shade was used to most people giving him a wide berth, but with Gavin, they practically froze, as if afraid a wild lion would break free of his cage, finding themselves on the dinner menu. What they didn't know was that unless he was protecting someone else, Gavin wanted to stay far away from them.

The brother who had been dragged out of the hellhole he had been forced to survive in wasn't the same one who he had served with in the military. Back then, Gavin had been happy and carefree, always ready for a good time, yet there had been no better to turn to when shit hit the fan.

The other soldiers knew that when Gavin was on a mission, he didn't go into it to fail. He wouldn't let any of the other men risk their safety without putting his own on the line first. Safeguarding others was such an intrinsic part of him, and the one that'd helped him survive his captivity.

Shade slid into the cab of the truck that Gavin borrowed to drive him back to the club. Neither of them spoke on the short ride. It was only when he was getting out that Gavin broke the silence.

"When does she leave?"

"Ginny?"

"Which of the men is their turn to watch her?"

"Rider at lead and Nickel."

Shade studied the brother. He had asked Gavin numerous times to take turns with various members who volunteered to guard Ginny. That the job was taking much longer than they had expected to find her stalker had built his own concern that the fucker was laying low, waiting for them to relax their guard. Viper felt the same way, which was why either he or Rider were sent.

"When does she go?"

This was the most words said in the last two months. Gavin never initiated conversations, and when he did talk, it was usually curt yeses or noes, if not outright ignoring a question posed to him.

"She and the band will be flying out at the end of the week."

When Gavin opened the truck door and got out, Shade did the same, walking toward the pathway to his house while Gavin headed in the direction of Viper's. But then Shade blocked his way.

"Rider could use a break."

"Then give him one. I don't give a fuck what you do."

Gritting his teeth, Shade stepped aside, letting Gavin go on his way, just like all the brothers did, not wanting to upset him whenever the subject was broached about him taking a turn.

Ginny was the first woman who had arisen interest in Gavin since he had come back to the clubhouse. Shade wished he had introduced the two of them.

Several years ago, Ginny worked for The Last Riders for a while. During that time, Shade picked up on several facets of her personality. She pretty much gave respect to those who deserved it while ignoring those who didn't. She had faced down more than one person who thought her polite personality would allow them to be disrespectful to her. She wasn't confrontational, but she didn't back down either.

It would have been interesting to witness Gavin's reaction if they had been introduced. He was also curious as to how she would have reacted to Gavin.

Going up the steps to his front door, he swung it open, expecting to see Lily. However, the empty living room had him going through the house in search of her.

Becoming concerned, he went back downstairs. Taking out his phone, he texted Lily.

Where are you?

I'm at Rosie's Bar.

What are you doing there?

Waiting for you.

CHAPTER 7

Lily wrung her hands as she stared out the window toward the parking lot, watching for Shade. The music Mick had turned on for her before leaving was playing, heightening the anticipation she was feeling.

She flushed, remembering the amused expression on Mick's face when she had shown up after calling him to ask if she could rent his bar out for the next two hours. Gratefully, he hadn't asked why when she arrived, just told her where the door key was for when they finished.

Running to the door now, her fingers fumbled with the lock before she quickly took off Shade's large raincoat that she had worn to cover what she was wearing. Placing it on one of the tables, she then rushed to the middle of the dance floor, pretending nonchalance as her husband strode into the bar.

Hiding her trepidation as she heard the sound of the lock kicking back in place, she frantically started focusing on the beat of the music as she twirled on the pole in the middle of the dance floor.

When he stopped at the edge of the dance floor, she seductively leaned back against the pole. "Have a seat."

Anger had been radiating from him when he entered, but she'd been married to Shade long enough to see he desired to watch her more than give in to his desire to spank her for stranding him at T.A.'s house.

As Shade picked up a chair, carrying it to the dance floor, she expertly hooked her arm around the pole. Twirling, she used a firm grasp to hold on while leaning her upper body away from the pole. With her free hand, she touched the floor as she made circles.

"What are you doing?"

Lily spun to a stop, leaning back against the pole once again. "Giving you your present. Do you like it?"

She saw her answer before he spoke.

"Yes. How did you get Mick to close up?"

"I rented it for two hours."

"For how much?"

"Does it matter?"

"No. I just want to know so I can tip him."

"You already did. I used your credit card."

She twined her long leg around the pole as she leaned backward, reaching out for the floor again as she watched his reaction upside down.

His eyes shifted to her breasts that were barely managing to stay confined inside the red bra that was under the mid-length, flimsy red nightie.

"Did you give him a generous tip?"

"Yes."

"Good."

Lily used her stomach muscles to raise herself, turning to give him her back. As the seductive music flowed faster, she then twisted her hips, scooching down until her butt rested on the heels of her feet before slowly rising.

"Come here."

Turning to face him again, she gave him a stern look. "No."

Baiting her husband, she scooched back down to the floor, trying desperately not to flush when his eyes went to the display visible between her thighs.

"You left me without a ride at the reception." His eyes flickered over to the thin coat that was laying on the table. "I expected you home when I got there."

Her confidence began to build at the low timbre of his voice.

"Are you mad at me?"

"I'm not pleased."

She provocatively walked toward his chair. "Good."

It was hard to keep appearing unaffected. The glittering desire she could see in Shade's hooded eyes had her nipples tautening. He was sprawled out comfortably on his chair. The thick bulge at the crotch of his jeans had her biting back a whimper. She wanted to sink to her knees and beg him to let her touch him.

She loved being submissive to Shade, being excited by the games they played. Putting aside her own preferences, though, Lily was determined to make it a day just for him.

Placing a high-heeled foot on the chair between his legs, she bent over, displaying her breasts only a couple of inches away from his mouth.

Shade reached out, brushing a knuckle across her peaked nipples.

"Uh-uh." She quickly struck her hand out, smacking his away. "There are three rules. Rule one: don't touch." She turned and sat on a hard thigh to twine her arms around his neck. "Rule two: no talking." Kissing the corner of his mouth, she let the tip of her tongue flick out before rising. Provocatively, she then slowly removed her nightie until she was standing in front of him in only her shoes, panties, and bra. "Rule three"—her lips curled in a sinful smile when the next song, "Kiss it Better" began playing—"you have to do everything I say, and I might, *just might*, give you a present."

"Which is?"

Tsk-tsking him that he had already broken rule number two, she started dancing farther away from him, returning to the pole. Looping her leg around it, she started climbing. Reaching the top, she stared at him mischievously as she slowly made her way back down the pole while the sexual lyrics played. Shade's face was etched in stone as he watched.

Reaching the bottom, she swayed back toward him. Licking her bottom lip, she saw his bulge grow under his jeans. Satisfied, Lily abruptly turned to stretch her left foot. Bending down, she gracefully touched her toe, listening to the beat of the music. She then stretched and extended her right foot, bending to repeat the same maneuver.

Gliding around, she caught his eyes as she clasped both her hands together behind her head, the action thrusting her breasts out. Dropping into a squat, she lowered her hands, planting them on top of his thighs. She used the momentum to raise herself before jauntily moving to his side. Raising her leg, she placed her heel back on the chair.

"Do you miss coming here to watch strippers before you married me?"

His eyes narrowed up at her.

"Good boy," she crooned, caressing his jaw when he didn't answer.

Lifting her foot, she swung her legs over his until she was standing over him. Bouncing on the balls of her feet, she rose up and down, rubbing her crotch over his dick in quick, teasing movements. Her long black hair tumbled over her face, thankfully hiding her expression. She could feel her center becoming slick and needy. Her movements were teasing her as much as Shade.

Rolling her hips, she gave a ragged sigh, forcing herself to get her own desire in check the way Shade was doing.

Sinking down on him with a last roll of her hips, she tightened her thighs around him as she reached for the floor. Situating her hands so they could bear her weight, she loosened her legs, flipping her lower body over.

On her hands, she tossed her hair back, glancing up at Shade. He was staring fixated on her bottom.

"Don't you want to spank me?" she goaded him, wanting to break his silence.

His lips went into a thin line. Despite her taunt, he stayed still.

"You're being so good."

Taking a deep breath, she bravely slid her hand intimately between her thighs to her crotch, running her hand over her panties twice before turning over and sitting on the floor. She then brought her hands to her hips, teasingly sliding her panties downward while jutting her hips upward so she could remove them. Lily was proud of her dexterity as she maneuvered the panties over one heel and then the other, flashing her crotch each time.

Gripping the panties in the hook of her finger, she fluidly rose to stand, taking the step necessary to bring her closer to Shade.

Hooking another finger inside the other leg hole, she slung the panties around his head to rest at his neck. Tightening her fingers, she pulled herself even closer to Shade's mouth, placing a lingering kiss on the sensuous curve.

"How am I doing? Am I being naughty enough for you?" she breathed the question against his lips. Then, draping herself over his body, she ground her pussy down onto his rock-hard bulge. "Or do you want more?"

JAMIE BEGLEY

His jaw tensed.

Giving him another kiss at his restraint, she left the panties hanging off his neck as she moved both her hands behind her back to unfasten her bra. Letting it fall to the floor, she slid down his body until she was back on her knees between his legs.

Carefully unbuttoning his jeans, she lowered the straining zipper. Parting the material of his jeans, she flicked her tongue over the head of his cock. Without giving him any warning, she then sucked the head inside her mouth as she stroked his thighs.

Through her lashes, she saw him grip the sides of his chair.

Parting his jeans wider, she gave swirls across the head of his cock before she slipped it out of her mouth, then kissed the tattoo on his pelvis.

"Did I do as good as Chasity?"

She smiled against his skin at his frustrated groan at not being able to talk.

"You didn't think I found out about her, did you? I've even seen her shopping in town a few times." Gliding her mouth to Shade's other hip, she pressed another kiss on the tattoo that had been inked into his flesh there. "She's even the reason you had the stripper pole installed in the clubhouse before you met me.

"Is it a sin I'm jealous of her?" Lily rested her cheek on the skin she had just kissed. "Because I am. I'm jealous of every woman you've ever made love with, because I'm waiting for the day that I wake up and find that our life and everything in it was just a beautiful dream. A dream that every day I wake up afraid to find out never existed." Raising her cheek, she skimmed over his skin back to his penis. "Then I touch you, and I'm given another day of my madness."

She lovingly slid her mouth down the length of his cock.

"I'd rather be insane"—she gave a self-mocking laugh—"in a padded room than living without you."

As she took his cock into her mouth, she felt the coiled tension in his body, his muscles in his thighs bunching under her hands as if he were restraining himself from reaching for her.

He wasn't the only one affected as she tantalized him with the slow stroke of her tongue, sucking him farther into her mouth.

Scooching closer to him on her knees, she rubbed the tips of her breasts on his thighs as she tried to drive Shade as crazy as she believed herself to be.

She looked up at him through her lashes. His expression rose alarm bells in her head as she sucked on his cock.

Shade was a master of control. Several times in their marriage, she had come close to breaking his control… or just as much as he would let her. This time, however, she somehow managed to bypass the control he exerted on himself.

Desire blazed down at her from his blue eyes, promising retaliation when her domination of him ended.

Deliberately, she let his cock slip out of her mouth. "Daddy looks mad at me."

His face went harsh. "I'm not your fucking daddy."

Giving a plaintive sigh, she stood up fluidly, stepping away from him.

"You talked, and I was having so much fun." Pretending to complain, she put a firm hand on his shoulder as she walked around him, her fingers going to the panties that were draped around his neck. Pulling them taut, she lowered her head to whisper in his ear, "Feel free to use my safe word if you want to. No? I thought Dom's liked to be called daddy? I know you're not my *daddy*. You're my *husband*. Or are you? I could be dreaming all of this. Am I?"

When he remained silent this time, she bit down on his earlobe.

"You're being a good husband."

Releasing the panties, she crouched down at his feet again. Curling her hand around his hard shaft, she took him in her mouth again. This time, she didn't tease and torment him.

Tightening her hand as she sucked on him, she quit playing, giving him the friction and suction he needed. He was gripping his chair so hard she was afraid he was going to break it into pieces.

"I love your taste."

Shade thrust his cock upward, telling her to stop talking the only way he could.

Going farther down on him, she adjusted to his thrusts, aware that he was holding back, not wanting to overwhelm her.

Loosening her grip on his cock, she moved her hand to his sack, giving a gentle pinch while at the same time grazing her teeth over him. He almost came off the chair.

Going faster, she started caressing his sack, taking him as deeply as she could. Squeezing him with her throat muscles, she felt him swell even thicker as he thrust harder into her mouth.

Glancing upward, she saw the unmistakable love staring back at her as he climaxed, his body convulsing underneath her touch.

Lily gave a satisfied smile as she got to her feet. "Are you ready for your present?"

Seeing the puzzled frown on his forehead, she laughed.

"The lap dance and blowjob weren't your presents. This is." Naked, she took a couple of steps backward, then lowered herself back to her knees. "I love you, and there isn't another man on God's green earth I would do this for... other than you."

Dropping her head, she was about to place her forehead on the floor when she felt herself jerked upward into Shade's arms. Automatically, she circled her legs around his waist as he kissed her with unrestrained passion.

Gasping, she tore her mouth free. She had never seen Shade so visibly shaken.

"You had to go in my private chest to get those panties."

"Yes, I did," she admitted, knowing exactly what kind of trouble she was going to be in with her husband. That was why she had done it. "What are you going to do about it?"

CHAPTER 8

Shade wanted to laugh at Lily's deliberate attempt to get herself a spanking. Any other time, he would have taken her up on the present she was trying to gift him, but the fear she had expressed about being insane had shaken him to his core.

He had overheard her once before talking to Jo.

"You're very happy, aren't you?"

Lily stopped jiggling a playful elephant at the wistfulness in Jo's voice that she hadn't been able to hide. Her violet eyes raised to hers. "So much that I get afraid sometimes."

"Why?"

Lily gave a graceful shrug. "That Shade will wake up one day and realize he doesn't love me, that another woman can give him what I can't." As she talked, she looked down and ran a hand over the delicate tattoo of forget-me-nots that was on the underside of her forearm. "It's kind of surreal how happy I am. It can't last forever, can it?"

Lily still didn't believe what they had would last. Couples that had been raised in loving families had the same fears about their relationships, but Lily's traumatic childhood magnified hers.

He hadn't been a boy scout either in his past. She witnessed what life he had lived, despite his attempts to shield her. Regrettably, it was inevitable that she still heard and was hurt by stories that were circulated around town.

Carrying her across the dance floor, he sat her ass down on the bar, using his boot to shove the barstools out of the way. Putting a hand on each side of her, he concluded he was never going to be able to convince his wife with words that what they had was going to last. He had to convince her another way, one she would know deep down in her soul that was real despite her anxiety telling her it wasn't.

Grazing her lips with his, he forced himself to step away from her.

"If you're in a padded cell, sweetheart, you're not there alone. I'm right there with you."

Backing up several more steps, he started to slowly unbutton the black dress shirt he wore with his suit to T.A.'s wedding. He had only taken the time to change his pants before running out of his house when he got the text to meet her.

"Chasity couldn't compare to you on her best day. There's no contest where that's concerned. You didn't have to give me a lap dance to prove that. Not only does she not have your ass, but she's not you either."

His shirt unbuttoned, he laid it meticulously on the table next to Lily's coat. Sitting down at the same table, he then removed his boots and socks. Standing, he took off his already loosened jeans to stand naked.

Walking back to her, he lifted his finger to a nipple, mercilessly twisting the nub between his fingertips. "Do you feel that?"

Her violet eyes went wide.

Watching her expression, he kept his own implacable.

"Yes."

"Really? I must be doing something fucking wrong then for you to believe you've been dreaming our marriage." He raised his other hand to her other nipple and started twisting it, too. "I've been too easy on you, Angel. When we walk out this door tonight, you'll have no doubt this is no fucking dream."

Without pity, he let a nipple go. Her gasp of relief was short-lived before his teeth were latching onto it, bringing another gasp to her lips.

Biting down, he exerted enough pressure, carefully gauging every nuance and sound to make sure he wasn't carrying her past a threshold she couldn't handle. He wanted to take her to a level she hadn't been to before, but neither did he want her using the safe word that would call a halt to what he was trying to prove.

"If we live for the next fifty years or die tomorrow, we'll do it together regardless. In a fucking dream or in real life, I can guarantee that. You can bank on it."

"You can't know that. You aren't God."

"I know I'm not God." He gave her a mocking smile. "That's not the first time you've accused me of thinking that. I guess we'll just have to wait and see, won't we? God might not give a damn about me, but He'll always want to make His favorite angel happy. Who will be there for you to fly with if I'm not there?"

Lily's luminous eyes stared up at him. "I love you so much."

Shade released her nipple, laving the protruding nub with a soothing stroke of his tongue. "Why do you think I love you any less than you love me? Do you compare me to other men?"

She rolled her eyes at him. "There's no comparison between you and other men."

"Evie, Bliss wouldn't agree. There's just no comparison in your eyes, and I feel the same toward women. Angel, that fucked-up world you had to live in when you grew up doesn't exist anymore. That's the part that's not real anymore. I can stand here until I'm blue in the face and make love to you a million times, but until you know that deep in your heart, you're never going to be completely free of that nightmare."

Lily lowered her gaze, unwilling to meet his.

Trying to convince Lily when she preferred to hide her fears even from herself was an exercise in futility. That was how Harvey had gained the upper hand with her. She had been hurt so badly when she was growing up that she couldn't stand to hurt anyone, even if they deserved it. Luckily, he didn't have the same problem.

Coming to that realization, he knew what he had to do.

Backing up, he placed a small distance between them. "Angel, look at me. There is no other woman in the fucking world I have done this for, nor would I ever even with a gun pointed at my head."

Making sure she was watching him, he went to his knees. Bending over, he then placed his forehead on the floor.

Ignoring her protests, he stretched out his arms and hands until he was prone like the perfect submissive.

"No, Shade! This isn't what I want!"

"Then what do you want?" Shade rose back to a sitting position to look at her. "Tell me what you want, and I'll do it. Anything, everything, and how you want it. I will do it to make you happy because, Angel, anything other than that doesn't work for me."

She stared at him enamored that the only thing he wanted was her happiness. It was humbling and so unexpectedly sweet coming from Shade, his words having the same effect as if he had written her a poem. "You've never done that before." It wasn't a question; it was a statement filled with awe.

It took every bit of his willpower not to go to her and wipe the tears that were sliding down her cheeks. "Never."

Lily held out her arms to him. "Come here, please."

"Don't ask. Tell me."

"Come here."

Shade stepped forward, feeling her arms enclose him.

"What do you want me to do now?"

"I want you to kiss me."

It was every fucking thing he could do not to fuck her.

Lily was watching him with a longing he recognized at gut level. She wanted him to take control, yet as much as he wanted to give her what she wanted, he couldn't.

Her fears were real in her head, and instead of decreasing the longer they were married, they had become worse.

His hand at her side clenched into a fist. The hard part was knowing he was responsible in part for exacerbating her fears.

Viper and he came to the conclusion in the last year that the stalker targeting Ginny was smarter than they anticipated. Ginny was surrounded by Mouth2Mouth security, but she remained under The Last Riders' protection, and they weren't about to let anyone harm the woman. He and Rider were always by her side.

The toll on their marriage had gone on so long that now he could no longer deny the repercussions. Something was going to have to change regarding Ginny's protection. Him spending time away from his wife and kids was over. He was loyal to The Last Riders, but if given the choice, Lily had to come first.

"How? Like this?" Shade placed a small kiss on her lips.

"Or like this?" The second kiss he gave her wasn't tender. It was hard, demanding, and anything but gentle.

Molding her mouth to his, he twisted his mouth over hers to delve deeper. Inhaling the exotic scent of her perfume was restoking the fire she just put out.

"Yes," she whimpered.

"What do you want now?"

"Touch me."

He had intentionally made sure that only his lips were touching hers.

Arousing his wife to show a more assertive side of her personality was arousing his own instincts to conquer. He started counting his drumming heartbeats to squash the desire to fulfill the need that was apparent in her expression.

"Here?" Shade laid a gentle hand on her breast. "Or here?" He moved his hand to the apex of her thighs, making the minimum contact before returning his hand to the bar by her side.

"There."

A muffled sob had his tongue swirling against hers.

"Which one? On your tit or your pussy?" His voice became ruthless. "Tell me."

"My pussy."

"Tell me."

Becoming frustrated, she dug her fingernails into his back. "Touch my pussy!"

Biting back laughter, he immediately brought his hand to her pussy. Rubbing the silken flesh, he felt her sudden inhale as she stopped breathing.

"Is this how you want me to touch you?"

"Harder."

"I can't hear you."

"Do it harder!"

He made his fingers firmer, giving her the friction she was craving.

"Is that better?"

"God, yes!" she whimpered.

With practiced fingers, he had her ass writhing on the bar top. Fucking her mouth with his tongue, he let his fingers breach the opening of her pussy. Driving a lone finger through the creamy flesh without hesitation to finger fuck her into an unrelenting desire that was taking its own toll on him.

Removing his fingers from her pussy, he rested his slick hand on her thigh.

"Don't stop!"

He moved his hand back to her, increasing the pace of his fingers inside of her. He could feel from her shudders that she was close to coming.

Again, he stopped.

"Don't do that!" she yelled at him, hitting him on the back with her small fist.

He went back to her pussy, only giving her three glides of his finger before stopping.

Grabbing his wrist, she put it back where she wanted it.

This time, she was only given one glide before he halted within her.

"Shade!"

It was hard to resist her pleas, but he did, wanting nothing more than to satisfy the desire that was tearing Lily apart into little fragments of need.

"Are you hurting, Angel?"

"Yes!" She grabbed his arm, trying to get him moving inside her again.

Shade ignored her efforts.

"Are you sure?"

"Yes!" she screamed out.

"Is this fucking real enough for you?" he gritted out, nearly at his own breaking point.

Her face crumpled as she started to cry. "Yes!"

Satisfied, he pried her hand off his arm and removed his hand from her pussy to jerkily lift her off the bar. At the same time, he sat down on the barstool nearest to him.

Meeting her eyes, he held her poised over his cock before slamming her down on him. Her long, black hair tumbled around them, forming a cocoon around their faces.

He swiveled the barstool until his back was braced on the counter as he raised and lowered Lily over him as she held on tightly to his shoulders.

Shade released her waist, stretching his arms on the sides of the bar, showing her that she was strong enough to keep herself from falling.

Shaking her hair back, violet eyes gazed at him with such a wealth of love that he knew soul deep he would never be able to go back to the shadowed world he existed in before her.

"I love you. There isn't a day that goes by that I don't thank God for you. And Angel, you know I'm not a praying man." His head fell back, trying to fight back the climax that was so close. He wanted to throw her on the counter and slam his dick into her so hard she would have no doubt it wasn't a fucking illusion.

Her uninhibited movements had him restraining himself from gathering her closer to him. It was hard not to shield her in his protective arms to keep her from falling, but Lily needed to realize she had grown strong enough to fly, that she was no longer the little girl terrorized by her mother.

Her movements became wilder and faster. Her breasts heaved with her exertion as she bounced on his lap. It was only when she stopped shaking, then sank down on his chest limply did he move.

Holding her, he slid off the stool, carrying her to the closest table. Laying her on the top, he stepped between her thighs, driving his cock inside her pussy. His hips plunged his dick as high as he could go before pulling out and ramming inside of her again.

"Don't you ever say this isn't fucking real again." He fiercely made love to his wife, driving her into another orgasm that had her legs wrapping around his waist, the tips of her heels stabbing him in the ass with each lunge.

"I won't."

Shade gripped her jaw in a firm hand. "The only crazy about you is that you love me."

Twining his fingers through hers, he pinned them beside her head on the table as he pounded into her body, reaching the climax he had been holding back.

"Don't think for one second that, when we get home, I'm not going to punish you for getting into my chest."

His arms gave out as he came, crushing her with his weight. He let the sensations surge through him.

Catching her gaze, Shade didn't hold anything back, letting her see how she affected him.

"There is no other woman that can compare to you. If I live a thousand different lives, not one of them would be worth living without you."

Sitting her up, he gave her a stern glance to stay put as he went to the table to get her coat. Standing in front of her, he held it open for her to slip on. Once she did, he closed it and buttoned it for her, attentively pulling her hair out from under the collar.

He dressed himself once he had her covered, then gathered the clothes she removed for his lap dance. He then meticulously straightened the stools and chairs and used a bleach bar rag to clean the counter before taking a wad of bills out of his wallet and putting it in Mick's cash register.

"I told you I paid Mick and gave him a tip," she reminded him as he came out from behind the counter.

Hooking an arm around her shoulders, he pulled her into the warmth of his body, bracing her for what he was about to tell her. "How long did you say you rented the bar for?"

"Two hours."

"Don't freak out, but the parking lot is full. Mick is out there trying to keep everyone out."

"How long did I go over?"

"An hour."

Lily buried her face against the side of his chest in embarrassment. "I can't go out there in front of those people!" she wailed. "They'll know what we've been doing!"

"Angel, don't worry about it. Most of them are Last Riders. They know I fuck you all the time."

CHAPTER 9

"Let me out of here! This is violating my constitutional rights!"

Shade heard the yells as he opened the metal door to the holding cells.

"Let me out!"

Closing the door behind him, Shade walked to the cell at the end to see the red-faced man who was trying to squeeze his face through the jail bars. His furious eyes glared hatefully at him when he caught sight of Shade.

"Motherfucker, I knew you were behind this. When I get out of here, I'll own the fucking Last Riders."

Shade gave him a mocking twist of his lips. "You think so?"

"I know so." Harvey shook the jail door. "I'm going to sue you fuckers for every dime you own! You'll have to use leaves to wipe your asses when I'm done with you. I've been stuck in here for two days. I haven't even been given my phone call."

"Your appointed lawyer hasn't shown yet?" Shrugging, he

studied the man who should be kissing the ground that he was still breathing.

"You know he hasn't!"

"How am I supposed to know that? Knox is the sheriff, not me. I just stopped by to see him when he told me you were here. Knox isn't even the one who arrested you. Greer Porter did. Knox is just doing his job. You're the one who's responsible for driving drunk and assaulting Greer."

"Because he pulled me over for no reason."

"You blew over 1.0. Not only that but you had an open container sitting next to you, and it's what? Your third offense." Clicking his tongue against the roof of his mouth, Shade gave him a grim smile. "You're the one that fucked up. I didn't pour those drinks down your throat."

Harvey shook the bars. When that didn't work, he reached out, trying to grab him. "You gave me that money—"

"I gave you money to buy a hamburger, not to get drunk," Shade cut him off. "You could have bought yourself the burger and took the change and spent it on your kid or your woman. Don't blame me because you're a dick."

Walking away, Harvey's curses filled the holding cells. Instead of leaving like Harvey thought he was, though, Shade picked up a metal folding chair and carried it back to sit down in front of Harvey's cell. Shade sat silently watching Harvey until the man ran out of steam.

"You finished?"

"Motherfucker!"

"You said that numerous times. Are you ready to shut the fuck up so I can talk? I don't give a damn what you call me, or how many times you tell me how to fuck myself. Personally, I think you're a stupid son of a bitch, but hey, if you want to sit here and trade insults all day, I can do that, or you can shut the fuck up and listen to me. Again, that's your choice. Hopefully, you'll make a wiser decision this time."

The cursing stopped.

"Cool." Shade leaned forward, watching for the reaction that he had bet Viper he was going to get.

"Who is it?"

Harvey's mouth flapped open, then closed before he warily moved away from the cell door. "Who is what?"

"Really?" Shade was disappointed the stupid fucker was making it easy for him. "Is this how you want to play it?"

"I don't know what you're talking about!"

Sarcastically, Shade folded one leg over the other, casually leaning back as if he was indifferent about being lied to.

"I don't!"

"Harvey, you're either the stupidest son of bitch in the world or someone paid you to antagonize me. Now, we both know you're stupid as fuck, which is how you almost fooled me for a second. But you're smart enough to get a free ride ever since you were fired, so why would you bite the hand that fed you just to take a stab at smearing Lily's good name just to blackmail me."

"I—"

"Shut up. I'm talking." Shade continued speaking coldly as if Harvey hadn't interrupted him. "You worked with me at the factory. You knew I wasn't going to pay. Like I said, you almost fooled me. You wouldn't be the first one to file a bogus lawsuit against the company or try to extort money from one of us. You almost had me. The thing is, fuckwad, unlike you, I love my woman, but the one thing you forgot about is that son of yours. I remember how much you showed that picture around when he was born. That boy, you give a damn about."

Shade gave him a satisfied smile when Harvey went pale.

"You wouldn't hurt my baby."

"No, I wouldn't. You are right about that. It's not the kid's fault that you're his father." Shade reached into the pocket of his jacket and took out a cell phone. Sliding it through the bars, he gave it to Harvey.

"Call Nicole. There're only two minutes on it. Make it short."

Harvey took the cell phone into his shaking hand. They stared at each other as it rang.

"She's not answering."

"No, she's not, and she's not going to."

"What did you do? If you hurt my—"

"I haven't touched them. I just made it possible that they'll never see your fucking worthless ass again."

"Where is he!"

"Your son? He's with his mother, of course."

"You just can't make them disappear. I have rights as his father!"

"Who says you're the father? Nicole certainly hasn't. You told her to keep your name off the birth certificate so she could get a check. If I believe correctly, her exact words to the public assistant worker were that she didn't know who the father was, that it was a one-night stand, and she had no way of finding out who it was."

"That's bullshit. DNA will prove he's mine!"

"You have to find them first, then you'll have to find a lawyer. How are you going to afford that? You don't even have a job. Even if the boy comes out as yours, you're going to have to reimburse the state for the medical bills and child support. In case you don't know, that's fraud."

"They can't prove that I knew. I could have just found out."

"Damn, you need to look over your head." Shade pointed at the camera angled at Harvey's cell. "Our conversation is being recorded. You knew that baby was yours, and you deliberately had Nicole lie. Like I said, that's fraud."

Harvey tried to reach through the bars for him.

Shade gave him an evil smirk. "You don't know how much I wish you could reach me. The only reason you're still breathing is because I have a better use for you instead of being worm food."

Harvey looked at the camera again.

"Don't worry that Knox is still listening. This part won't be a part of the tape that he hands over to the D.A."

Harvey slumped against the cell door. "What do you want?"

"I want to know who paid you to use Lily to get to me?"

When Harvey started to open his mouth, Shade could tell he was going to lie.

"Before you start lying your ass off, let me stop you. I know for a fact that new trailer you put a down payment on last month didn't come from you working. Nor did you make it selling pot or drugs on the side. Greer Porter knows who's selling what and where, so don't bother going that route. You have two options. Only two. Tell me what I want to know or you're never going to see that son of yours again. You will be sitting in this cell until hell freezes over."

"He said he'd kill me if I told."

"Give me a name."

"I don't have one." Harvey woodenly went to sit on the side of his bed.

"How did he give you the money?"

"It was sitting in the seat of my truck when I came out one morning."

"How much did he give you?"

"Ten grand. Told me that he'd give me the same amount every month that you don't go back to Nashville."

"How did he contact you?"

"He called me."

"How'd he get your number?"

"I don't know. I didn't ask. At first, I thought it was a joke until he gave me the money. I was so broke I really didn't care. I just wanted the money. Can I go home now? I told you everything."

Shade stared at him unfeelingly. "You don't have a home anymore. Didn't they tell you? Whoever hooked your trailer to the gas line did a shit job. There's nothing left. I hope you had insurance. If you didn't, sorry about your luck."

Harvey's jumped off the bunk and within three steps his body hit the cell bars so hard they shook.

Shade gave a smile that belied how angry he was.

Unafraid of the hand that was reaching for him, he stood and struck out his hand, grabbing the top of Harvey's prison jumpsuit, then smashing his face into the iron bars.

"You little shit, I would have paid for that trailer in full and gave you ten grand a month if you had come to me. All you had to do was tell me someone wanted you to harass Lily to keep me here and I would have taken care of you." Shade pushed him back, then smashed his face into the bars again like a rag doll. "Doing the right thing never occurred to you, because you're a piece of shit. I hope you took plenty of pictures of your son, because he'll be grown before you see him again." Smashing him into the bars one more time, he flung him backward.

Shade didn't even wait for Harvey to hit the floor before striding away.

"Wait! You can't just leave me here!"

"Watch me."

Shade raised his fist to knock on the door for Knox to let him out when Harvey broke.

"Tell me what to do and I'll do it!"

Shade paused at the shouted plea.

"I'll do anything you want."

Shade moved back to the cell.

"You're useless to me. Whoever paid you will have seen Greer bring you outside. He'll know you talked to me.

"When I leave here, I'm going to the diner and will make sure I drop a hint or two that I'm going to pay for a lawyer for you. Let's hope whoever paid you isn't a man of his word. If so, you're fucked."

"He'll kill me."

"Why are you afraid of someone you don't know? You know me, and you weren't afraid to take me on."

"That's different. He promised to protect me. He said he would have my back."

"You can't be that stupid."

"I fucked up! Don't you think I know it? Just tell me what you want me to do to fix this and I'll do it!"

"You think you can take back the way you treated my wife? That you threatened to show fake nude pictures of her to a community that Lily loves? I could have turned the other cheek if you had just kept the target on me, but you didn't. You used Lily as a pawn, well aware of how much she means to me. Those are consequences you're going to regret for the rest of your shitty life. I'll make sure of that. Until I decide to bring your misery to an end, you're going to do exactly what I want for exactly how long I want. Do you get my meaning? If not, it's fair game who's going to kill you first: me or whoever the fuck paid you."

Shade turned and started walking away again.

"Aren't you going to get me out?"

"No, I'm going to go have lunch at the diner with Greer. You're going to sit here until I make sure everyone in town knows who's footing your legal bill."

"You'll get me killed for being a snitch!"

Shade heartlessly knocked on the door, wanting out. "That's the plan."

CHAPTER 10

S hade crossed the street to the diner. Entering, he flicked his eyes over the busy restaurant, spotting the men he was looking for.

Taking the chair next to Rider, he met Viper's grim expression with a curt nod.

"Did you tell Harvey that The Last Riders would be taking care of his legal bills?" The president of The Last Riders made no attempt to keep his voice low.

"I did. He was crying with gratitude when I left him."

"The Last Riders always take care of their own." Viper motioned for the approaching waitress to refill his and Rider's cups, his comment placing a target on Harvey's back. "You want a cup?"

"Yes."

The waitress left to get him a cup after refilling the two on the table. They remained silent until the waitress returned, then moved on to wait on her other customers.

"Did you ask Greer if there was anyone new in town?" Viper asked the question so only the ones at their table could hear. Shade did the same.

"He said, *take your pick*. That the town is full of strangers for Dalton and T.A.'s wedding."

"Whoever it is obviously sees you as the main obstacle of getting to Ginny."

Both he and Viper glanced at Rider, who was spooning the last of his chocolate sundae into his mouth.

Shrugging, he gave them an arrogant smirk. "I told you that being a clown has its advantages."

"I wouldn't be so smug." Viper shoved his coffee cup away. "When he can't get rid of Shade, he'll go for you. I'm actually surprised he didn't go for you first. Jo is as accessible as Lily."

Rider continued eating, unperturbed by Viper's warning. "No one comes to her house unless it's one of The Last Riders to visit us, and she only works on our vehicles. No one gets close enough to her to make trouble. Even if they tried, it wouldn't work with Wizard watching her and the baby when I'm gone."

Shade clenched his hands over the spoon by his coffee cup. Rider had done a better job of protecting Jo than he had Lily.

The realization felt as if someone had ripped his chest open and removed his heart with one jerk. Harvey had slipped through the crack, one that would never be accessible again.

"I won't be going back to Nashville. One of the other brothers will have to take my place. I'm done. I'll do what I can here, but count me out for anything more."

Shade starkly waited for Viper's and Rider's reactions.

All the brothers were good, but the methodical thinking that only another killer could outsmart like he and Rider would leave Ginny vulnerable.

"I want to help Ginny, but Jo and I being apart continuously so I can take Shade's place is a no-go. We want it over as much as you do, but there is no fucking way I'm going to be gone month after month. Wizard can take Shade's place. I'll find another brother to watch Jo when I'm gone."

"Wizard is good enough to handle anything that fucker throws at him," Shade agreed.

"Being good isn't getting the job done. I'm tired of this bullshit. I made Wizard the new president in Ohio for a reason. I need him always there, not every other month. I can't send Moon back to Ohio; he makes more trouble than he's worth, and he's just as bad when I send him to Nashville. Kaden has already said he doesn't want him back."

Shade had tried to keep Moon away from Kaden's back-up singers without success. He was catnip to women, and he didn't have a problem taking full advantage of every opportunity given.

The men sat, each lost in their own thoughts as to how to best keep Ginny safe while at the same time returning to their normal lives.

"We all know who you should send." Shade was the first one to voice his thoughts aloud.

Viper shook his head. "He won't do it. I've already asked."

"Don't ask. Order him."

"I agree," Rider inserted. "Gavin could shake the tree and put Ginny's stalker off guard."

"Telling Gavin anything is difficult. He just goes to his room or rides off."

Shade was tired of tiptoeing around a touchy subject. Nothing was going to change where Gavin's behavior was concerned until the right person spurred Gavin into giving a damn again. That person was sitting next to him.

"I'm glad you agree. You go tell him."

Rider dropped his spoon into the parfait glass. "No, you go talk to him."

Shade stared at him pitilessly. "The only one that could

ever get Gavin to do something he didn't want to do was you. It has to be you."

"I said no."

"Then you might as well move to Nashville, because Ginny won't move back here until she's sure Willa and the other women are safe. She's already said she won't go back to Queens City when Mouth2Mouth's contract is up in four months. She's searching for a new place to live without telling anyone her intentions. She's tired of looking over her shoulder."

"How do you know?"

"Penni. She thinks that she'll cut and run as soon as the contract is up, if not before then."

"Fuck," Rider growled. "She'll run right into the stalker's hands if she does."

"She's willing to take that chance to protect the people she loves."

"You're not just saying that to get me to talk to Gavin?"

"Get Knox to show you her checking account. For the last two weeks, she's been taking out large of sums of money that she was saving for a house. She's hoarding her cash so she can disappear."

"Fuck me." Rider threw his napkin on the table. "I'll take this month again. I'll come up with a plan—"

"Talk to Gavin."

"He won't talk to me anymore than he does to Viper. The only ones he talks to is Colton, Peyton, and Diamond."

Shade could tell from Rider's stubborn expression that he wouldn't try to sway Gavin into helping.

He was tired of beating his head against a stone wall to get Rider to open up about the real problem between him and Gavin.

The club was going to have to solve this problem themselves. Lily was his main priority. He wasn't going to give someone another chance to use her as a pawn, despite how much he wanted to protect Ginny.

The stalker had accomplished his goal.

Viper picked up the ticket that the waitress left on the table as they rose. Outside, the men were getting on their motorcycles when they saw Greer Porter crossing the street from the jailhouse.

Shade was tempted to start his bike and ride away, especially since Greer's grumpy attitude always gave him a headache. Already having to talk to him once today, he was determined to stay quiet and let Viper handle the obnoxious asshole.

"Afternoon, Viper."

"Greer."

"I remembered something after Shade left. He asked if I noticed anyone new around town. I told him that, with that fancy pants that T.A. married, newcomers have been in and out for the last couple of weeks."

"So?"

"About a month ago, Knox asked me to drop a part off to Jo for the motorcycle she was working on for him. As I was turning in her driveway, I saw a black Xterra sitting across the street. I thought someone had parked there to go hunting in the woods. They had backed in far enough I almost didn't see them."

Rider's usually carefree countenance underwent a dramatic change. "Who was it?"

"How in the fuck am I supposed to know? I was going to check it out after I dropped the part to Jo, but it was gone when I came back."

"You should have checked it first!" Rider shouted.

Shade shook his head at Rider, trying to get his attention. It was too late. He had offended Greer by yelling at him, and you didn't want to offend Greer. It just made him a bigger ass.

Greer gave Rider a *fuck you* with his finger, then started walking across the street.

"Wait, Greer! Ignore him. He's just worried about Jo and Crux," Viper called him back.

Greer gave Rider the evil eye as he returned. "He yells at me again, that shotgun in my truck is going to do some damage."

Rider clenched his handlebars. Shade knew it was killing him to do what he was going to have to do next.

"Sorry," Rider mumbled.

Greer gave Rider his patented shit-eating grin that more than one brother wanted to stomp off his face.

"Like I said before I was *rudely* interrupted, it was gone when I came back. I figured they were just out hunting or looking for ginseng. That part of the woods has several places they can dig up the root. It won't be the first time I've seen people coming out of there with their baskets filled."

"Do you think that's what they were doing?"

"I thought so, but after I talked to Shade, I remembered something else."

"What?" Rider snapped when Greer didn't explain what he remembered right away.

Shade knew it was a bad sign when the mercenary Porter hitched his gun holster farther up his waist. He wasn't disappointed.

"I haven't been able to take Holly out to a good steak dinner for a while. King won't let me back in his restaurant."

"I'll talk to him," Rider ground out.

"You do that. Of course, even if he does, I couldn't exactly afford one of those fancy dinners anyway."

Shade had to look away before he burst out laughing at

the sight of Rider trying to keep himself from strangling Greer.

"It'll be my treat."

"I enjoy a couple of beers with my dinner."

Steam was practically coming out from Rider's collar.

"Order whatever you want. It'll be my pleasure."

Shade thought Rider had gone overboard with the pleasure bit, but he stayed out of the negotiations. His wallet had taken the hit too many times when he needed Greer's help. Rider could fork over his own cold hard cash for the information.

"Naturally, I can't take my woman out not looking my best. I'm going to need a haircut."

"Naturally, I'll take care of that, too. Give Knox the bill, and I'll reimburse you. Anything else?"

Greer hitched his gun belt up again. "Now that you mention it, Bubba got fired from the bread store. He could use a job. I'd be much obliged. Jessie's cousin is about to eat us out of house and home because he doesn't want to tell his pa he was fired."

Shade was about to say *fuck no* to that demand when Rider answered before he could.

"Tell him to come to the factory tomorrow, and I'll make sure we find a job for him."

Finally satisfied that he had the last concession out of them, he offered the information he held back.

"I remembered the Xterra had a sticker on the bumper. It was one of those that Muller puts on his rental cars. I already called Muller's; they'll have a list of names of those that rented cars out that day waiting for you."

Greer had done most of the work for them.

"Thanks, Greer." Rider begrudgingly forced the words out.

Greer shrugged. "I would have given the information for

free if you hadn't yelled at me. Next time, mind your manners."

The three men watched the middle Porter walk away with varying degrees of irritation.

Shade couldn't hide his laughter any longer.

"I tried to warn you," he goaded Rider's anger even more. Rider couldn't stand being outsmarted.

Rider's hand was shaking as he started his motorcycle. "I had a horse when I was growing up. It was so mean no one could ride it. It bit anyone that came too close. One day, it took a chunk out of my father's hand. It took sixteen stitches. He was so mad that he shot it when he came home from the emergency room. I couldn't understand then why. Now I do. If Greer pulls that crap on me again, he's going to be crossing over that rainbow bridge the same way that horse did."

CHAPTER 11

"Mom! Clint keeps smushing my lunchbox."

"Clint, leave your brother's things alone." Lily ran a comb through her younger son's hair. "I told you that I packed you the same things in your lunchbox that I did John's."

She smiled as the three-year-old fidgeted under her hand, attempting to reach for the dark blue lunch bag on the counter. He was always trying to outdo his big brother.

"He took the last banana," Clint complained, standing on his toes to reach for it again.

Lily pushed the bag farther back, knowing it was bothering John. "He didn't take it. I put in it his bag. You don't like bananas."

"I do, too," he argued stubbornly.

"He can have the banana if he wants it, Mom. I can take the apple," John amiably tried to put an end to Clint's temper tantrum.

"You'll both eat what your mother put in your bags."

"Yes, sir," John acknowledged their father's order, going into the living room to get his things ready for school.

73

Lily watched with mirth-filled eyes as different emotions chased across Clint's face as he debated obeying like John or trying to argue.

"Now, Clint."

It was a short-lived battle.

"Yes, sir."

Lily held Shade's coffee as Clint ran into the living room, making a face when a second later she heard the beginning of another argument.

Her husband gave her a kiss before carrying his coffee out to stop the brewing fight.

Happy that he was dealing with the squabble, she finished zipping the lunch bags closed, including her own, before going into the other room when she saw a text message lighting the front of her phone.

"Beth is ready." Handing John his lunch bag, she gave him a quick kiss on his cheek. "I love you."

"Love you, too."

Holding the door open, she watched as John ran outside where Beth was waiting to drive him to school with Noah and Chance. She would drop off Clint at his preschool before going to work at the thrift store.

Closing the door, she turned to see Clint sitting on the couch, snuggled next to Shade. Both boys adored their father. She had no doubt of their love for her, but they were their father's sons.

John was like a miniature replica of his father. He wasn't as outgoing as Clint, who had more of his aunt Penni's personality than either of his parents. He also shared the same features as Shade.

She worshiped her sons, but she ached for a little girl.

When she was pregnant with Clint, they expected a girl. They had even decorated the nursery in frilly pink. They were both surprised with another son instead.

"Can I stay home with you today?"

"Not today. I have to work at the factory. If Jessie gives me a good report for the rest of the week, you can stay home with me on Friday."

"Yipee!" Clint jumped into his father's lap to hug him tightly.

Lily put on her coat and buttoned it closed. "If you don't want to go to daycare, you can spend the day with me at the store," she offered, putting on her gloves. "You can help me unpack boxes."

"That's okay. I'll go to school." Clint hopped up to put on the jacket that she held out for him.

Lily tried to hide her disappointment. "You used to beg to spend the day with me."

"It's my turn to pick out which book Ms. Jessie will read before naptime."

Resisting the urge to ask him again, she slid his stocking cap over his black hair.

Raising her eyes when she finished, she flushed at Shade's perceptive stare that easily read how she wanted Clint to spend the day with her.

She gathered her and Clint's things together as Clint waited by the door. She missed Shade when he was away from her, wanting to spend extra time with Clint because he couldn't understand why his father had to be away. She had even been letting John stay up an extra hour at night to lay beside him on his bed, just talking to him about whatever he wanted.

With everything gathered in her hands, she went to give Shade a goodbye kiss. Bending over, she gave a quick kiss and was about to pull away when he brought his hand to her neck, holding her in place. The kiss he gave her was anything but quick.

He parted her lips with a sweep of his tongue, diving

75

inside to swirl around provocatively. She was gasping when he released her.

"I have to train a new employee this morning, but how about I stop by and take you out to lunch?"

She happily stared down at him. "I would love that. Who did you hire?" she asked curiously as she walked to the door.

"Bubba Hayes."

Lily stopped short of the door, stunned.

"You hired Bubba!" Her husband had just made her day. "I love Bubba!" Going back to her husband, she gave him a big hug. Shade, on the other hand, looked like she had ruined his.

"Love is a strong a word to use for a man you don't know."

Lily lovingly rolled her eyes at her husband's jealous tone.

"I know Bubba quite well. I've been so upset since I found out he was fired. I think he was fired because he donated the bread for the Thanksgiving and Christmas baskets. The rolls he made weren't stale either. He made hundreds of them. And you've met him several times."

"I've seen him at the bread store," he agreed.

Lily looked over her shoulder toward Clint before turning back to Shade. "He volunteers at Christmas to dress up for the kids." She wagged her eyebrows to get her meaning across.

"He's San—"

"Shh!" She happily hugged Shade again. "See? You love Bubba, too!"

"I wouldn't say *love*." Shade was beginning to look even more jealous.

"Oh, you will the more you get to know him." She waved off his jealousy, then gave him a stern look. "Be *nice* to him."

"I'm always nice."

"You're polite when you want, but I want you to be nice

to Bubba. Please. You'll hurt his feelings if you say something mean to him. He's very sensitive."

Feeling indecisive, she didn't know if she should stay or go. "Perhaps I should take Clint to daycare and come back. I could introduce Bubba to everyone and make him feel more comfortable."

"Lily, go to work. I'll be *nice*."

She looked at him skeptically.

"I promise."

"All right, that makes me feel better." Relieved, she went to open the door. "Make sure everyone else is nice to him, okay?"

Shade looked like he had eaten something sour, but he nodded.

The bright sunlight outside lightened her footsteps.

"It's a beautiful day, isn't it?" she chatted to Clint as they walked down the path toward the parking lot.

"It's okay. Mama, do you love me as much as Bubba?"

Lily laid a hand on his shoulder. "I love you more than Bubba."

There was one trait that Clint did inherit from his father. Her son was very possessive about her affections.

"I love Bubba like a friend or like a big brother. You're my baby. You'll always hold a special place in my heart."

"I'm not a baby anymore."

Lily opened the back door of the car for him to climb in, making sure his car seat was securely fastened. Then, after putting their lunch bags in the seat beside him, she got in the front seat.

"No, you're not," she continued the conversation after starting the car.

Waiting until she was on the road toward town, she darted a quick glance in the rearview mirror, still seeing a frown on his forehead.

"No matter how old you get, you'll always be my baby. Just like John is. When I say *baby*, it doesn't mean a little baby; it means, despite how old you get, I'll always love you the same way I did the first time when the doctor handed you to me."

Reassured, Clint began talking about which book he was going to pick for naptime. Lily listened indulgently as she drove.

Reaching town, she came to a stop at a red light. Attentively, she glanced in the rearview mirror again at Clint as he talked, seeing two motorcycles come up behind her SUV as she waited for the light to change.

Recognizing the bikers, she waved at Wizard and Nickel. Neither men responded, their dark helmet guards concealing their features.

When the light turned green, she saw them following her until she reached Jessie's daycare. Then they turned into the parking lot of the diner.

It only took a few minutes to take Clint inside, where Jessie was busy getting the rest of her students settled. When she came out, both Nickel and Wizard were still sitting outside. Wondering why they weren't going inside the diner, she drove to the thrift store.

She juggled her lunch that she no longer needed since Shade was coming to take her out—she would save it until tomorrow—and a small bag of canned food she picked up on sale.

Turning the lights on as she walked through the door, she turned to close the door and saw Wizard and Nickel sitting at the end of the parking lot.

Confused as to why they would be sitting there, she was going to ask them, but the phone ringing had her rushing to the counter.

It was an hour before she had time to catch her breath,

dealing with phone calls and three customers coming in who she fielded questions on how to qualify for their services.

She was hanging coats when she remembered Wizard and Nickel.

Looking out the window, she saw they were no longer there. Thinking she was making a big deal out of nothing, that the men seeming to be watching over her had been her imagination, she went back to work.

"The whole world doesn't revolve around you, Lily," she mocked herself out loud.

She was bagging clothes that were in too bad of shape to be of any use to anyone when the bell over the door rang.

Fear raced up her spine and her blood went cold like ice over a lake when she saw the man who came inside, walking toward the counter. She reached out for the phone to call Knox, but then her courage kicked in. If she could be brave enough to dance in front of Shade like she had never believed herself capable of and order him around, then she could handle Harvey.

"Out."

He stopped in the middle of the store. "I just want to talk—"

"You have nothing to say that I want to hear. The services of this store are no longer available to you or Nicole. I no longer feel comfortable being in the store with you, and I requested to Nicole that she no longer send you. Since you are here, none of the church services will be accessible." Prepared to defend herself physically and verbally, she was stunned when Harvey didn't attempt to move closer.

"I can understand. I came to apologize for my behavior. Nicole has taken the baby and left me. She moved away, so you won't be seeing us again. You don't know how bad I feel about how I treated you. I'm sorry."

Lily didn't relax her guard, moving her hand within reach

of an iron curtain rod. If he took one step nearer to her, she would brain him.

Mutely, she watched him leave, relieved she would never have to see him again. She only hoped that Nicole found a more loving environment to raise her son in.

Relieved that he was gone, she picked up the iron curtain rod to take it to the home section when she bumped into a hard body.

She gave a startled scream of terror, raising the rod to hit the man who had frightened her.

"It's me, Lily!" Pastor Dean barely managed to catch the rod before she could hit him with the heavy metal.

"You scared the death out of me!" Shaking, she dropped the rod to the floor as she started shaking at how close she had come to hurting him. "When did you come down?"

Was that why Harvey apologized?

The feel-good moment when she had stood up to Harvey began to fade.

"I just got here." Puzzled, Pastor Dean stared back at her sharp question. "Are you all right? I needed my old laptop that's in the storeroom, but I can stay if something is wrong."

At his innocent response, she shook her doubts off. "I'm fine. I'm just being ridiculous."

"Are you sure?"

"I'm sure."

Nodding, Pastor Dean went to the storeroom as she finished bagging the over-worn clothes. She was tying the bag when he came back with the laptop.

"I'm going back to my office. If you need anything, just text me, okay?"

"I'm fine. I'm sorry I almost hit you."

"I should have told you that I was here. Next time, I'll be more careful about walking around you." Winking, he went up the steps to the church.

Lily used the lull to straighten the racks and process new clothes. She had just finished when Shade arrived.

"You ready?" he asked when he saw her coming out between two large racks.

"Yes." Going to him, she reached up to give him a kiss. "I just need to get my purse and put the sign out that I'll be back in an hour."

Taking the sign out from underneath the cash register, she remained unmoving as he expectantly waited.

"Harvey came in today."

His piercing blue eyes settled on hers. "Why was he here? Did you call Knox or Lucky to stay with you?"

Lily observed his reaction carefully. "No. I didn't have to. He apologized and left. It took two minutes."

"He apologized? Good, then I don't have to kill him." He said it in a joking manner, but she wasn't quite sure he was.

"Did he come in here to apologize to me because you made him?"

"Why would you think that?"

"Because his face was in bad shape. He looked like he had been in a fight. Did you get in a fight with him?"

"I did not get in a fight with him."

"He looked beaten up."

"I did not beat him up."

"Are you sure?"

"Lily, I would know if I did or not."

"Did you make him come in and apologize to me?"

Shade raised a brow. "You know me better than that. I don't want him near you, whether apologizing or not."

That she believed.

"I have to admit, I'm relieved. Maybe he's turning over a new leaf because Nicole and the baby moved away."

"She finally got a brain?"

81

"Apparently." Taking his arm, she reached up to give him another kiss. "I'm glad you restrained yourself with Harvey."

Locking the store behind them after she put the sign up, she remained holding his arm as they walked toward the diner.

"How is Bubba's first day going?"

"His is going good. Mine, on the other hand, has been a disaster."

"Why?"

"Because you made me be nice instead of firing him after he broke the popcorn machine."

"You weren't mean to him, were you?"

"Me? Mean? I don't know how to be mean," he joked, holding the door open for her.

"For having such a bad day, you seem like you're in a good mood."

His good humor was infectious. Smiling up at him, she thought again how much she loved her husband. He was so sweet and kind when he wanted to be.

"I look at it like this: it can't get worse."

CHAPTER 12

Two hours later, Shade was cursing himself for saying his day couldn't get worse. It had gone to hell in a handbasket.

It had become apparent that he tempted fate when he returned from lunch to have Jewell waiting for him. Bubba had gotten into an argument with another worker who had stormed out, threatening to sue The Last Riders for hiring a maniac.

Looking up from the desk when he heard the door open, he saw Jewell come in, shutting the door, then furiously putting her hands on her hips.

"Bubba broke the lift on the delivery truck."

"How in the fuck did he do that?"

"He overloaded it. Several of the packages were damaged and will have to be repacked. We'll be lucky if we're able to get them out today. It'll also put us behind tomorrow. Fire him."

"I can't. I told you that Rider hired him as a favor for Greer."

"The way he's going, Bubba will send the factory in bankruptcy within a month."

"I can't fire him. Lily found out that Bubba started today. She *loves* him."

"What fuckwad told her? I'll kick—"

"I did."

"We are so screwed!" she shrieked at him.

"Calm down. I'll text Train and get the lift repaired. You call Nickel and Moon. Tell them, if they get those packages repacked, I'll give them a bonus."

Jewell cooled down. "That's not going to solve the underlying problem. What are we going to do about Bubba?"

"I'll find another job for him to do. One that doesn't involve machinery."

"Good luck, because if he breaks one more thing, I'm going to break him." She picked up a stress ball that was sitting on her desk.

"Put that back," he ordered her, knowing she wasn't taking it to relieve herself of the frustration of dealing with Bubba's mishaps.

"Come on. I won't hurt him too bad. His talking about little green men is driving me nuts. I just wanted to shut him up until quitting time."

"Put it back."

"He won't even let me put him on payroll. He wants cash."

"Then give him cash. Lay it back down. If you hurt him, he'll tell Lily. Then she'll get upset, and then I'll get upset. Do you want me to get upset?"

Jewell laid the ball back down.

"Whatever you find him to do, make sure it's where I don't hear about those fucking green men again."

"I'll have a talk with him."

"The sooner, the better."

He winced when she stormed out of the office, slamming the door.

Opening the drawer by his side, he took out a bottle of ibuprofen. He started to take two, then decided on taking three. Texting Train next, he asked for him to come fix the lift, then he texted Razer. Satisfied when both answers were yes, he settled back in the office chair and resumed working on the inventory that needed to be reordered.

When the door was slammed open again, he looked up, glad he had taken the extra pill.

Leaning back in the chair, he crossed his arms, waiting for Gavin to tell him why he was so angry.

"Viper wants me to take over watching Ginny." Placing his hands on the desk, he towered over Shade threateningly. "Find someone else."

"No." Shade stayed still. He didn't want to get in a physical fight with Gavin, but the fucker needed a wake-up call, and he was tired of pussy-footing around him. "All the brothers have been carrying your weight long enough. Everyone in the club pulls their own weight. It's time you started pulling yours again."

"Then I'll start working in the factory or taking turns in the security room."

"I don't need you to work in the factory. We're overloaded right now anyway. I don't need you working the security room—Rider and I can take care of that. What we can't do anymore is leave our women and children unprotected while you run around on your bike, shirking your responsibilities."

"She's not my responsibility."

"She is now. If you don't do it, then Rider or I will go. If something happens to Lily or Jo, do you want that *responsibility?*"

"No," he answered reluctantly.

"Then I guess you'll be packing your bags."

"I won't do it!" With a swipe of his large hand, the contents on the desk were wiped clean.

Shade still didn't move.

"That was unnecessary, and you will clean this mess. If that computer is broken, you will buy another one."

"Go to hell!"

It was hard, but Shade managed to control his expression. The tortured expression on Gavin's face was difficult to take without caving in and letting Gavin off the hook.

"Ginny's a sweet kid. You'll like her."

Gavin used a booted foot to kick the computer against the wall.

"If I couldn't protect myself, how in the fuck can I protect her?" he shouted at him.

"You're older and wiser. No one could get past you before. You were the first one that saw through Rider. You knew what I was capable of after meeting me for two minutes and warned Viper. You saw through Delara and warned Rider. If you hadn't realized what she was going to do, a lot of soldiers wouldn't have made it back."

Gavin picked up the massive desk and dropped it back down.

Shade had had enough. Something bad had happened for Gavin to react so strongly. He was so furious he had lost his grip on reality.

Shade didn't give him an opportunity to react, plowing into Gavin so hard he was shoved back against the wall, sending pictures falling.

"What the fuck?" Jewell started rushing in, hearing the sounds of the fight.

"Get out!" Shade yelled at her.

She barely made it out, closing the door again when Shade found himself thrown against the center."

"I'm not going!" Gavin shouted.

Shade took a running jump at him, shoving him down on top of the desk. Pinning him with an arm on his throat, he unmercifully used his weight to cut off his oxygen supply.

"You're fucking going!" Snarling down into his upturned face, Shade made his demands clear.

"I don't know what the fuck set you off, and I don't fucking care! Viper ordered you to go, and you're going to fucking obey his order just like every one of us do! You think you've been through hell?" He pressed down harder. "Your disappearance nearly destroyed Viper! He blamed himself. He still does! Every time he looks at that fucked-up haircut, the scars on your back and wrists, it kills him. I'm fucking sick of watching him pay for your mistake.

"Yes, brother, you made a big one. Own up to it, figure out why you made it, and don't ever make it again!" Shade raised his arm, but only long enough to slam his head down on the desk.

"Now get your ass out of my sight and get your bags packed, or so help me God, I'll tie you up and put you on that fucking plane myself! You fucking got me?" With another head slam, Shade released him.

He moved away from Gavin, expecting the man to jump up and attack him again. He didn't. He just lay there, staring up at the ceiling, blinking, frowning.

Shade was beginning to think he had hurt him by banging his head on the table, but suddenly Gavin staggered off the desk, going for the door.

Shade was surprised when he didn't go to the door, but instead leaned against it face first, his hand on the knob.

"I can't do it."

Shade steeled himself. It wasn't easy, but he wasn't going to pull back and let Gavin get out of going. He already had too many chances to fix himself. It was time to take it out of his hands.

"You can, and you will. Viper trusted you once before when you came to Treepoint to start the factory, even though he wanted you to wait for him," he reminded him heartlessly. "He's trusting you again to do this job for him, and you *will not* let him down this time."

Shade saw him nod his head against the door.

"I won't." Straightening, he opened the door and left, leaving the door open.

Shade walked to the doorway, watching him leave.

"Is he okay?" Jewell asked, coming to his side.

"No," Shade answered. He didn't know if his friend would be okay ever again. Gavin was a broken man. His body and mind still bore the wounds of his torture and always would. Until the wounds both mentally and physically scarred over and they couldn't hurt him anymore, he would continue to battle a non-existent fight.

All his captors were dead. He had no one left to fight except the ones who still existed in his memory. Only when he accepted that truth would Gavin finally be free.

"Do you want me to clean the mess he made?" Jewell volunteered, seeing the destruction behind him.

"No, let Bubba do it. There's nothing left to break."

CHAPTER 13

Lily entered her front door, expecting to see Shade, John, and Clint playing in the living room, waiting for her to get home. The only one there was Shade, sitting on the couch, staring at a dark television set.

She was used to laughter and the raised childish voices, so the silence in the room was deafening.

Taking her coat off, she then hung it up, afraid that something bad had happened from Shade's deadened expression.

"Is something wrong? Has something happened?" Dropping her purse on the chair, she wanted to go to him, but something held her back, sensing that he didn't want to be touched. "Where're the boys?"

"I asked Razer if the boys could stay with him tonight."

"Why?"

"I needed the night away from them. I want you to go spend the night there, too."

Lily bit her trembling lip. Shade had never asked her to spend the night away from him before.

"Did I do something wrong?"

"No, I did." Shade turned his eyes away from the television set to meet hers. "You told me the other day that you're afraid I'll stop loving you. Angel, you should have never loved me in the first place. You have no concept of the man I am. You can't because you're everything I'm not."

"Shade…."

"I'm not kind, I'm not nice, I don't care about anyone but us. How fucked up is that?"

"It's not fucked up. It's why I fell in love with you. I knew you would put our children and me first."

"I haven't put you first since I started watching Ginny. I let that that snot-nosed kid think he could get away with harassing you. I let you doubt yourself again."

"Shade… please don't. All of us have sacrificed to keep Ginny safe. We all voted. We chose to keep her safe, and we have."

"I didn't even realize you were pregnant until we had lunch."

His hoarse voice had her blinking back tears.

"How did you figure it out?"

"You didn't drink coffee for lunch. You always have coffee with your pie. Both times you were pregnant, I knew. This time, I had no fucking clue."

"There was no way you could have. I only found out yesterday. That's why I wanted to spend the day with Clint. I want to spend as much time as I can with them before the baby comes and they have to share me. My men are a little overpossessive."

Shade didn't smile at her attempt of humor.

"Are you angry that I'm pregnant? We talked about having another baby…."

He shook his head at her. "No, I'm not angry at you. I'm sick at what I just did to Gavin."

"What did you do?" she whispered.

"I forced him to take over watching Ginny. Rider and I

will be staying here. We won't be switching out anymore. He didn't want to go."

"If Gavin didn't want to go, he wouldn't have."

"I didn't play nice to make him go."

"I didn't assume you did. This may come as a shock to you, but I know the only ones you play nice to is me and the boys.

"Shade, why do you think I fought falling in love with you? Anyone with half a brain can see you're a dangerous man. I've seen women cross the streets with their children when they see you walking down the sidewalk."

"When you came into the clubhouse that night and saw the party, you should have run farther than back to college. You should have run until you were out of my reach."

"Would it have done me any good?" she asked softly.

"No, because I'm a heartless bastard."

"You're anything but heartless. Are you dangerous? Yes. But heartless, you're not. If you were heartless, you wouldn't haven't waited until I fell in love with you before making love to me. You wouldn't have cared that my mind was screwed up; you would have taken advantage. You didn't. I've watched you leave every other month to protect Ginny, knowing how much you were hurting to leave us. I can count a hundred times, you sacrificed what you wanted to help the others in the club. Not only the club, but also the people in town. No, sometimes you didn't play nice, but you *always*"— she raised her voice vehemently until she was practically yelling at him— "*always* did what you thought was right. I'm never going to believe that you didn't do what was the best thing to do for Gavin, despite how much you wanted to stay here with us. If you truly don't believe it isn't in his best interest, then call him and tell him to come back. If you don't want to leave us here alone anymore, then the boys and I will go to Nashville with you."

"I can't ask you to leave the store. You'll worry yourself sick about the people that depend on you. You'll miss Beth."

"I will, but the boys and I will adjust."

"I won't uproot you and the boys because I'm putting The Last Riders over my family."

"You're not. You wouldn't be uprooting us. Our family isn't tied to any ground. Our family isn't a house you built or possessions. Don't you know how much we love you?" She started plucking at her dress, raising the hem so she could pull it off.

"Angel…."

Letting her dress fall to the floor, she reached behind her to unsnap her bra then slid her panties off.

Shade watched as she picked her dress and undergarments up and laid them neatly on the coffee table in front of him.

Going to the middle of the floor, she stared at him, unashamedly displaying all the love she felt for him in her eyes. "Where you lead, I will always follow."

Sinking down on her knees, keeping her back straight, she kneeled before her husband. Laying her forehead down on the carpet, she stretched her arms before her, submitting to Shade, giving him complete control over her and her life. Not because he was stronger or demanded it, but because she finally understood deep in her soul that Shade's love wasn't going anywhere.

He wasn't going to wake up one day and discover he didn't love her. His love was true and faithful. It didn't harm nor seek to master. It put the control in her hands to follow him. With one word, she could release herself when she wanted to go in her own direction.

Shade's love was steady, strong, enduring. Forever. Like hers.

"Sir, do you want me to go to Beth's?"

Shade gruffly cleared his throat. "No, follow me."

Lily obediently followed behind as he climbed the stairs. Coming to a stop in front of their bed, she waited patiently for his instructions. There was no fear in her for what he would do or ask as he removed his clothes.

She traced his tattoos with her eyes as Shade went to the chest where he kept his toys. There wasn't a piece of skin that wasn't covered with a tattoo. Her husband lived in a shadowed world of his own making. The only time she truly believed he stepped out of the shadows was when he had to protect someone that he cared about or when they were in their bedroom. Then the real Shade came out. Ruthless and unwaveringly, he would drive her over a brink into a realm that she only wanted to find with him.

Finding out that they were expecting a baby and that he hadn't known sooner that Harvey had been pestering her shook him, since they had slipped past his notice. Gavin taking over his job to protect Ginny was just as hard to accept. Shade didn't do a job halfway, and not being able to find the stalker was irritating to Shade's pride. But she knew why he had wanted her to go to Beth's.

The men loved Gavin. They had been in protective mode since he was recovered. That Shade had stepped in and ripped off the shield that everyone had been protecting him with couldn't have been easy. Not only had he exposed Gavin's vulnerably to get what he wanted him to do, but Shade had also exposed his own. He had stepped out of his shadowed world to get Gavin to take the first steps toward healing. Like when he needed to be stern with Clint and John, he'd done what he believed was in the best interest of Gavin.

Being loved by Shade had its advantages and disadvantages. He would always do what was right, no matter how much it hurt, both the person he was trying to help or himself, because intrinsically, Shade was a protector. He had thrown Gavin out of his safe nest so he could fly again. And he would fly again. Shade would see to that, even if he fought him every inch of the way.

He had saved her sanity, giving her wings that she didn't even know how to use.

"I might have been busy the last few days, but I haven't forgotten about the punishment I owe you."

"Punishment?" Perplexed, she took her eyes off Shade's firm behind. "I've been good."

"Did I say you could talk?"

"No, sir." She bowed her head, watching him from underneath her lashes. She waited expectantly for him to open his armoire.

"How did you get in my *locked* chest to take your panties out?"

"I took your keys when you were in the shower." She had known when she did it that there would be punishment when he found out. It was another Valentine's Day present to him.

"You just can't stay out of trouble, can you? First, you steal my keys to take something that belongs to me."

She knew when she spoke it would make her punishment worse. "Technically, they were mine."

Her husband loved it when she pretended to be a brat.

He clicked his tongue at her, closing the first drawer he opened the one on the bottom. Shade took out several items before closing the drawer, then placed them on the bed before he moved to stand in front of her. Crossing his arms over his chest, he studied her.

It was hard not to fidget, but she remained still, knowing it would give him another reason to punish her. Valentine's Day was over; there was no need to go overboard and spoil him.

"I've had a terrible day. I found out I'm having another baby, and my wife had several opportunities to tell me. Had to be *nice* to a man that's trying to put The Last Riders out of business his first day on the job. And then, to put a cherry on top of this clusterfuck of a day, I had an argument with a man I would have rather cut off my right arm for than fight. Do you know which was the most irritating?"

Lily waited until Shade gave her a curt nod before responding.

"Bubba. He's a little out there."

"Angel, he's so out there he's no longer on planet Earth."

Lily had to bite her lip to keep from laughing. He pretty much summed up how everyone in town felt about Bubba. She didn't mention that Bubba's brothers were just as out there as he was. She didn't think Shade would want to hear that. The chance of any of them getting a job from The Last Riders were between nil and non-existent after he spent the day with Bubba.

"Did you know he freaks out when he sees anyone wearing green?"

Again, she waited until he nodded before answering.

"I should have probably mentioned that fact."

"*Probably*," he said sarcastically. "He nearly ripped Rex's head off when he arrived to pick up the orders. Then, because he was so scared of Bubba, he refused to go near the truck and made Bubba load it himself."

"Is he the one that's vertically challenged?" she asked curiously before she could stop herself, regretting it as soon as she did when Shade picked up one of the items on the bed.

"He's short as fuck, and Jewell said that Rex is going to file assault charges and wants physical and mental compensation before he comes back to work."

"Bubba reacts without thinking when he's frightened."

Shade used the handle of his paddle to raise her chin.

"That fucker wasn't scared. You want to know how I could tell?"

Lily tightened her lips, praying to God she wouldn't laugh at Shade's disgruntled expression.

"He wants to be paid only in cash. Now tell me one thing: what color is cash?"

She waited for his nod before answering.

"Green."

"That's right. Fucking green." Shade used the tip of his paddle to turn her around to face the bed. "And I had to put on a smile the whole time instead of firing him because I promised you that I would be fucking *nice*. Get on the bed."

Lifting a knee, she climbed on the bed.

"Stop."

He stopped her at the bottom of the bed, her body barely on the mattress. Unable to see him in the position, butterflies fluttered in the pit of her stomach, anticipating the crack of the paddle on her bottom.

She tensed when she felt the paddle follow the line of her spine, then go down her arm to be laid down on the bed beside her hand.

She watched as his hand went to the other items on the bed, licking dry lips when she saw what he chose.

"Spread your legs wider apart," he ordered as he placed one manacle on her ankle, then latched the other end of it to one of the bedposts. Taking another manacle off the bed, he placed it on her opposite leg.

"Now, isn't that a pretty sight."

Feeling him take the length of her hair into one hand, she tried fruitlessly not to turn around to see what he was doing.

The palm of his hand landed on her bottom. The warmth from the smack sent a matching warmth between her thighs.

"Eyes forward."

Shade continued to do what he had been doing with her

hair. She finally figured out he was braiding her long hair with something he had taken from the bed.

Concentrating, she felt the thin strip of leather being entwined in her hair. When he ran out of hair, Shade ran the leather strip under her body, crisscrossing each breast until they were tightly encased in a circle of leather.

As he leaned over her, she could feel his breath fanning across her back, each of her nipples prickling in arousal in response. Shade traveled his hand farther down her body and between her thighs, wrapping each of her thighs.

Shade was harnessing her, using the long leather cord to restrain movement.

She jumped, startled when he laid the other end of the cord over her shoulder. Glancing down, she saw that the end had slender tassels.

Shade rested his palm on her naked backside, squeezing a cheek before giving it a gentle tap. His hands became rougher as he positioned her exactly the way he wanted her.

"Don't move," he growled when she started shaking as he moved his fingers from her mound to stroke her clit. She was unable to prevent her moans when he speared her opening with one finger at the same time that he lifted up on the harness that had been looped over her breasts like a bra. Her breasts felt as if they fire as he tugged on it while he finger-fucked her.

Just as she was beginning to enjoy it, he released the harness and removed his finger.

"Do it again."

A sharp smack on her bottom was her penalty for talking.

"I have something better."

Lily was trembling so hard she could barely hold herself up on her hands, wanting to sink onto the bed. The feel of his cock surging inside had her nails curling into the blanket.

Once seated fully inside of her, Shade reached for the

JAMIE BEGLEY

other end of the leather rope, sensually dragging it off her shoulder, down her back, to hold it teasingly over her ass.

Each movement of the leather tugged at her thighs, breasts, and hair. The cascading sensations with Shade's cock inside her had her wanting to fervently beg him to go faster instead of the slow pace he had set for them.

She wanted to move passionately back on him, but every time she did, he would hit her with the tassels, sending stinging pain that made her want to do it again so he would do it more. Over and over, she raised her hips just to feel the sting of the leather.

She was so lost in what he was doing that he had to repeat his question twice.

"If you could fuck anyplace you wanted to, where would it be?"

When she couldn't think fast enough, he pulled the leather tighter, using it swat her other butt cheek.

"Mick's bar."

"You enjoyed it the other night?"

"Yes," she whimpered.

"So it was worth the money *I* spent on it?"

"Oh, yes! Can we do it again next Valentine's Day?"

"Not if Bubba bankrupts me before then. The way he's going, I won't be able to afford college for one kid, much less three."

Her gurgle of laughter was cut off by another swat on her butt.

"It wasn't funny."

"No, Sir." Meekly, she attempted to soothe him, more interested in what he was doing to her than Bubba. She would worry about him getting fired after Shade let her come, if he ever would.

Shade prolonged the exquisite agony of tightening and

releasing the leather strap until he had her unable to hold back her pleas.

"Please, Shade...."

"Are you sorry you stole my keys?"

"So sorry...," she apologized, giving a scream of frustration when he stopped moving inside her.

"I don't believe you."

"I'm sorry. I'll never touch your keys again!"

He started moving his cock again, tightening the strap in his hand and sending her head rearing back at the same as her breasts were pushed upward.

"Did you put the panties back?"

"Yes, right after I washed them."

"How did you when it was locked? Let me guess, you took them when I was in the shower?"

"Yes, Sir."

"You do know that will be the last time I shower alone?"

"Yes, Sir." She didn't tell him that was a punishment she could live with.

Shade pressed his chest to her back, enfolding her in his arms and bringing his hands to cover her abdomen.

"Thank you for giving me another child."

Lily had to blink through the sudden shimmer of tears. "You're welcome."

She felt the harness loosen, giving her free range of movement.

Shade raised his body off her to roll her over and stare down into her face as he positioned himself back inside her. His thrusts quickened as he hooked one of her thighs over his as they lay side by side on the bed.

He gripped her butt cheek to move her closer to him, their pelvises grinding together to find the fulfillment that was just out of reach. She broke first, her pussy constricting him as he impaled her as deeply as he could, sending her soaring into oblivion and taking him with her.

The euphoria that Shade had given her finally dimmed enough that she could raise her lashes to look at him.

"You take my breath away," he murmured, staring down at her.

Winding her arms around his neck, she slid her lips along his jaw. "That's the way I feel every time you tell me you love me."

Kissing her, he rolled farther onto her until her back was on the mattress.

Wrapping both of her thighs around his hips, she felt him getting hard again. She was about to joke that she needed to regain her breath when she heard the front door slam and running footsteps in the living room.

Both her and Shade's eyes darted to the open bedroom door.

"You didn't lock the door?" he whispered, jumping off the bed.

Frantic, Lily didn't bother answering, trying to dive off the bed, sending Shade's toys flying. Horrified that one or both of the boys would come into the bedroom, she brushed her hair out of her face to see Shade leaning naked against the closed door.

He looked at her as if she was as looney as Bubba. "You should have gone for the door, too! What if I didn't make it in time?"

Lily plumped up a pillow, shoving it behind her back while pushing a wooden paddle off the bed with her foot. "There was no way you were going to let the boys see your toys." Lily used a pink fingernail to twitch a turquoise plastic toy away from her hip. "What is that?" she asked curiously. "I haven't seen that one before."

Shade locked the door, treading toward her with silent feet. "Let me show you—"

"Mom!" John yelled out from the opposite side of the door. "Clint spilled Noah's Kool-Aid on his shirt."

"Go in the bathroom. I'll be there in a second," Lily called back, flipping the blanket off her.

"Stay put. I'll take…." Shade gave her an anticipatory grin, eyeing the toy. He looked like John when he had gotten his Xbox for Christmas.

"Mom!"

"What!" Shade yelled in frustration, trying to pull on his jeans over his hard cock.

"He spilled some on me, too!"

"John!"

"I know, go to the bathroom."

Lily waited until the boys were moving away from the door before looking at Shade questioningly. "Would you like me to put the toys back for you?"

"No, I'm going to get them in their pajamas before sending them back to Razer. Then I'm going to text him and make sure he keeps them there this time, no matter how many cups of Kool-Aid Clint spills."

"What then?" she asked breathlessly, seeing he was still having trouble getting his jeans zipped.

"Then, Angel, I'm going to show you exactly how that toy works."

CHASING RAINBOWS

CHAPTER 1

"Have you seen Ice?"

Grace turned as her brother Dax entered the formal dining room of her father's new home. "No. The last time I saw him was this morning when he left to get his tux. I've been helping Willa and Ginny set up for the reception."

Dax frowned. "The photographer wants to get started taking pictures of Dad's groomsmen.

"I'll text him and see where he is—"

"Just call; it'll be quicker."

"I left my phone in the kitchen." Conscious of her brother following her, she kept her expression neutral as they headed toward the kitchen. If she told her brother she didn't want to talk to her husband, it would raise alarms in both him and their father. Although, neither of them had missed the growing coldness between her and Ice.

For the last year, they had subtly tried to find the reason for it, but she had been keeping them in the dark, evading their questions as much as possible when she could. When she couldn't, she would use a variety of excuses that pointed away from the real reason her marriage was falling apart.

Giving Willa and Ginny quick smiles, she reached for her phone on the counter, then nervously pressed Ice's number. They fought that morning when they woke up. When Ice hadn't been willing to end the argument, she stormed into their private bathroom and slammed the door on him. If they had been in their own home, he would have never let her get away with it. But because they were in her father's home, he left, slamming the bedroom door on his way out. She sat on the side of the bathtub and cried at the sound.

He was furious and, truthfully, she couldn't blame him. She had created this problem in their marriage, and she wasn't willing to give in. She couldn't.

When her call went unanswered, she felt a crushing dread that Ice was so angry with her that he returned to Queen City without telling her.

"He didn't answer," she was forced to admit to Dax, self-conscious that Willa and Ginny were listening. "He'll probably be here any minute. Tell Peyton to start taking pictures, and I'll text you as soon as I hear from him."

Sensing her embarrassment from having the two other women in the room, Dax nodded. "Just send him on to the church when you hear from him. That's where Peyton is waiting for us."

"I will." She started texting Ice to tell him as Dax left the kitchen, leaving her with a worried glance. Before she could finish the text, though, Ice's name flashed across the screen.

Accepting the call, she started walking to the bedroom that T.A. had given them during their stay. Grace walked inside the room that was situated off from the kitchen, closing the door behind her.

"What did you need?"

She clenched the phone at the abrupt way he had answered it. "Killyama's mother wants the groomsmen for pictures at the church."

"I'm already here."

Grace licked her dry bottom lip. "I'm sorry I yelled at you this morning."

"I was over the fighting a couple of months ago. I'm sorry just doesn't cut it anymore, Grace."

Walking toward the bed, she sank down onto the mattress to keep from collapsing on her shaky legs. "Are you saying you want a divorce?"

"No, I don't want a fucking divorce," he hissed from the other end of the phone. "What I want is for the fighting to stop."

"I do, too," she said achingly. "This fighting is tearing me apart."

"I'm not the one that starts them."

"I know," she admitted, then heard his sigh of frustration when that was all she was willing to concede.

"Grace, Dax is coming in the door. I have to go."

Her hand holding the phone dropped to her lap when the phone went dead.

Their fights were escalating to the point that, if they didn't stop, the marriage was going to be irreparable. If it wasn't already.

Grace stared blankly at the wall in front of the bed. She hated herself for being the one who was sparking their disagreements, but unless Ice was willing to give in to her pleas, she couldn't see their arguments ending. Divorce might be the only option left for her if Ice wasn't willing to walk away from Desmond Beck.

Desmond was the owner of Beck Industries. Wealthy, handsome, and charming, the man was a favorite bachelor in Queen City's society. But behind closed doors, he was ruthless, cunning, and formidable at the power he held.

The truly frightening part to her was when she had found

out that her husband was the one who enforced Desmond's power.

She had turned a blind eye to the strip club that he protected by placing Jackal and Buzzard inside as bouncers. What she couldn't turn away from, though, was him placing his life on the line every time a deal went down by making sure the agreement was met without the fear of the buyers or the sellers being double-crossed, all the while making sure that Desmond received his cut of the transaction.

Of course, the affluent friends he had accumulated not only provided a smokescreen but were also another layer of protection Desmond used to surround himself. He was able to stay safe and warm in his mansion, hiding behind the façade of being a legitimate businessman, while Ice did whatever dirty work he was ordered to perform.

Naively, she hadn't asked too many questions, and those she did, she had accepted the ambiguous answers he had come up with. She had told herself repeatedly that he would get tired of the job and move on like normal men did as they grew older and wanted to start a family. Except, Ice had no intention of changing his job, whether they started a family or not.

That fact had finally registered to her when she became pregnant two months after her mother's death. She had looked at the baby as a bright spot in the grief she had been dealing with, happily planning to turn one of the guest rooms into a nursery. That was the same time their arguments began.

Dealing with the overwhelming grief of losing her mother, it occurred to her: What if something happened to Ice? No one could do anything if misfortune happened, such as an accident, but the job Ice did was laced with danger that could be prevented.

That was when the truth about her husband finally hit

home: he had no intention of changing, regardless of how many children they had.

Each time they fought, his only response was the exact same—she had known what type man he was before they had married. And she had.

Another blow to their marriage had been when she suffered a miscarriage. During that year, Ice had been supportive and loving. Everything a woman could need from her husband was there, except for what she needed the most. She needed Ice to pick her and the child she hoped to have in their future over being Desmond's henchman.

That was over three years ago, and they were no closer to a solution that would make them both happy.

To make matters worse, she had no one she could confide in. She didn't want her father and Dax to know what Ice did, nor could she talk to Penni, who was her best friend. Penni was married to Jackal, who was Ice's sergeant-at-arms in the Predators. He was right beside Ice when the deals went down.

It didn't seem to bother Penni that her husband took risks, or that he worked at the Purple Pussycat, protecting the women during encounters with their customers. Penni's brother, Shade, belonged to The Last Riders motorcycle club, so she was used to turning a blind eye to the jobs the men in her life carried out.

Rising from the bed, Grace smoothed down the dress she was wearing. The knee-length, rose-colored chiffon skimmed her body lovingly.

Catching sight of her reflection in the bureau mirror, she was tempted to throw something at it, to break the image that was staring back at her.

She might look the same as when she married Ice, but she'd changed. Losing her mother and the child she wanted had altered something inside of her. Now something was missing, and unless she discovered what that void was, Grace was deathly afraid that it was going to swallow her whole.

Ice had said he didn't want a divorce, but she didn't know how much longer she would be able to say the same if what she suspected was true.

Tucking a stray wisp of hair back into her chignon, she took a deep breath to steady herself. Today was Valentine's Day, she reminded herself, and her father was getting remarried in a few hours.

Both his and T.A.'s happiness glowed on their faces whenever they were in a room together, highlighting just how unhappy she and Ice must appear.

Valentine's Day was supposed to be filled with love. So far, hers was totally sucking. The only bright spot she was looking forward to was the wedding. As much as she was anticipating the wedding, she dreaded the oncoming evening when she and Ice would be left alone.

After the reception, her father and T.A. were flying to Florida to retrieve a motorcycle he had left with a friend. She and Ice would stay the night, then fly back to Queen City in the morning.

She wasn't under any delusions that they wouldn't spend the night arguing, despite the romantic nature of the holiday. No pink cardboard heart was going to be able to heal the rift between them. It was going to take something that Grace was beginning to doubt Ice still felt for her.

Love.

CHAPTER 2

Grace stared down at the wedding ring on her left hand as T.A.'s and her father's guests mingled while waiting for the newly married couple to arrive from the church.

"It was a beautiful ceremony."

Startled at the soft, feminine voice, Grace looked up to see Lily standing in front of her.

Shade's wife was gorgeous in a violet, tea-length dress that emphasized her eyes and black hair.

"Yes, it was," she agreed, her attention switching to Ice who was talking to Jackal, Penni, and Shade across the room.

Lily turned her head to see what she was staring at, then turned back with a smile. "They look handsome all dressed up, don't they?"

"Yes, they do." Grace's hand shook as she lifted her glass to her lips.

"Are...?" Lily began, then cut her question short, blushing.

"Are what?" Grace asked.

"Nothing. I was about to ask if you're okay, but I didn't want to be insensitive. I'm sorry. I'll leave you alone."

Grace placed her hand on Lily's arm, stopping her. "You

couldn't be insensitive if you tried. You were about to mention my mother, weren't you?"

Lily nodded. "It has to be difficult to see your father getting remarried."

"I miss my mother badly, but I'm glad Dad isn't alone anymore. My mother and Dad had a very happy marriage. They were best friends. The thought of Dad not having that relationship was almost as bad as losing Mom." Her lips curled in a smile. "T.A. will keep him on his toes."

"Yes, she will." Lily laughed with her. "She has a quality that a lot of people don't have anymore. When she cares about you, she'll stand by you until hell freezes over. She loves children. I wouldn't know what I'd do without her at Christmastime. She always volunteers to wrap the children's presents for the baskets I do for the needy our church puts together."

Grace smiled, finally managing to relax with Lily's friendly chatter that took her mind off the problems going on in her marriage. One of the best things about being friends with Penni was that she had been introduced to Lily. She had even accepted a couple of invitations when Penni came to visit Shade for just that reason.

Lily was warm-hearted, sweet, and would give the shirt off her back to anyone in need. She was the exact opposite of her husband. When she thought of Shade, warm-hearted and sweet did not come to mind.

"You don't have to convince me. She has my dad laughing and smiling again. And she convinced him to take an acting role that he would have never taken unless she talked him into it."

"I'm glad, too. I saw his movie. It's really good."

"I think so, too." Grace watched proudly as her father and T.A. came into the room to cheers. She didn't rush to their side, letting the rest of their friends go first.

Grace felt a pang in her chest at how happy they looked, remembering how happy she had been the day she and Ice married.

She felt Lily touch her arm. "Are you okay? You look like you're about to cry."

"I'm fine. I was remembering when Ice and I were married."

"I remember when Shade and I were married. He gave me my dream wedding. I didn't even know he planned it until the morning of the wedding."

Shocked, Grace took her eyes off her father to stare at Lily. "You didn't plan your own wedding?"

"No, Shade did. He knew that I wanted an outdoor wedding with snow, and a snowfall had come in the night before. It was beautiful. The next time you come for a visit, I'll show you the video. He made my dreams come true. He still does."

Lily was staring at Shade as they talked, and Grace noticed that Shade was watching her back. He had no idea what they were talking about, yet they were communicating in a way that only those truly in love could.

It brought another pang to her chest, this time much sharper and it didn't go away.

Setting her champagne glass down, she reached for another. "Ice doesn't want any part of my dreams."

Lily turned to her in surprise. "That can't be true. Ice loves you very much—"

"He used to. Right now, I don't know how he feels."

Grace couldn't believe she was airing her laundry in front of Lily. She couldn't even understand why, other than the fight they had this morning had been the worst, or Lily was just the type of person that she could talk to—one who wouldn't make snap judgments.

"I understand."

Grace frowned. "You do?"

Lily blushed at her own disclosure. "I think all women, whether they're married or not, at one time or another have doubts if their partners love them the same way they did at the beginning of their relationship."

"It's evident that Shade does. Ice? I'm not so sure. We've been fighting a lot lately." Grace finished her drink, mentally blaming the three glasses of champagne she had for revealing the state of her marriage.

Unable to stop herself, she divulged even more, like a dam had broken free within her, and the pain she had been holding in came spilling out.

"I want to have a baby, but I want Ice to find another job. I don't like the person he works for now."

"Are you worried about his job security if you have a baby?"

"Not that. I don't like who he works for."

"Does Ice like him?"

Grace frowned at her question. "I've never thought to ask."

"If Ice likes him, that might be why he doesn't want to quit. Why don't you like his boss?"

"I can't say." Grace twisted her wedding ring on her finger, unable to meet Lily's eyes.

"I see."

Grace saw that Lily was also twisting the wedding rings on her own hand.

Lily started to say something, then seemed to change her mind before deciding to say what she wanted.

"Ice and Shade seem to have similar personalities. I've noticed that when you two come for a visit with Penni."

"I've noticed that, too," Grace acknowledged.

"When I met Shade, I was terrified of him."

Grace thought back to when she met Ice. "I wasn't afraid

of him. More like wary of him."

"That's because you're more confident and stronger than I was back then."

"I can't believe that. When I came to visit, you handled all your guests and their children like a pro."

"I used to be afraid of my own shadow," Lily said ruefully. "Becoming friends with Penni and falling in love with Shade gave me more self-assurance. He taught me how to be stronger and confident. It's wonderful how people can affect your life." Lily gave her a wide smile. "If not for her, I wouldn't have met you."

"I was just thinking earlier that being friends with you is one of the best things in my life."

"Penni isn't afraid of anything. I met her in college. She talked me into doing things that my own sister couldn't have." Lily laughed. "Not that Beth would have tried to talk me into pole dancing or going to sorority and frat parties. I used to freak out if people drank around me."

About to reach for another glass of champagne, Grace jerked her hand back.

"It's okay. Unless someone is drunk, it doesn't bother me as badly."

Lily might have said that, but Grace noticed she was the only one who didn't have a glass in her hand.

Changing the topic from drinking, she teased Lily, "What did Shade teach you to be more confident and stronger?"

"That evil doesn't always win."

Grace swallowed hard, looking away from the secrets in Lily's eyes. Only someone who had faced and conquered evil could understand. And like Lily, she had. She and two of her friends had been kidnapped when they had gone to New York with her parents. Her friends hadn't made it out alive. It took a lot of years to come to terms that she had.

"No, it doesn't."

"I should go congratulate your father and T.A."

Grace could tell Lily wanted to get away from her memories.

"Lily…" Grace stopped her before she could move away. "Could I ask you a question?"

She didn't answer yes or no, waiting to hear the question first.

"I'm not… I'm not sure how to ask this."

Lily smiled. "Just ask. If I can answer, I will."

"Does…? How do you…?" Grace bit her lip. "Does Shade ever do anything he shouldn't do? God, this is coming out all wrong. I don't know what I'm trying to say. Just ignore me…."

Lily didn't move away.

"Do you mean, does he cheat on me?" Her face went pale. "Has Penni told you something I don't know?"

"God, no!" Grace frantically waved her hand. "That wasn't what I was trying to ask. Oh my God! Never mind. That thought never occurred to me."

"That's a relief," Lily said, giving a shaky laugh. "Then I don't understand?"

"Can we just forget we had this conversation?" Grace was painfully aware she was making an idiot of herself. "I was just trying to ask how you deal with it when Shade does something you don't like. It came out totally wrong."

Understanding dawned on her face. "You're asking me if Shade does something for The Last Riders that I don't agree with?"

Grace started twisting her wedding ring again. "Basically. But it doesn't have to be the club he's doing things for. Just something you wished he wouldn't do."

Lily stayed silent. Grace could tell she was thinking over her reply.

"I shouldn't have asked something so personal. I'm sorry.

Ice and I had a terrible fight this morning, and I don't want my dad and brother to know how bad things are getting between us. Instead, I've made a fool of myself in front of you."

"You did not make a fool of yourself. Don't say that." Lily's gentle smile relieved some of her tension. "I'll try to answer your question as best I can with the details you've given me.

"I trust Shade. I love him based on how he treats me. I love him because I see what he does for not only me and our children but also for others. The church store doesn't make a dime. The Last Riders fund it. The majority of our clients would go to bed every night with an empty stomach if not for them. Shade is responsible for that. I'm not saying The Last Riders wouldn't help without him talking them into it, but he's gone beyond what I hoped to achieve.

"Every year, he picks out two students from the families and gives them a full-ride scholarship to the college of their choice. The only stipulation is that they have to come back here and work three years in their field of choice to give back to the community. He's trying to save Treepoint from dying like the other towns surrounding us.

"Since the moment I met Shade, I realized he wasn't a normal man. He has his own sense of right and wrong.

"One time, I was so angry that I accused him of thinking he was God. I was wrong. Shade doesn't think he's God, but he does believe that men and women are responsible for their own actions. If those actions lead them to hurting others, then he has no hesitation in using his abilities to even the playing field.

"He's leveled the field not only for me but for some of the people in this room. My sister, Willa, Pastor Dean—" Lily broke herself off. "If I can trust that my husband did what he thought was best to save my life, then I have to trust that he does the same thing to save the lives of those I love, too.

Sometimes those measures are extreme. Shade isn't a gentleman. Sometimes those measures are harsh and have left marks on his soul. He doesn't have my faith, yet a part of him believes that God will punish him for some of the things he's done. That he'll never be forgiven."

Grace saw the heartbroken expression on Lily's face as she exposed a part Shade's character she never knew existed. If a man could be made of Kevlar, it was Shade.

"You don't believe that, do you?"

Lily shook her head, her eyes still on Shade, almost as if she wasn't standing beside her. "No, I don't think he'll be punished. I think Shade is one of the precious few that God chose to be one of His warriors."

"I don't think that Ice could be classified as one as God's warriors." Grace looked at her own husband, startled to see he was observing her the same way Shade was watching Lily. He must have noticed that she had been staring at Shade. His frown showed he wasn't happy.

At her comment, Lily switched her attention back to her. "Ice was for me. He was responsible for me being able to restore a part of my life that I thought was gone forever. If he hadn't, I wouldn't have met you."

Taken aback, her gaze returned Lily's.

"It's true, Grace. A true warrior doesn't always walk the path of righteousness. They follow the path that their conscience leads them to take. I believe we will all end our journey at the same destination; we just have different ways to get there."

A movement out of the corner of her eye had Grace nodding toward to Willa. "I think Willa needs you."

"I better go see what she wants." Lily gave her a quick squeeze of her hand before taking a step toward Willa.

"Thank you, Lily."

"I didn't do anything to deserve your thanks. I was

returning a kindness that Ice gifted me with. He wouldn't have been able to achieve it by following a straight and narrow path, but the one I will forever be grateful that he made his way through...."

A bundle of energy threw herself into Lily's arms as she was talking. Laughing, she bent down, picking up the little girl into her arms. Her black hair fell to her shoulders. Grace was struck by how similar their features were.

"Mama won't let me have another piece of cake." The childish hand patted Lily's hair.

"What am I supposed to do about that?"

"Make Daddy make her." The child gazed up at Lily adorably.

Grace swallowed hard as Lily stared down at the little girl in her arms with just as much adoration.

"How about if I ask Evie if you can have another small piece?"

"Yes, please."

The resemblance between Lily and the little girl was too close for them not to be relatives. They shared not only the same hair color, but the purple eyes that were unusual enough that she looked like a miniature version of Lily. She would have to ask Ice what the relationship was between them.

Thinking about Ice had her wanting to talk to him. Maneuvering around several of the guests, it took several minutes to realize that he wasn't there. He had left.

CHAPTER 3

"Want another beer?"

"No." Ice took another drink of his mostly full beer. The bar had only seven customers in it. Three men and a woman were sitting at the side of the bar, spaced out so they could enjoy their beers alone.

Celebrating Valentine's Day had never been high on his list of priorities, even before he was married.

Thinking about the state of his marriage had him taking another drink. It was hot as piss. Beer had never been his favorite liquor to consume. He preferred his alcohol to have a bite. Like most of the women he fucked before he fell in love with Grace, once you had the real thing, nothing quenched the thirst for what you really wanted.

Reaching for his beer, he saw the screen on his cell phone light up on the bar top. Disregarding the message from Grace, he reached for his wallet, taking out a ten.

"Give me another beer." He laid down the ten on the counter.

The bartender brought him a cold beer, setting it down in

front of him, then lifting a wondering brow when he took the still full one away.

Ice took a sip of the cold beer. It didn't go down any easier than the hot one after he saw Grace texted him again.

The crack of a shrill screech had the same effect as nails against a chalkboard. The woman sitting with the men shrieked when the one sitting closest to her must have done something that she hadn't liked.

Beer bottles and glasses clanked together as the table was jostled underneath. Ice could see the glare from the woman's eyes when she pulled a hand out from under the table, slamming it down on the table. "Cut it out!"

The lone woman in the bar had all the men glancing toward the table, including him.

Ice could understand their interest. Amber-colored hair and finely arched eyebrows were her best features. Not that he could see distinguishing features from where he was sitting. She wasn't too thin or too plump. She didn't seem the type of woman who could garner the attention she was getting from the three men, yet she had all three regarding her closely. But then, she was the only woman in the bar.

The one who attempted to get a handful of her pussy had been rebuffed, and the other two men were giving warning signs that they weren't going to tolerate the woman's snatch being grabbed by the lone one who was roaring his head off in laughter, as if he expected the other two to egg him on.

Ice shook his head. The dimwitted one didn't realize the other two were getting angry while the woman did her best to scoot her chair away from the table, but she was blocked in by the wall.

Taking another swig of his beer, he kept his eye on the building tension at the table.

He was setting his beer back down on the bar top when

the phone rang behind the bar, and the bartender went to answer it not far from where he was sitting.

"Hello?"

Ice listened with only half an ear as his gaze remained on the four across the room.

"Hey, Lily. What can I do for you?"

Hearing Lily's name coming out of the bartender's mouth had Ice's sharp gaze shooting to the man who was standing just a couple inches from him. Lily was the name of The Last Riders' enforcer's wife.

"It's not really busy. It's pretty slow right now. I don't expect it to get busy until later tonight."

The music played in the background as the bartender listened to whatever Lily was saying.

"No, I can't do that." He looked at the phone like it had turned into a snake while he was listening. "Wait. How much money we talking about?"

The phone had turned into a pot of gold from the expression on the bartender's face.

"Give me an hour, and it'll be yours." He hung up then yelled out, "Last call!"

"What the fuck, Mick!"

Ice recognized the man yelling out as one of The Last Riders.

"Chill, Moon. It'll only be for two hours. I'll give a free beer to anyone who comes back when I reopen. Lily wants to give Shade his Valentine's Day present without you yahoos around."

Moon's beer bottle toppled over when he set it back on the bar top too hard. "Motherfucker. How does that fucker get so motherfucking lucky?" Moon snarled, righting his beer. "He scored the best-looking woman in town, and she's closing down the bar for him?"

Ice felt for the brother when he looked like he was going to cry.

"There is no fucking justice!"

"Tell me about it," Ice muttered beneath his breath. After the argument he and Grace had this morning, he would be lucky to get laid tonight, even if it wasn't Valentine's Day.

Picking up his cell phone, he was about to send a text to her when the bar door opened. As if his thoughts had put her there, his wife walked inside.

Grace had changed from her dress, which she had looked hot as hell in, to a pair of skin-tight jeans and a baby blue and dark blue tie-dye top that fit her tits like a glove. Wearing a fuzzy, baby blue coat, she looked around the room before spotting him at the bar.

Where in the fuck had his wife gotten that outfit? He had never seen her wear it in Queen City.

Feeling his tongue get dry in his mouth, he lifted a shaky hand to his beer to take a drink as his wife sat down next to him.

"I've been looking for you."

"I was on my way back. I needed a break."

Grace nodded as if she understood. "I did, too. Can I have a beer?" she asked the bartender when he approached.

"Sure, but the bar's closing in fifteen minutes."

When Grace gave Mick a curious frown. Ice explained, "Lily rented out the bar for the next two hours."

She poured the beer into the glass that Mick set down in front of her. "Of course she did."

"What does that mean?" Ice turned on his stool to see his wife blushing at the fact that he had heard her comment.

"She has the perfect marriage. It just makes sense that she's the perfect wife, too."

"How much champagne have you had?"

"Too much."

Ice tensed at the danger she had put herself in by driving after consuming too much alcohol. "And you drove here?"

"Relax. Beth and Razer dropped me off on their way home."

"How'd you know I was here?"

Grace slid her hand inside the fuck-me coat, taking out her phone and laying it next to his on the bar. "You're the one that put *find a friend* app on my phone."

"I put it on yours, not mine."

"You're not the only one that knows how to install apps."

He started to get angry, then remembered he had done the same. Biting his tongue, he decided to play fair this time, even though it galled him that she had gotten one over on him.

"Dad and T.A. left for Florida."

"Sorry, I was…."

She waved off his apology. "I don't blame you. I've been such a bitch lately that I don't want to be around myself."

She had been a bitch, but he couldn't stand the defeated expression that was on her face.

"Grace…."

She waved off his apology. "I have been a raving bitch to you, and I know that."

Ice saw that her bottom lip had gone white with her biting down on it.

"I hate myself every time I open my mouth to you, but I can't seem to stop myself, no matter how hard I try."

Her admission had him feeling as if she just ground her high-heeled boot down on his heart, then picked up what was left to squish in her hand like silly putty.

"Grace, I think it's time to—"

"Don't… Please. Just give me a minute to say my peace before you tell me you want a divorce. I want to tell you that—"

"Ten minutes!" Mick's voice boomed, startling them both, her hand going to his thigh.

"I need to use the restroom. All the champagne I drank has my bladder going on overdrive."

"It's in the back on the left. Hurry up. I told Lily I'd have everyone out before she got here," Mick broke in after hearing the last part of their conversation.

Standing up, she squeezed his thigh tighter. "Please don't leave. I'll be right back." Releasing the grip on his leg, she unsteadily went in the direction of the bathroom.

"Brother, I hate to kick a man when he's down, but I need you and your woman to get the fuck out."

Ice paid for the beer, expecting Grace to come right back as the others in the bar left.

When Mick went to stand at the window, he gave him an exasperated look. "Lily's here. If she sees you, she'll call it off."

"I'll go see what's taking so long," he said, rising from his stool.

"I'm going outside. Get your woman and use the back door. It's on the other side of the bathroom."

"Will do."

Ice strode toward the restroom, wondering why Grace was taking so long to take a piss. He didn't bother knocking on the door, going inside to see his wife leaning against the wall, crying.

"What's fucking wrong?" he asked, taking a quick look around the room to make sure nothing could have hurt her.

"I'm such a bitch!"

Dumbfounded, Ice let the stall door that he had opened swing closed. "Quit saying that. You're not a bitch."

"I am." Shuddering, she went to the sink to grab a handful of paper towels then wet them under the faucet. Dabbing her eyes, she stared at him in the mirror. "I can't even blame you for leaving me. I've been such a witch to you."

"Grace, you're not a bitch or a witch," he said, trying to calm her down so he could get her out of the bathroom.

"Who starts a fight with her husband on Valentine's Day?" she muttered, talking more to herself than to him from the reflection in the mirror. "I should have made you your favorite meal and a cake."

"I'm sure there's a fuck-load of cake left over from the reception."

Grace shook her head dismally. "Rider packed most of it up to take back to the club, said he was working tonight and needed it as a snack. It doesn't matter anyway. It wasn't your favorite flavor that I always bake for you on Valentine's Day." Grace gasped out, taking a deep breath before continuing on with her tirade. "While Lily rented out a bar for Shade. Lily's the perfect wife, and I suck!"

"We can talk when we get out of here." Ice started to open the door but stopped when Grace started dabbing her eyes again.

"Look at me. I look ridiculous."

"You look hot as fuck."

She dropped her hand to the sink. "T.A. said you would like it when she talked me into buying it. Even T.A. knows what you like, and she isn't married to you."

Ice moved to stand behind her. "There isn't a man alive that wouldn't want to fuck you in that get-up."

"Then, why do I feel as undesirable as a dishrag?"

He was unaware his wife felt that way.

"If you're feeling like that, it isn't on you. That's on me."

CHAPTER 4

"How is that your fault?"

He trailed a line from her beating pulse to the curve of her breast. "If you're feeling neglected and not sexy, then I'm in the wrong. That's not being a good husband. Was that why you were staring a hole in Shade at the reception? Does he do it for you instead of me?"

"Huh?"

Her astounded look quieted the jealously, which was what had him making the excuse to leave the reception.

"I couldn't be attracted to Shade in a million years. He's not my type."

"I don't believe you." Ice used his knuckles to shove down her top, curling a possessive hand over her wispy blue bra.

"I was only looking at him because Lily was talking about him. She thinks he's God's warrior."

The sound of Ice's laughter ricocheted off the bathroom walls. "Shade and God shouldn't be used in the same sentence. I would say he's more like the devil's minion, but Shade is no one's minion."

"He can't be that bad, or Lily wouldn't love him."

Ice rolled his eyes at that innocent statement. "Then she's blind as fuck where he's concerned."

Grace's head fell back to rest on his shoulder when he started squeezing her tit, pushing the plump flesh out of the thin material that was holding it confined. "Lily's not blind. She's in love."

"I really don't care if she is or isn't. The only woman I care about is mine."

"Do you...? Do you still love me?"

He brought his hand to her shoulder, jerking her around to face him. "What kind of a question is that? You know I do. I'm getting sick of this bullshit. You blow hot on me one fucking second, and the next, you ask if I love you? If I didn't love you, can you tell me why I would be putting up with this bullshit?"

She gripped the sink as if she was about to fall to the floor.

"Would my ass be sitting in a marriage counselor's office if I didn't?" He ruthlessly moved away from her touch when she would have reached out to him. "You need to get your head on straight and figure the fuck out that it's not me that's the problem."

"What do you mean?"

"You know what I mean. Winston is going for reevaluation in two months, and it's scaring the fuck out of you."

"They'll never let him out."

"They won't, but for the last four years, every time that yearly reevaluation comes up, we go through months of hell until he's denied. We get a few months break before we're notified again. It's torture for you, and it sure as fuck is on me, having to watch you go through that. Even if he gets out tomorrow, he's paralyzed from the neck down. I'm fucking sure you can take him."

"Our fights are over Desmond and the job you do for him, not Leon!"

"Really, Grace? Fool yourself, not me. You think those dirtballs that I make sure Desmond gets his part of their profits are worth this fighting back and forth? At least the people in Queen City know that what they're sticking in their noses and arms won't put them in a casket. You can't be that naïve as to think that shit won't be going down whether Desmond takes his part or not?"

"You take your part, too!"

"Damn right I do! I sleep like a baby, too! You think I'm going to lose sleep over that? I'd have a hard time sleeping knowing shit was hitting the streets that is taking over other towns. Read the fucking papers. Some police departments are volunteering to check out people's stash because so many people are dying. I've only had one shipment almost get past me in the last two years, and the fucker that tried it left in the truck he attempted to bring it in."

"You're risking your life! You're risking it all for nothing!"

"It's not nothing! It's Gert's nursing home payment. You think Max can pay for all those kids on his and Casey's salary? Cole might be better now, but he has a shit-ton of medical bills that they're all trying to pay off. And I'm not even talking about the other brothers in the club and the baggage they have on their shoulders. Braces, school supplies, child support payments, clothes, food. Don't tell me it's not for fucking nothing, because it's a big fucking something to them."

"There are other ways to do that legally."

"It may have gotten past you that I don't exactly qualify for big, high paying jobs. Nor do the other brothers. We do what we do best—protecting our own. And if that doesn't make you happy, then I guess we don't have anything else to say, do we? Now, I'm going to take a leak and get the hell out of here before Mick comes back and I have to beat the fuck out of him for telling me to hurry one more time."

Slamming his fist against the stall door closest to him, it swung open so fast that Ice had to bite back another curse when he saw Grace run out of the bathroom with her hand pressed to her mouth. Unbuttoning his jeans, he raised his other fist to hit the thin metal.

He was washing his hands, considering punching the mirror, when his eyes widened in the glass when he remembered that he and Grace were supposed to go out the back door.

"Fuck!"

CHAPTER 5

R ushing out of the bathroom, Grace came to an abrupt stop when she saw what was going on in the front of the bar. Frozen in place, the dark lighting prevented her from being seen by the couple.

Thrown off balance by what was going on in front of her eyes, she didn't know how to react without making a fool of herself. There was no way she was going to be able to traverse the length of the bar and slink out without being seen. Not only was she was going to be humiliated, but Lily would freak out if she found out that the pole dance she was giving her husband was being witnessed. The only reason she had avoided being seen so far was that Lily was swinging on the stripper pole.

Deciding to shout out that she was there and give Lily the opportunity to cover herself, and then run out hell-bent for leather, Grace opened her mouth. But before she could manage a squeak, a hand covered it.

She had been so disconcerted at Lily's performance that she forgot Ice was in the bathroom.

JAMIE BEGLEY

Raising her chagrinned eyes to his, she saw that he had seen the predicament they were in.

At the silent nod of his head, she realized he was using his chin to motion toward the side. Nodding her understanding, Ice removed his hand from her mouth, then turned to look to where he was indicating.

She was still thanking God that Ice had known how to get them out without being seen when she started to push the metal bar of the side door that would get them out of the bar. Before she could push down, though, Ice pulled her back.

Puzzled, she looked at him to see he was gesturing at the sign above the door.

Swallowing hard, she read the note that said an alarm would ring if the door was opened.

Feeling frantic, she was willing to take the chance when the music changed. She darted a glance toward the front and saw what was going on with Shade and Lily.

Seeing that Ice was staring just as hard, she hit her husband's shoulder, redirecting his attention.

If she had needed further proof that Lily was perfect, she was seeing it now without Lily's knowledge. No woman should look like that. It just wasn't fair. Especially with her looks.

She hit Ice again, ignoring his mouthing of, "What the fuck?"

Her body was nothing to sneeze about, but Lily's boobs and ass were perfect, which were the sore points on her own body. That she could see the appreciation in Ice's expression had her wanting to pop him to make him stop watching. The jerk wasn't stunned in place, not knowing what to do to get them out of the situation they found themselves in because of her bladder.

If she hadn't just taken care of the situation, she would have peed herself when she saw what was happening now.

132

Her jaw dropped open when Shade rose from the chair and put Lily on the bar. Afraid she was about to been seen, in the gloominess of the back room of the bar Grace hastily took a chair at a small table that was close to them. Fearfully, she looked to see what Ice was doing and realized her husband's ass had found a chair at the same time hers had.

"*What are we going to do?*" she silently mouthed at him.

She narrowed her eyes on him when he just shrugged and continued watching.

She hit him again.

"*Quit doing that,*" he mouthed.

She was about to bury her head in her hands when she saw what Shade was doing. Gaping, she could only stare at him in wonder as he started taking his clothes off. Damn, they were the perfect couple.

Grace winced, shooting Ice an irritated glance when he swatted her hand for watching. It was okay for him to appreciate Lily, but she wasn't allowed to appreciate Shade?

Sparks from their eyes went back and forth among them when Shade knelt on the floor.

She was rising half off her seat so she could see when Ice's hand on her shoulder made her sit back down. Ice shook his head warningly at her.

Her disappointment was short-lived because, then Shade rose and went to Lily.

The passion between the couple nearly set the bar on fire.

Unconsciously twisting on her chair, what she was witnessing had launched a grenade in her own body. Grace had never felt like that before.

Unaware, she had taken Ice's hand and was squeezing it tightly.

Unblinking, she watched Lily and Shade, her heart starting to hammer when Shade's eyes seemed to pierce them through the shadows. Terrified for a second that they had been spotted, Grace reacted instinctively, sliding off the chair in a hunched over position, then making her way toward the restroom, feeling Ice doing the same.

When she reached the women's bathroom, she started to push the door open, then changed her mind, going for the men's.

Ice stopped her by clutching the bottom of her jacket, trying to tug her back to the women's. Shaking her head, she tried to bat him away, but a sharp smack on her bottom had her twisting like a contortionist to smack back at his hands.

Grace gave up when Ice's furious eyes met hers.

Backpedaling to the women's restroom, she opened the door barely enough to squeeze through, afraid that Shade or Lily would see the light spilling out into the darkened hallway.

She dropped to the floor once she and Ice were safely inside, fearfully watching the door as if Shade or Lily would barge in to ask what the hell was going on.

"Why in the fuck were you trying to go to the men's restroom?" Ice huffed, sitting down beside her.

"Shh! They'll hear us!" she hissed. "I don't want Lily to see us if she needs to use the toilet."

Ice stared at her as if she was deranged. "You'd rather be caught by Shade?" he hissed back.

"Shh! They'll hear us!" Grace wheezed out, afraid she was about to have a panic attack.

"They aren't going to hear shit. They're out there fucking their brains out!"

"Shut up. Don't say that!"

"Well, they are," he huffed, settling his back against the wall.

"I know, but you don't have to remind me. We are so dead if we get caught," she moaned, curling her knees to her chest. "Can you take him?"

"What do you mean *can I take him?*"

"I mean, I don't want to die!" she whispered plaintively. "Can you take him if he goes over the rails and finds out we watched."

"You're being ridiculous. He won't kill us."

That Ice didn't seem as sure as he sounded didn't inspire confidence in his abilities.

She whimpered. "We're going to die."

"We're not going to die."

At least Ice sounded more sure of that.

"He'll beat the fuck out of me, but you should be good."

"It's all your fault we're in this situation! You should have let me open the door!"

Ice rolled his eyes. "Yeah, that would have been so much better."

"I could have run. Now, if Lily comes to the bathroom, we're trapped." She was appalled at the thought of Lily entering the bathroom. "What if she comes in here naked?"

"God, I can only hope," Ice muttered.

Grace punched him on his arm.

"Fuck, I was only joking. Quit fucking hitting me!"

"You weren't joking. Don't think I didn't see you looking at her boobs."

"Are you fucking serious? If I hadn't looked, that should be a trigger for you. There is no red-blooded man that wouldn't get turned on by her."

Hurt, she dropped her eyes from his.

"Don't give me that hurt look! I wasn't the one twisting on my chair when you got a good look at Shade's body. For a second I thought you were going to knock Lily off the bar and hurl yourself up there."

She looked at him in confusion. Had she?

She gave a haughty sniff out loud. She couldn't remember.

"*Please.*" Ice snorted. "You were looking at him like he was a snow cone and you were in a heat wave."

"Don't be crass."

"I'm not being crass. I'm horny as fuck!"

"Well, you're not getting any in here," she snapped.

"What's new?" he snapped back.

"Are you trying to act like you don't get any?"

"I'm not acting. I'm saying it like it is."

Grace cupped her palms over her knees. "We have sex all the time."

"When's the last time you let me fuck you, then?"

"Uh… the other day."

"More like three weeks ago."

"That's not true. It's just been a couple of days."

"It's been three weeks, Grace."

"Really?" Surely, he couldn't be right. She racked her mind, trying to remember.

"Really."

CHAPTER 6

"You haven't let me touch you since the day we received the letter that Winston's hearing was rescheduled."

Numbly, she stared at the sink, focusing on a drop of water at the edge of the faucet, like it was hanging on for dear life. The way she had when she was kidnapped, her life hanging on the balance every time Leon Winston walked down those wooden steps.

"I didn't think it had been so long."

"Well, it has."

Feeling like a complete failure as a wife, she continued to look at the stupid droplet of water, waiting for it to fall. "I keep hearing him coming down those steps. During the day, when I'm at work. At night, even when I know you're there and Winston's in the psychiatric hospital. How am I supposed to make myself stop hearing them when he really gets out?"

Ice laid a comforting arm around her shoulders, shifting closer to her. "He can't walk anymore. Maybe you should go back to therapy."

"I did two months ago. It's not helping, I still hear those

footsteps." She brought her hand to her hair, her forehead resting on her knees. "I'm never going to stop hearing them."

"You will. He'll never get near you again."

"I know you think that you can protect me against him, but you can't. Sooner or later, he will get out. His doctors keep writing those letters for him that he's not a physical threat. His body might not be able to move, but there's nothing wrong with his mind. He's skilled at finding people's weaknesses and taking advantage any way he can."

"They won't let him out. They'll move him to a prison cell."

"Somehow, someway, he'll get out. His doctors like him. They're underestimating him. He's pretending he's sorry. He will eventually get out, and when he does, he'll manipulate someone into finding me. He said he would never let me go, and he meant it."

"The sick fucker will not get within breathing distance of you. I swear, Grace, I swear on my grave that he won't get near you."

Grace raised her head to stare at him. "I'm afraid of that, too. When he finds out we're together, he'll kill you. How can you protect me if you're not here?"

"Fuck. Is that why you've been on my case about working for Desmond?"

She hadn't seen the correlation before, but Ice could be right.

"I think so. I don't like you working for him. But yes, part of it is because I need you alive, Ice. I don't need you buried six feet under because of a shady deal that Desmond needs you there for. What if something goes wrong?"

"Something could go wrong anytime I ride my bike or step out in traffic."

"That's true. But you don't have to be a target for anyone wanting to take Desmond out either."

He held her tighter to his side. "Even if I quit, stayed home, and lived in a bubble to make you happy, I could drop dead of a heart attack from boredom. I can't live my life afraid of shit that could happen, any more than you can live in fear that Winston will have hurt or kill someone to get back at you."

"I know. What are we going to do?"

"I'll tell you what we're going to do. We're going to live our lives like Winston doesn't exist, that none of the deals will go down wrong, and I won't crash and burn on my bike. You don't think I'm just as afraid for you? Your mother was dying of heart failure when they found the breast cancer. You think that shit doesn't ride on my shoulders for you? You think I want to raise a kid on my own if something happens to you? Fuck no! But we're not going to live in fear that one of your checkups will come back anything but negative."

She nodded. "I'm trying."

"Fuck trying. You've been trying to forget Winston since he was arrested. Maybe that's the problem. You've gone to those hearings and talked about what he did to you and your friends. Fucking tell him everything you've been holding back, get it off your chest, and let it go when you walk out, because my dick's not getting any younger. I don't know if I can get it up anymore."

She jabbed him in the ribs with her elbow, knowing he was ready to change the subject from Winston. "You didn't have a problem getting a hard-on when you saw Lily dancing." She gave him a reproachful glance, letting him know she was aware of the bulge under his jeans when he tugged her into the restroom. It wasn't like she could have missed that huge bulge pressed against her ass as she sidled inside the bathroom.

He gave her a rueful smile in acknowledgment. "She would have gotten a rise from a dead man with the way she went up and down that pole. You should ask her where she took lessons."

She jabbed him again. "Shut up while you're ahead."

"No need to be jealous. She can't hold a candle to you. I prefer my women blonde…."

She arched a brow at him. "Women?"

"I prefer my *woman* to be blonde," he corrected himself. "She has too much junk in her trunk for my taste…."

"You're lying to make me feel better."

"Is it working?"

"Yes."

"Then it's all good. But seriously, you need to learn how to do that pole dancing. It's sexy as fuck."

"You go in a strip club almost every day in Queen City; it's not like pole dancing is a foreign concept to you."

"Those strippers are tired of twitching tails. Henry needs to hire some new ones. Besides, it's different seeing a good girl being bad. Gets my libido stirring, you know?"

"I can't say I do. I wonder if it works the same with men? Several very sweet men are clients of Zoey's. Maybe one of them has a bad boy side. I'll have to ask for her opinion."

Ice looked like he didn't appreciate the comparison.

She laid a hand on his thigh, and he laid one on top of hers.

"You trying to play nice after trying to get me jealous?"

She started to argue with him, then stopped herself, realizing the pattern she'd let fester.

"I guess I was just seeing if I could still make you jealous."

He gave her a crooked smile as if he was thinking about a joke only he could understand.

"What?"

"You don't have to make me jealous to find out if I feel the same way about you. You want to know something funny as fuck? I never expected our relationship to last."

She didn't find his confession funny.

Hurt, she tried to pull her hand back, but Ice forestalled her, linking his fingers with hers.

"I expected you to get tired of my ass a long time ago. You could have any man you want, someone smarter, has a decent job, or a decent family you wouldn't be ashamed to be a part of. I only married you because, once I put that ring on your finger and you swore on our marriage vows, that if I fucked up, you wouldn't walk away. When you say something, you fucking mean it. You're everything I'm not. I counted on you loving me despite me not being able to hide the fact I'm not the best man you could have chosen to be with."

"I don't want to change you."

"You do, but I can't. That's why I married you. I've been banking on that fact, when you realized it, you wouldn't leave me. How could I blame you when I couldn't cash in the promises you expected me to?"

"This whole time you've thought that the only reason I've stayed with you is because of a ring and a piece of paper?"

"Yes."

"If we had a marriage license or not, I wouldn't stay if I didn't love you. That's what divorce is for."

"Since I'm putting all my cards on the table, there will never be a divorce. I'll never let you go."

She squeezed the hand in hers. "I don't want you to. I think both of us have been so afraid of losing each other that we've been pushing each other away. We have to start fighting for what we have, and I have been more to blame than you. I'm sorry.

"If you want to keep working for Desmond, then go ahead. I won't interfere again. I have to trust that you'll do what's best for our marriage, even when I'm not there. And since we're laying our cards on the table, don't think that crap you just spilled about you not being smart, having a regular job, or a decent family was an effort to pull on my heartstrings. You're smart enough to know how to do that, and you know I don't give a damn about the other two."

Laying her head down on his shoulder, she relaxed against him for the first time in what felt like forever. "How much longer do you think we have to stay in here?"

"Want me to sneak out and see if they're finished?"

"No, I don't need you getting any more ideas."

"Too late. It's Valentine's Day, and I know what I want."

"Does it involve a pole?" she teased.

"No, it involves that jacket, those boots you're wearing, and a lap dance."

She was about to tell him that wasn't going to happen when they both jumped at the bathroom door being swung open.

The bar owner stood there, staring down at them grimly. "You were supposed to leave."

Ice stood, helping her to her feet. "We tried, but we didn't want to set the alarm off."

"That fucking alarm hasn't worked in ten years."

"That would have been good to know an hour ago." Grace blew a tuft of blue fur from the corner of her mouth.

"It's been over three hours since you went to the bathroom."

"It didn't seem that long, did it?" she asked her husband, seeing the man's skeptical look as he stared them down like they were peeping toms.

That he didn't agree with her had her jabbing him in the ribs.

"Yeah, sure," he finally conceded, even though he clearly didn't.

"How'd you know we were still in here?"

"Other than your rental car is still out front?" Sarcasm

rolled of his tongue. "Shade gave me your cell phones that you left sitting on the bar to return to you."

Grace's throat went dry. She gave Ice a killing glance because he didn't seem as embarrassed as her.

"What did he say?" Ice asked, taking the phone from him.

"Happy Valentine's Day."

CHAPTER 7

"I've never been so embarrassed in my life! Shade knew we were watching them!"

Ice took his eyes off the road to see Grace's face planted in her hands. "It didn't seem to bother him," he teased, trying to lighten her anxiety.

She raised her head to look at him. "Do you think Lily knows?"

"No."

"You don't think he told her?"

"If he had, he wouldn't have told us Happy Valentine's Day. He would have kicked my ass."

"I'm glad we're flying back in the morning. I'll never be able to face Lily again if she knows we saw them."

"You're being a little overdramatic, aren't you?"

"That's easy for you to say. With women, it's different. We get embarrassed about stuff like that. Especially Lily. She's very shy."

"She wasn't shy tonight," he said, then cautioned, "Don't hit me. I'm driving."

Grace huffily gave him an angry glare but kept her elbow

to herself. "Keep it up and it'll be four weeks until we have sex again."

"Don't hit a man when he's down."

"I truly didn't know it had been so long."

"Grace, I could have said something. I didn't. I knew Winston's hearing was coming up, then your dad getting remarried. The last thing you needed was me hounding you for sex."

"I don't know whether to thank you or be worried that you didn't."

Ice put the blinker on to turn down the street of Dalton's home. "There's nothing to be worried about."

He felt her eyes on him in the darkness as they pulled into the driveway.

"You haven't asked me to come to the clubhouse lately."

He tilted his head to the side, trying to study her expression in the shadows.

"You've been working late, and the mood you've been in, I didn't think you would want to."

"Me being a witch is over, Ice. I mean it."

"I know you do."

Getting out of the car, he took her hand when she held hers out to him as they walked up the sidewalk to the house.

"I'll be glad to be home tomorrow. I miss our dogs."

"Stump will be ready to give them back, and Zoey will try to keep them."

"It won't do her any good. I'm selfish when something is mine."

Ice gave her a quick glance as he inserted the key in the door. He had heard a subtle hint of possessiveness in her tone but thought she was overreacting.

Zoey would give the dogs back. To tell the truth, he probably would put up as much of a fight where the little shits were concerned.

Turning the lights on, he deactivated the alarm system that Dalton had shown him. The house was wired like Fort Knox.

"Looks like the caterers cleaned before they left." He expected to come back and have to spend the rest of the night helping Grace clean.

"They did. I told Willa and Ginny that we would, but they wouldn't let me lift a finger. I even wanted to pay them, but they wouldn't let me."

"I'm sure Dalton took care of it." Removing his jacket, he was going to take Grace's from her to hang it up, but she skirted from his touch. "Don't you want to take it off?"

"No, I won't be wearing it in the morning. I'm going to pack it in my suitcase before I forget it. I'm dreading packing. Our room is a mess."

Locking the door and resetting the outside alarms, he went to her side. "Come on, I'll help you pack."

"Don't you want me to make you something to eat?"

"We'll find something when the packing is done. I'm sure there're plenty of leftovers. You look exhausted."

"I am tired," she confessed.

Concern filled him for his wife. She had been through so much emotional turmoil lately that she was like a violin string wound too tightly.

"Come on; get what you need for tonight and the morning, and I'll do the packing. While I do the packing, you take a shower."

"That's okay. I can."

They walked through the foyer, then through the kitchen, toward the bedroom. He flicked the light switch on as they rounded the corner, both stopping when they saw what was sitting on the counter, waiting for them.

Moving forward, Grace laughed when she read the card left in plain sight.

"It's from T.A. and Dad. It's their Valentine's Day present to us. She said there're steaks and potatoes in the oven."

Ice took the champagne out of the ice bucket.

"Damn, I like T.A." Tearing the foil off the top, he reached for the wine opener sitting beside the bucket.

"I do, too." She picked up the glass he filled first for her before pouring his own. "I thought I'd resent anyone Dad would marry. Mom and I talked before she passed away, and she made me promise that whomever Dad picked that I'd show her as much as love and respect as I gave her."

Ice choked on the drink he had just taken.

"Oceane must have been high on pain meds when she said that." Skeptical, he didn't think his mother-in-law would ever give Dalton the go-ahead to remarry unless she had been stoned out of her mind.

"She wasn't. She told me when they found the breast cancer and she had been taken off the transplant list. Then she told me again two days before she died."

He paused, reaching for a spear of strawberries and pineapple. "Did you tell your dad?"

"Not yet. She gave me a letter to give to him when he remarried. I gave it to T.A. this morning to give to him tomorrow. Today should be about them."

"You learn something new every day. That Oceane gave her approval for Dalton to get remarried blows my fucking mind."

"She didn't give her approval. My mother was too jealous and possessive of Dad to do that. She told him that she loves him and that she still expects him to be buried next to her. That his new wife can be buried on the other side. She had Dax buy the cemetery lots before she passed away."

"That's the Oceane I knew."

The introspective look on her face told him that she hadn't told him what else had been in the letter. Ice didn't press her, getting the impression that she was leaving something out that she didn't want to discuss.

"You go take a warm bath, and I'll get our clothes packed."

Graced nodded going to the bedroom as he finished the skewer of fruit, giving her a few minutes alone.

Ice knew how close she had been to her mother, and despite how much she had come to love T.A., she still missed Oceane.

Walking into the bedroom, he saw Grace sitting on the bed with a jewelry box in her hands. Sensing he was there, she tore her eyes from the striking bracelet in her hands.

"It's beautiful." Her voice wobbled as she held out her hand for him to put it on. "When did you have time to get it?"

"I've had it for a couple of weeks. Dalton's been keeping it for me. I didn't want a repeat of Christmas. You're terrible about opening your presents."

During Christmas, he caught her rewrapping a present that he had wrapped and put under the Christmas tree. She was worse than a child when it came to presents. She couldn't resist the temptation.

"I can't help it."

"I know." Fastening the bracelet, he knew he had chosen well. The dainty jewelry came alive against her skin. The gold metal gleamed with the small, jeweled hearts flashing fire, catching the light as she raised her hand to stare down at it.

"It's beautiful. Thank you."

"You're welcome."

"I have a present for you, too." Going to the closet, she took out her suitcase. Unzipping the compartment in the front, she took out an envelope and hesitantly gave it to him.

Opening the envelope, Ice took out a Valentine's Day card. Inside was a receipt.

"I bought you a bike like Colton's."

"I asked him to sell me one. Now I see why he wouldn't."

She gave a sigh of relief. "I knew you needed another bike. Colton said he would refund the money if you had another you wanted more."

"Are you kidding me? That bike is kick-ass. Shade was trying to buy one off him, too, when we were outside."

"So, you're happy?"

Ice looked up from the receipt. The unsureness in his wife's face had him reaching for her. "I was happy before you gave me the bike."

She nuzzled the side of his throat poignantly, burying her face in the crook of his neck. "You were?"

"I am," he assured her.

Turning her toward the bathroom, he swatted her on the ass to get her moving. "Go take your bath, and I'll get everything packed so we can enjoy the rest of the evening."

"Yes, sir," she mocked.

"Damn, that sounds good. You should ask Lily for a few of those less—Ouch!" Ice dodged the empty jewelry box still in her hand.

"You know that's not going to happen."

"Babe, let a man dream."

"Okay, you can dream about it when I'm in the bath, but when I come out, you better be back in reality."

Positioning Grace's suitcase on the end of the bed, he started working on packing their clothes as the sound of running water came from the bathroom. Confident that Grace was occupied, he took out his cell phone, making sure there weren't any missed calls. There weren't any, but without a doubt, Shade would be shooting him one when he wasn't occupied.

The Last Rider wouldn't give a fuck that he had been seen doing his wife, but what the brother would care about was Lily never finding out.

Finishing the one suitcase, he pulled the smaller one out of the closet, filling it with his things. He was lifting it from the bed when he heard Grace getting out of the tub.

Shoving the two suitcases back in the closet, he was thinking of lying down and stretching out on the bed when the door opened and Grace came out with a towel wrapped around her.

"Your turn," she said, running a smaller towel through her hair. "I'll heat us up something while you take your bath."

Determining that once he lay down, he would be out for the count, he nodded tiredly, then went around her and into the bathroom. He preferred taking a shower, but Grace had already drained the tub and was refilling it for him. Taking his clothes off, he sank down in the warm water. She had even laid out a washcloth.

Washing off, he then relaxed, resting the nape of his neck on the end of the tub, too lazy to get out. He promised himself that he would get out in a minute.

"Ice." He was so tired that he hadn't heard Grace come into the room. His eyes landed on her, startled to find her kneeling by the tub.

"I'm coming. I dozed off."

He brought his hand to the side of the tub to pull himself out of the water, but she pressed him back down with a firm hand on his shoulder before reaching for something by her side.

"Stay still."

Curious, he took the champagne glass she handed him, then watched as she reached down again before placing a plump strawberry at his lips. He took a bite as she deliberately ran a hand down from his shoulder to his chest.

"When we married, I swore I would never be the type of wife that would make excuses for not making love."

"Grace, it's not a big deal," he tried reassuring her, setting the glass on the other side of the tub.

Caressing his chest, her sad eyes collided with his. "I don't know which is worse: that you think it's not a big deal, or that you didn't call me out on it."

He nearly knocked the glass off with his elbow as he raised up in the tub. "I haven't been fucking around on you."

She continued stroking his chest as if he hadn't said anything. "How could I blame you if you had? I've certainly not been there for you the last few weeks. Honestly, I haven't been there for you since I lost Mom and the baby."

Her forthright admission had him snaking his hand out to wrap around the back of her neck.

"Look at me. You think I don't know that? You didn't even have your balance back before you were knocked down again. You weren't the only one who lost the baby. I lost him, too. I never planned to have kids—it's not like I have any redeeming qualities to pass on—but I convinced myself that, with you in the picture, he might have a chance of having a normal life."

"Except he didn't."

Ice could tell she was trying hard not to cry.

She lifted her chin and gave him an inviting smile as she reached for another strawberry. "I don't want to talk about this anymore tonight. The rest of the night is just going to be about you."

Chewing on the strawberry as she shrugged out of her robe, he forced himself to swallow the berry. Then she leaned over the edge of the tub to glide her hand under the water before wrapping her hand around his cock.

"Anything you want tonight is yours for the taking."

"Uh… How many glasses of champagne did you have while I was napping?"

"I'm not drunk. I sobered up when you reminded me that it's been three weeks since we had sex."

"I don't want to fuck just because you're feeling guilty."

"I'm not feeling guilty. I'm horny."

He wasn't stupid enough to keep arguing, especially when her hand was wrapped around his cock like a fist. How could he be sweating while sitting in a tub of lukewarm water? He'd had more pussy than most men had in their whole lifetime.

When he fucked a slut at the Predators' clubhouse to prove a point to the brothers when their relationship had first begun, he lost Grace. The only way he had gotten her back was to swear never to do it again. He kept his word.

One thing that fucking Brandy had done for him was to show him that no snatch was worth losing Grace over. There was always fresh pussy that the brothers kept around to relieve their itches with, but he was never tempted, despite them making their eagerness known.

One in particular was beginning to be a pain in his ass. He hadn't paid any attention to Porsche when Lizard introduced her to the club, and he still didn't. But the more he ignored her, the more she was determined to capture his attention. He told Lizard before he had left for Kentucky that the woman was on borrowed time.

The morning he and Grace were leaving for Kentucky, he stopped by the club to make sure there was enough money for Jackal for emergencies while he was gone. When he went into the office, Porsche was sitting behind his desk with only a tiny pair of shorts on and a bra that her huge tits were pouring out of.

Swinging the chair to the side, he told her to get the fuck out, but instead of running scared, she brought her hands to his belt buckle. "You look like you're in a bad mood. Let me suck your cock." Pouting up at him, she ran her tongue suggestively over her lips. "Come on, baby. I can make you feel so good," she crooned.

*He stared icily down at her, his eyes narrowed. "I bet you could."
He clasped her chin so hard that her skin whitened under his
fingertips. The bitch didn't even realize how close she was to him
strangling her. "But so could any other bitch in the other room.
You're like a two-dollar bottle of cheap wine that I can have
anytime I want. When I want it, I take it. There isn't anything
about you that I want to fuck. Not that mouth or that pussy you've
been begging me to take."*

*Sliding his hand to her neck, he tugged her out of his chair, then
forced her toward the door. "Open it," he snarled.*

Whimpering, the woman opened the door.

*When he tossed her out of his office, she had to catch herself on
the wall in the hallway.*

*"The only thing I want from you is to tell Lizard to get his ass
in here."*

*Slamming the door on her, he went back to the desk to take care
of the business he had come for.*

It didn't take long before he had a knock on the door.

*"That bitch is trouble." Ice made no bones about voicing his
displeasure.*

"Which one?"

"Don't play fucking stupid. You know who I'm talking about."

"She has a thing for you—"

*"She doesn't have a thing for me. She wants to get to Desmond.
She just wants to use my dick as an introduction like she used
yours to get to me."*

*"She'll be gone before you get back," Lizard said, turning to
leave.*

*"She better be, or when I throw her ass out, yours will be right
behind hers."*

CHAPTER 8

Grace saw the conflicting expressions chase across her husband's face. Had she waited too long to try to save her marriage? She didn't have to be told she had taken Ice for granted, lost in her own pain. Every time she tried to find her way out, it returned like a boomerang, driving her farther and farther away from Ice.

"Anything?" he asked huskily.

"Anything but me kneeling down to you, which is never going to happen."

She teasingly pressed a kiss to his lips, then removed her hand from his cock to stand. Taking a towel from the towel rack, she held it open for him.

The sight of him rising from the water had heat rising between her thighs. His body was gorgeous. Even Killyama's mother, Peyton, had asked her if she thought he would model for her. T.A. told her that she was a gifted artist, but as much as she liked the woman, she didn't want Ice to model. She didn't want anyone but her seeing the body that promised sensual pleasure just in the way he walked across a room.

His brown hair was shorter than when they first met. His compelling gaze made you feel as if he was aware of the indecent fantasies she was imagining, even in broad daylight. Sinful, dark passions lurked just beneath those ice-blue eyes. Sexually, he was a magnet for any woman, much less the women who had no hesitation in going for what they wanted.

She wanted to scream at herself. If she lost him, she would have no one to blame but herself.

She didn't wrap the towel around him and let him dry himself. Instead, she attentively dried him off herself. Starting at his shoulders, she rubbed the towel over his body, taking extra care at his chest, then his waist before sliding it down to the nest of curly hair above his thighs. Going lower, she dried the cock that was swelling upward, smiling when she heard him hiss.

Moving on, she slid the towel down his legs, soaking up the droplets of water, then moving to his feet before standing. Going behind him, she dried his back, intermittently placing kisses on each of his shoulder blades, then trailing down his spine. She appreciatively dried off his ass before returning to his legs.

Satisfied that he was dry, she walked around him to face him again, noticing his cock was so hard that she could see the veins through the thin skin.

"Who needs a towel warmer when I have you?"

"You like?" Amusement filled her at Ice's reaction. "Any time you want, I'm at your service. I enjoyed it, too," she admitted thickly.

Dropping the towel over the side of the tub, she showered Ice's chest with the same attention she had his back. Pursing her lips on one of his nipples, she laved at the sunken nipple until it rose into a tiny bud. Then she slid her tongue across his chest and did the same to the other one.

"I can be or do anything you want, Ice," she murmured against his skin.

"Shut the fuck up," he rasped out as he tunneled his hand through her hair. "All I've ever wanted was you, even before I met you." He roughly enclosed her in his arms, tilting her head back by her hair, forcing her to meet his eyes. "Rainbows are beautiful while they last. I was fucking lucky to catch you before you found out what kind of man I was. I fucked up and almost lost you. I am never going to put myself in that position again."

Tipping her nose upward, she bravely didn't try to pull away from the hand pulling at her hair.

Ice wasn't the only one aroused. Being in such contact with her husband had her hands going to his shoulders, her nails unknowingly leaving half-moon prints in his flesh. Her nipples beaded as heat flared in her center, coiling tighter when she saw the reciprocal passion in his gaze.

Ice was experienced enough to know she wanted him that it wasn't just make-up sex; the desire, banked with grief of losing her mother and baby, was still there, waiting to flare out of control again.

Ice slid his free hand down to her bottom, kneading her buttock with his rough palm, insinuating his fingers between her cleft.

"I might be taking you up on that offer of doing what I want."

Grace gulped at the image of Ice the Predator being given free reign.

"Are you going to take it back?" he asked, raising a brow at her, giving her the chance to rethink her offer.

Feeling frantic, she thought about the way he was looking at her, only the yearning within her own body wouldn't let her. She wanted him as much as he wanted her. She had been trying to put restraints on Ice for so long that it had nearly destroyed their marriage. She was done with that. Limits sucked.

Ice was a biker used to breaching the speed limits. Striving to tame the thing she loved most about him, she tried to turn him into a four-door sedan.

She wanted her biker back. She wanted him back badly.

"Ice, fuck me."

Bracing herself for what her husband would do next, she stood there gaping when he released her butt and strode out of the bathroom.

"What are you...?" Grace started to ask, coming to the doorway, then wished she hadn't. She should have used the opportunity to lock herself inside.

She would never describe Ice as a playful lover. He had never wanted to play games like most couples do to spice up their sex life. The only spice he needed to get him hard was a sultry look. She hadn't needed it either, because Ice did two things really, really well: riding a motorcycle and having sex. Tonight, though, it appeared that Ice wanted to play. The problem was that she felt like a lamb and he was the big bad wolf.

He was pulling the shades down and drawing the thick drapes closed. Then he went to nightstand that was closest to him and turned the light off. The way he stalked around the bed to the other lamp had her shivering.

"Ice, when I said anything, I *really* didn't mean *anything*."

"Trust me; come here."

Unexpectedly, she felt herself growing slick as she walked across the bedroom floor to him.

"Turn around."

Turning around, she complied to his thick voice, hearing that Ice was getting excited about what he had planned.

"Shouldn't we have some kind of safe... word?" she asked haltingly.

"You know the word *stop*, don't you?" he asked.

"Yes."

"Then we're good."

She laughed nervously, turning her head to look over her shoulder, wanting to see what Ice was doing.

"Don't look at me and close your eyes tight."

Turning her face back around, she closed her eyes tightly.

"Keep them closed." Taking her hand, she could feel him tugging her somewhere in the room. "Keep them closed," he repeated., stopping her.

Staying still, she waited for what he would do next. The sound of the lamp being switched off had her nervously shifting back and forth on the balls of her feet. She wasn't afraid, just curious about what he was going to do.

"You can open your eyes now." The sound of his voice was barely a whisper. "Find me."

Her eyes flew open. The bedroom was pitch dark. Twirling in the darkness, she couldn't see where Ice was.

"Since when did you want to get kinky?" She started to laugh but couldn't.

Had he discovered the pleasure of playing games with another woman and now he was trying to spice up their marriage?

She tentatively shuffled around the room, going to the place she had heard his voice. She extended her hands in front of her in a sweeping motion to keep from bumping into the furniture.

When he didn't answer, she knew he was making sure his voice wouldn't lead her to his hiding place.

Feeling her knee brush the bed, she used it as a guide to navigate. When her fingers brushed the lamp shade, she knew she was going in the direction she wanted.

Sidling around the nightstand, she held out her hand, searching for the wall. She thought he was in the corner beside the bathroom door. She came up empty, though, and had to keep sliding her hand along the wall.

When her naked belly came to the doorjamb, she knew he wasn't in the corner. Turning around, she stared fruitlessly around the dark room. Squinting, she waited for any small movement that would give her a telltale sign.

"You don't have to be afraid of the footsteps you can hear. It's the ones that you can't hear that you have to be afraid of."

She jerked her head to the side, in the direction of his whisper. Then she reached out for the bathroom doorknob, wanting to open it and turn on the light.

She didn't, though. She knew it was Ice in the room, and she could never be afraid of him.

Skirting to the side, she made her way across the wall, trying to keep her own movements soundless. Using the memory of the bedroom in her mind, she was almost at the bedroom door when she felt fingers trail down her spine.

Jerking around, she swept her hands out, sure that Ice was within reach. However, all she felt was the swoosh of air as her hands flailed around.

"How did I not know my husband could be so sneaky?" she asked when she futilely came up empty.

"I've been keeping a secret from you."

Her heart dropped. Was he using this method to tell her that he had been cheating on her, unable to see her face when he told her?

"What's your secret?"

"I've always been a sneaky bastard; you just didn't know it."

CHAPTER 9

"That's no secret."

His low laughter had her stomach clenching in need.

Grace moved in the direction of his laughter, leaving the safety of the wall. Stepping in unknown territory, she cautiously took a small step forward, then another.

"You're going the wrong way."

She spun around, hearing his voice behind her.

"Jerk."

His laughter had her spinning around again. It came from the direction she had originally been going.

"What would you say to Winston if you could?"

Grace stopped dead in her tracks. "I have a therapist. I don't need someone else to talk to."

"I don't want to talk about it. Just pretend I'm him. What would you say?"

"I don't want to do this."

"Then say stop."

She opened her mouth to say the word.

"We both know you'll go into the hearing and repeat the

same two pages you wrote the last time. Tell me what you want to say without having to look at him."

"No."

"No, you don't want to, or no, you want me to stop?" His voice was moving closer.

Instead of going toward him, she backed away in the dark. "I have a therapist…."

"Who is a woman. I'm a man. Tell me one thing you wished you had told him during the last hearings but didn't because either the board was listening or because he was there, staring at you."

Her spine finally came up against the wall. Spreading out her arms, she started sidling to the side, looking for the light switch.

"Do it, Grace. Just one thing."

"I hate you. God, I hate you so much." She stopped moving, turning to face the room.

"I don't care. I'm never going to care."

Those are exactly the words that Winston would say, even though they had been uttered from Ice.

He was right; Winston was never going to care about the damage he had done. Avril and Simone had lost their lives because of the madman, yet he never showed an ounce of remorse.

Unsettled that she really wanted to get all the pent up fury off her chest without the board considering her a hysterical victim, she started talking, imagining it was Winston in the darkness and not Ice.

"No, you don't care. You never have. You're responsible for taking the lives of two beautiful girls that had their whole lives in front of them. You don't deserve any hearings the doctors and lawyers apply for on your behalf; you don't deserve another chance. You didn't give Avril one, and she was so terrified. All of us were. But the more frightened we

161

became, the more you enjoyed it. That's what your psychiatrists will never get about you. Your body might be broken, but your mind is so twisted they can't fix what's wrong with you!"

Her voice strengthened as she talked. "If I could kill you without going to jail, I would. The only reason I don't is because I won't let myself be locked up again because of you. I wished Ice killed you, but he didn't and I won't lose him by asking him to finish you off.

"You had no intention of ever letting either me or Simone live. I saw that the day you looked at me when you found Simone dead. The only thing you cared about was that she did it herself instead of giving you the pleasure. You screwed up by killing Avril first, didn't you? God, I bet you were sick to your stomach when you realized that, weren't you?

"She was the one who was most frightened of you. Simone was like a fragile flower; you crushed her the first day. Me?" Grace gave a bark of bitter anger. "You knew if I could get a hand on a weapon, I would kill you, and I would have.

"Neither me nor Simone were any fun for you. If you hadn't been caught that day, you would have been out hunting for another victim. Just like you will be if they transfer you to a regular prison. The only reason you're still in that mental hospital is because you haven't figure a way out, when your body is tied to that bed. Someway, somehow, one day, you'll find a way to hurt me. I was the one that got away, wasn't I? And you can't stand that. I bet it eats at your soul that I'm still alive."

Running out of steam, the burning hatred she bottled up didn't matter anymore. It took her own words for her to convince her of that.

"That's what I've been missing, isn't it? For five hundred and four hours and thirty-seven minutes, you held that power over me. But the clock hasn't stopped ticking for you, has it?"

She brought her hand to her forehead, rubbing her temple. "Jesus Christ, it hasn't for me either. That's why I keep hearing your footsteps, isn't it?

"*No more*, Winston, *no more* will I let you have one more second of my life. It's mine, and you can't have it. You'll never have it. Even if you have me killed, you'll never have it, because Ice has a part of me that is beyond your reach. My soul will be his forever. You could hurt the shell of my body, but what's underneath is already gone. It was gone the moment I met him…."

Warm arms enclosed her. Crying, she laid her head on Ice's shoulder.

"I've been such an idiot," she sobbed out, wrapping her arms around him.

"No, you haven't." He soothed his hand down her back as he pulled her closer to his body.

"I love you so much…."

She raised her head, searching for his mouth passionately.

"I love you." His mouth found hers, ardently driving his tongue through her parted lips.

The warmth of his body seeped into hers, smothering the hatred she felt for Winston, the hatred that had ruled over her life since she, Avril, and Simone got into that cab. The loathing she had for him had been unconsciously affecting her, even though she thought she'd come to terms with it and moved on with her life. His petitions kept the memories fresh like a festering wound.

The honest admission to herself was a burden taken off her back.

Compressing her lips harder against Ice's, she fought for control of the kiss, wanting to take everything he could give her. Panting sounded in the darkened room as they tried to catch their breaths without breaking the passionate kiss.

She used her hands to lift herself until she could circle her legs around his hips. Ice cupped her bottom as he took a few steps to push her against the wall.

Unrestrained desire ran through her veins, as if she was running to catch something just beyond her reach.

"Please don't ever leave me…"

"It would take a SWAT team to make me leave you."

Ice lifted her higher up the wall, making her whimper when his mouth covered her nipple. Her body felt as if her insides were melting.

His lips constricting around her nipple brought another surge of warmth to her vagina. Her slick center wanted him so badly that she tried to wiggle downward so he could fuck her.

A low, hungry growl had her beating on his shoulders when he switched to her other nipple. "Please, Ice. I need you…."

"I know what you need."

His erect cock pressed into her waist.

"You don't, or you'd be inside me!" she moaned out, trying to wiggle down again.

Crossing her ankles behind his back, she used the heels of her feet on his ass to push his hips closer to her.

"Uh-uh. I know what you're trying to do."

"Ice…."

He let a scant inch separate their bodies, just enough room to slide his hand between them. He moved it unerringly to her slick folds, the sensitive flesh becoming even wetter as he deliberately manipulated her desire to a nearly unbearable level. She felt like a cat in heat, searching for a mate to satisfy the primal urge that he was building inside her but was refusing to satisfy.

When he moved his mouth to return to her other breast, Grace lowered her head to bite down on his shoulder. "Quit playing and fuck me," she demanded. Frustrated, she moved her hand to between her thighs to make him move faster.

"Is that better?"

"Hmm…," she hummed, within reach of her climax.

"Oh no, you don't." Ice removed his hand, lowering her to the floor.

"Ice!" She swept her hands out to find him, attempting to pull him back.

A second later, she was blinking at the glare of the bedroom light.

When she was able to focus, she saw a slumbering passion in her husband's eyes that set her bloodstream on fire. The sexual vibe exuding from him was palpable. She wanted to drop to her knees and beg him to take her.

Barely able to stand, she put out her hand to brace herself.

Circling around the bed, Ice lowered the comforter to the bottom. "Come here."

Walking jerkily forward, she moved toward the bed as he watched her every step of the way. When she reached the bed, she started to lie down.

"Wait."

Grace paused in place.

"If you could have me do anything you wanted, what would it be? Think hard, Grace. I'll never offer again," he warned without expression.

She swallowed hard, knowing instinctively what he was asking. He was offering to quit working for Desmond to make her happy. She had the chance to change their lives for the better or the worse. However, she would never risk coming so close to losing her husband again. She was going to blow the chance Ice was giving her.

"That you never stop loving me."

"Get on the bed."

She lay down, opening her arms wide for him.

He placed his knee on the bed as he rested his hand on the pillow beside her head to hold himself over her.

"You chose wrong. There was never a chance in hell that I would ever leave you."

Grace stared up at him with her heart in her eyes. "Some chances aren't worth taking."

CHAPTER 10

The feel of Grace's soft body almost undermined the control he was exerting over himself not to pound every inch of his cock into her pussy until she was left with no doubt that they would never be separated.

Pushing his cock against her soft belly, he raised her hands over her head, then cuffed her wrists together with one of his hands. Her naked body shook under his, her tits heaving with every breath she took as her eyes pleaded with him.

Ice laid his palm roughly over one of her luscious tits, squeezing it hard. Letting her nipple slide between his fingers, he trapped it between two digits. Then, scooting his hips downward, he made room for himself between her thighs, the movement placing his cock right where he wanted it—between her pussy lips.

Gritting his teeth to keep from climaxing, he stayed still, letting the sensations in his cock ease before he tried to move. The only thing he wanted to do was immerse himself in her, sink his body into hers so far that the only thing she could think about was him.

"What are you waiting for...?" she moaned, writhing under him.

He tightened his hand over her wrists, controlling her movements with another steely hand on her hip. His cock was so hard it felt as if the skin was stretched too tight. The barbell on the tip of his dick wasn't helping, giving an edge of pain that had his gut twisting with his own need.

"I'm waiting for you to tell me how you want it." Separating her folds, he swirled his finger over her clit. "Do you want me on top?" He gave another swirl, making sure she was ready enough before he plunged his cock inside. His lips curled upward sensually when she arched under him. He only gave her two pounding thrusts of his cock before slipping out. "Or do you want to be on your stomach?"

Lifting his body off hers, he flipped her over onto her belly before pinning her to the mattress where he resumed fucking her.

"Oh, God... Ice."

"Which one?"

Grace urgently squirmed under him. "Yes! Like this," she screeched.

"Or..." He let the word drip off his tongue for a brief second before slipping out of her again, hearing her screech of frustration before he rolled onto his back and pulled her on top of him. Holding her poised over his cock, he then slammed her down on it while lifting his hips to meet her halfway.

Grace's head lolled back, her tits trembling under the strain of her harsh breathing.

"Like this?" His eyes were slit in passion, hiding how close he was to losing control. "Ride me, baby, until you make up your mind... or I make it up for you."

As Grace began moving up and down on his dick jerkily,

he had to bite back his lust as he watched her pussy slide up and down his dick.

It took all his willpower to move his hands behind his head as he lazily watched her do all the work. He had fucked Grace enough times to know which position she preferred. His wife liked to be ridden and leave the riding to him.

"Come on; you can do better than that." Inciting the passion she was still holding back, he swore to himself he would give her only a couple more minutes before taking over and giving it to her the way she wanted.

She narrowed her eyes at him spiritedly. "I'm going to make you regret that."

"Bring it on, baby. Because right now, you're not showing me anything you haven't given me before."

His taunt stirred the flames in her eyes as she glared at him.

"You're such a prick," she moaned out raggedly.

Ice thought his skull would split open when she started moving on him faster.

"Now that's the way I like it," he groaned out. "Give it to me."

"Oh, I'm going to give it to you."

She was the one taunting him now, raising her knees until she was squatting over him, bouncing on dick.

"Goddamn! That's better than fucking pole dancing!" he grunted out. Watching his wife getting raunchy with him had his dick swelling further. "Fuck," he hissed through bared teeth.

"I thought you'd appreciate that." She moved her hand to her breast teasingly before sliding it down to her pussy, letting him watch her play with her clit.

"*Appreciate that* aren't the words I would use. I fucking love it."

Any thought of riding his wife's sweet ass had gone out of his shell-shocked mind. He enjoyed the position too much to switch. Damn, it was so good he didn't want it to end, but his cock was at a bursting point.

When her expression changed to one of rapture and her pussy started contracting on him, he lost it.

"Motherfucking hell!" he shouted as his climax hit him like a ton of bricks. Rising, he grabbed her hips, slamming her down on him. Losing her balance, Grace's scream drowned out his curses as her pussy crashed against his pelvis.

Taking her thighs in each of his hands, he pulled them to his sides as he rocked forward, pushing her to her back, fucking her so hard that he felt his dick banging against her womb.

Raising her hands over her head, he stroked out his climax in her spasming cunt.

"You are fucking mine."

"I know," she whimpered. "I know."

He ruthlessly let their climaxes start to play out, then flipped her back onto her stomach and started fucking her again before he lost his erection. He adeptly drawled her orgasm out, moving his hands to her hips to bring her to her knees before sliding a hand around her waist to find her clit, keeping the tremors of ecstasy going.

She fucked back on him, not wanting it to end either. The slaps of their flesh hitting each other had him lunging forward, trying to catch that fleeting moment of anticipation at building another climax.

He placed his hand on her shoulder to pull her back farther on his dick. Grace stole a heart she already had when she clutched his hand.

"Don't stop. It feels so good."

Ice bent over her back, using his chin to see her face. He would never be the perfect match for Grace, he shouldn't even be allowed to touch her, but she was a lifeline that either God or whichever twist of fate had brought into his life, and he was going to make damn sure she never thought about him leaving her again.

Inexorably, he kept lunging forward until both their bodies were covered in a sheen of sweat. She wantonly surged back on him. driving what was left of his brain to mush as they each tried to outdo the other on how much pleasure they could give each other.

The first climax they had shared had just been an appetizer, not quenching their hunger that the three weeks of abstinence had built. Now, the climax he was building in their bodies was one that would not only alleviate the remnants of what was left, it would also consume them in a fiery blaze.

Stroke by stroke, Ice drove them closer to the edge like a sailboat anchored to shore, waiting until he felt the flash of need that signaled he was getting close to coming before using the heel of his palm to crush down on her clit, setting her free to sail toward her own climax.

The aftershocks had them crashing down on the bed together, neither of them able to move.

"Ice...," Grace plaintively mumbled underneath him. "I can't breathe."

Groaning, he managed to roll over onto his back. "Damn, woman, that was good."

He winced when she smacked him on his chest, then grinned down at her when she tiredly climbed on top of him, resting her cheek on his chest.

"Are we dead?" she asked sleepily.

"No." Running a hand down her spine, he then grabbed an

ass cheek, giving it a loving squeeze. "But the night isn't over yet."

"It is for me. I have nothing left."

As she burrowed into him, Ice saw she was already half asleep.

"Take a nap. I'll wake you when I want to fuck you again."

Her lips curled in a satisfied yawn. "Do that and I'll make you regret it."

"If you think that's going to deter me, you chose the wrong threat."

"It wasn't a threat; it was a promise."

Turning her face into his chest, she put her hands under her chin to stare at him seriously. "I'm not going to the hearing."

"Grace... I wasn't—"

"It has nothing to do with you. This is a part of my life that has to be over. It's poisoning me just as surely as the poison Simone drank to escape him. I'm never going to forgive him."

"I don't expect you to," he said, rubbing a knuckle across her cheek.

"I'll write a new letter, but I'm not going to give him one more minute of my life. Not one. I've been so afraid of him getting out that I've only focused on that. The *only* revenge I could get was to keep him where he didn't want to be. I hope he gets out, because he *will* come searching for me. And when he does, I'll be waiting."

"Are you sure?" Ice didn't try to sway her either way.

"I'm sure. I need to stop listening to footsteps from my nightmares and start listening to the patter of little feet."

Ice could feel her eyes drilling into his soul.

"Is that a hint?"

"It's a request. That is, if you still want to have one with me?"

At the sight of her trembling bottom lip, his curled salaciously. "I thought you were tired."

Scooting down his body, she reached for his already rising cock. "We can sleep on the way home."

CHAPTER 11

Grace sleepily stretched out in the bed, reaching out with her hand to search for Ice's warmth. Feeling only the cool sheets, though, she lifted her eyelids to find the bed empty.

"Ice..." She turned over, seeing the bathroom door wide open, but he wasn't in there.

Brushing her tousled hair from her face, she looked toward the clock on the bedside table and then hurriedly flipped the covers back, jumping out of the bed to get dressed.

Rushing in the bathroom, she took a quick shower. They were supposed to meet Dax at the airport for the flight back to Queen City.

Expecting to find Ice in the bedroom when she came out of the bathroom, she sent him a text as she got dressed. Anticipating that he was in the kitchen or the living room, she assumed he would come to the bedroom when he got her text.

She was taking the suitcases out of the closets when she heard a text *ping* on her phone.

Give me five. Having breakfast with Shade.

Disappointed that he hadn't asked her to go, she shrugged it off, too happy in the aftermath of spending the night in Ice's arm to resent him for taking a break for masculine company.

Wheeling the suitcases into the living room after checking that they weren't leaving anything behind, she was about to go to the kitchen to make a pot of coffee when she heard a key in the door.

She gave him a beaming smile when he came through the door with a large cup of coffee.

"I was about to make me some."

"Then I'm glad I saved you the trouble." Giving her a kiss, he saw that she had the suitcases ready to go. "Did you double-check that we have everything?"

"Of course," she said, taking the lid off the steaming coffee cup.

Ice gave her a know-it-all look, then went around her to head into the bedroom. Grace trailed after him as far as the kitchen to get some milk for her coffee.

Stirring her coffee, she flushed when Ice came out of the bedroom, carrying her favorite sneakers.

"Thank you. I would have missed them when I got home." Taking a sip of her coffee, she flashed him a grateful smile.

He didn't return it, coming to stand beside her at the kitchen counter.

"There's something I need to tell you." The seriousness in his voice had her hand trembling around the Styrofoam cup and her heart plummeting to her feet. It was everything she could do not to beg him not to leave her before he spilled the bombshell she had been expecting.

"I won't be going back with you."

This was it then. What she had been expecting to happen.

"I see." She set the cup down, then turned toward him,

waiting for him to speak the final words, to say their marriage was over. Feeling desperate, she promised herself she wouldn't beg. Then she immediately decided she wasn't going to give him up without a fight. If she was hurting this badly now, how was she going to survive without him in her life? It wasn't humanly possible to live with this pain and survive.

"Grace…." His snapped voice dragged her out of the pain-filled well she sank into. "Listen to me. I'm only going to be gone for a couple of weeks. I have to take care of some business for Shade that he asked me to do."

Relief had her sagging, and she braced herself on the counter. "Okay."

He frowned at her. "That's it? You're not going to ask what it is?"

She quickly shook her head. "I trust you. Can I have a kiss?"

He put his hand behind her neck, pulling her toward him. "You're getting as crazy as T.A.'s friend."

She smoothed her hands over his chest. "Probably. I've heard love does that to you."

"That's for fucking sure. My head hasn't been on straight since I met you."

She put her arms around his shoulders as he kissed her, committing it to memory until he got back to Queen City.

The sound of her phone ringing had Ice trying to break off the kiss.

"It's Dax. I'll call him back. I'm going to miss you."

"I'm going to miss you, too. Just think of the sex we'll have when I get back."

"Hopefully, I'll be recovered from last night," she said, finally forced to answer the insistent ringing of her cell phone.

"I'm on my way," she told Dax when she answered.

"I was beginning to get worried," his voice sounded from the other end.

"Don't be. I just woke up late. I'll be there in twenty minutes."

Disconnecting the call, she placed it in her pocket so she wouldn't forget it, then took the shoes from Ice.

"We better be going, Dax is waiting."

She put on a brave face when Ice put her suitcase in the rental car, leaving his suitcase behind. Getting in the passenger seat, she took his hand when he got behind the wheel, holding it all the way to the small airport.

When he pulled into the airfield, she didn't immediately get out, even though she could see Dax waiting by the plane with the door open.

"Please take care of yourself," she said, turning to face him when he stopped the car.

"Grace, don't worry." He raised a lone finger to rub away her frown lines. "Baby, you know I would be on that plane with you if it wasn't important."

"I know." She turned her face, resting it on the palm of his hand. It was calloused and hard, yet he touched her with the gentleness of holding delicate porcelain.

"I'm not happy about staying behind either. I don't like you flying without me."

"Dax is an excellent pilot," she assured him.

"Baby, I know. Or your ass wouldn't be getting on that plane."

When he kissed her, she didn't want to let him go. It was Ice who finally had the strength to pull away.

Reaching for the door latch, she stalled. "When Mom died, I couldn't truly understand the grief my dad was going through. Stupidly, I thought he was going through the same type of grief I was, that Dax and I were both going through. It was different, though. I see it now." A tear rolled down her cheek. "I'm thankful to T.A. She makes it more bearable for him in a way that Dax and I can't. I'm happy he found her.

"Mom told me that, with Dad, they fell in love at first sight, and when she got home, she told her chaperone that she was going to marry him. I asked her how she was so sure. She said she knew because, when she always looked at other men, she imagined chasing after a rainbow with them." A sob slipped through her lips at the memory of her mother's words. "She said, with Dad, not only could she see them chasing after rainbows, but that he would do his damnedest to catch them for her.

"You're like my father where that's concerned.

"Stay and help Shade. You wouldn't be staying unless it was important, and when you come home, I need your help catching a couple of rainbows, but I'd rather have three if I can talk you into it."

Gathering her emotions, she sprang out of the car before Ice could say something, seeing that Dax was walking toward the car, concerned that it was taking her so long to get out.

She didn't want to look back at Ice. She was crying too hard and didn't want him to see her makeup smeared to hell and back.

"Grace!"

She kept walking, afraid that if she didn't, she would want to stay.

"Dammit, Grace!"

At the authoritative tone in his voice, she turned and walked straight back into his waiting arms. Enclosing her in them, he rubbed his unshaven cheek against hers.

"Baby, when I get home, you can have as many rainbows as you want."

CHAPTER 12

THE DAY GRACE RETURNED TO
QUEEN CITY

I ce quietly put on his boots before standing up from the chair in the corner of the bedroom. Walking to the side of the bed, he stood looking at her sprawled out naked. Her beautiful face was relaxed, and for the first time in a long time, she looked as if she was sleeping peacefully.

Pulling the comforter over her, he couldn't resist placing a soft kiss on her lips. Then he straightened and stood silently a moment longer before forcing himself to leave, making sure to close the bedroom door quietly as he left.

He didn't live in Treepoint, but he knew where he was going. It was hard to miss the main street of the small town.

He was pulling into a small parking lot when his cell phone rang.

"I'm here," he said, answering.

"You're late."

The unknown number on his phone had been unidentifiable. Shade's voice wasn't.

"I overslept."

"Me, too."

A brief silence came over the phone, both waiting for the

other to mention the night before. Ice wasn't about to open his mouth.

"It's a go. The deputies are all on patrol, and Knox gave the front desk clerk the day off."

"Okay. Thanks." He paused.

"About last night…."

Ice forestalled what he was sure Shade was about to say. "Grace and my mouths are zipped. We spent most of the night in the ladies' restroom."

"That wasn't what I was about to say, but it's good to know."

Ice could hear the amusement in Shade's voice.

"I was going to ask if you recognized the redheaded woman at the bar last night."

Ice frowned. "No. Is there a problem?"

"No problem that I'm aware of," he said cryptically. "I just left. I don't want to keep him waiting."

"Me either," Ice said grimly, disconnecting the call.

I ce heard the metal door close behind him. He had once been locked up when he took a job from Desmond to get Yo-Yo out of prison. The best part of the job had been meeting Grace. The worst part was being locked in the small cell. It could fuck with a man's mind. He sure as fuck hoped it did Harvey's.

Walking to the cell at the end, he saw a man stand up from a lone bunk.

"Who the fuck are you?"

"I'm here to give you one chance, and one chance only, to save your life… at least for a few more days."

"Go fuck off! I don't have to listen to a damn thing you

say. When I get out of here, I'm going to let the whole county know how I've been treated!"

"Shade told me you were a stupid son of a bitch. He nailed that one on the head." Ice stared at the face that already bore the marks of the enforcer's wraith. "He also told me I'd be wasting my time trying to talk to you."

"Shade sent you?" Harvey stared at him distrustfully through the bars. "Is he finally getting me out?"

"For about ten minutes, then you're coming right back."

"I don't want to come back. I want to go home!" he yelled.

Without pity, Ice was unmoved by the man's anger.

"You don't have a home anymore. You went after what belonged to Shade. Instead of hauling ass out of the state as fast as you could, you tried to blackmail him with fake pictures of Lily. There're two men in the world I would never try to piss off, and Shade is one of them."

Ice could tell that Harvey still had no idea of the gate he opened and the consequences he was going to have to pay.

Ice took one step back from the cell when Harvey looked like he was going to vomit in fear.

"Who's the other one?"

Callously, Ice refrained from answering. "You're going to have to get it in your fucking head that there isn't any clean way to get out this shitstorm you made for yourself. Man up and brace yourself for the impact of what you did, and you might live to see another two weeks. Or, you might as well have the funeral home on the top of your contact list, because the box you're headed for is smaller than the cell your ass is standing in now."

Feeling sick, Harvey grabbed one of the bars of his cell. "What do I have to do?"

"First off, I'm going to escort you to the thrift store and you're going to apologize to Lily. I'll watch you go in while Lucky will be there to make sure that, this time, you treat her the way she should have been treated at the start. Then, when you get back, Knox is going to lock you back in this cell."

Ice could tell Harvey was going to go off again, so he squashed him with the truth.

"It's the safest place for you. Not only can Shade not kill you in here…" This part he had to lie to Harvey about. If Shade wanted him dead, Fort Knox wouldn't keep him from accomplishing his mission. "But the man that was smart enough to get you to take the blowback for him might not be afraid of taking you out as he was of Shade. You're actually easy pickings where that's concerned.

"After the thrift store, make yourself comfortable for a few hours. I have to take care of a few things, but when I come back, I'm going to tell you exactly what you're going to do to keep breathing."

"Why not tell me now?"

"We're on my timetable, not yours. I'm going to get Knox so he can get your clothes."

Before he could move away from the cell, Harvey tried to reach out for him through the bars. "Is this going to get Shade off my back?"

Ice almost lied to him, but the good conscience part of his brain that loved Grace wouldn't let him.

"The only thing I'm able to offer you is a couple of weeks where you won't have to look over your shoulder. You committed a cardinal sin where Shade is concerned. The only good news that I can give you is that the other man I wouldn't piss off doesn't know what you did. If he did, I wouldn't be standing here talking to you. There wouldn't be anything left."

This time when Harvey met his eyes, Ice let him see the stark truth in them. There was no way around what he had done. Harvey had bet that outsmarting Shade and letting greed blind him outweighed the ramifications if he failed. Not only had he failed, but he had failed hard. Fortunately for Ice, Harvey's failure played right into his hands.

Moving away from the cell, he went to the door, knocking on it to alert Knox that they were ready.

The door opened, the sheriff on the other side.

Ice wanted to roll his eyes every time he saw the brother in the uniform. The citizens in the small town obviously had no conception of who the man really was who guarded their homes and businesses. They might believe he was no longer a Last Rider, but the club would have his loyalty until his dying day. Just as the Predators had his.

"Did he go for it?"

"I didn't give him the choice," Ice said, taking the clothes that Knox held out to him. "Give us ten, and then we'll get this show on the road. I need to get back before Grace wakes."

"Have you told her that you're not going back with her?"

"Not yet."

"You sure you want to do this? It's not too late to back out."

"I'm sure." Pivoting, he strode back toward Harvey.

Ice knew what he signed up for. Thankfully, the other man had no clue about the nightmare heading for him. By the time he did, it would be too late.

This wouldn't be the last time Harvey was used as a pawn. This Predator had a use for him, too.

CHAPTER 13

Grace looked at the corner of her computer screen, seeing what time it was. Taking her purse out of a drawer, she then pushed her chair back from underneath her desk.

"Can I get you something for lunch while I'm out?" she asked Penni, who was sitting at the desk close to hers.

"If you wait until I finish this email, I can go with you."

"I wasn't going anywhere in particular. I was just going to hit a drive-thru. I have an errand to run so I might be a little late coming back."

Penni lifted her blue gaze to hers. "Where are you going? I don't mind waiting for you to finish your errand."

Grace knew her friend and boss wouldn't let her leave until her curiosity was appeased. "I need to stop by the club, and I want to go alone."

She could tell that Penni's curiosity had risen even more.

Grace moved toward the door, wanting to get out before she was asked more questions. She didn't make it. Penni caught up with her in the outer office where Stump was working.

"You never go to the club unless Ice is there, or if Sawyer, Vida, or I go with you. What's up?"

"Nothing. If it was important, I would tell you. I'll be back in an hour or two."

Grace left before Penni asked any more questions.

She should have stayed home today. Penni told her she could have the day off since she just came back from Treepoint the day before, but since she had taken off so much lately she wanted to get caught up with the work that she knew would be waiting for her. Besides, the house was lonely without Ice there.

It was going to be a long two weeks.

Driving to the Predators' clubhouse, she thought of several ways to accomplish her errand and finally concluded that she would just wing it.

Lizard was smoking a cigarette outside the door when she got out of her car.

"What's up?" he greeted her, taking a drag on his cigarette.

"Not much." Seeing the same curious expression on his face that had been on Penni's and Stump's, she hastened inside before he could say anything.

Hiding her nervousness behind a cool mask, she looked around the clubroom. Surprised, she saw Max sitting at the bar with Griffin. The woman behind the counter paled as she walked toward Max.

Grace ignored both Griffin and Rita.

"Hi, Max."

The burly biker looked over his shoulder at her. "Whatcha doing here? Ice isn't here."

Grace barely kept herself from rolling her eyes, conscious of the other men in the room.

"I know. I'm not here to see Ice. I want to talk to Porsche. Is she around?"

"In the kitchen." Max nodded toward the door behind the bar.

"Thanks."

Grace was thanking her lucky stars that Jackal wasn't there as she went around the bar.

Feeling the whole club's eyes on her back as she went into the kitchen, Grace saw the woman she was looking for standing at the old four-burner stove, cooking something.

Grace didn't let the disdainful glare deter her from walking closer.

"What do you want? If you want a grilled cheese, you can make it yourself."

"No thanks. I just stopped by so that I could talk to you. Do you have a minute?"

"No, I'm busy."

The woman's breasts were bulging out of the push-up bra she was wearing under a white tank top. If T.A. hadn't told her what purpose she was used for in the club, her clothes made it self-explanatory.

Steeling herself for the confrontation she was determined to have, Grave reached out and turned the stove off.

Porsche turned around, giving her an irritated glance.

"It won't take a minute." Grace gave her a cold look back. "Ice won't be back for two weeks."

"Bitch, tell me something I don't know."

Grace wanted to smack the look off her face but restrained herself, continuing as if she hadn't heard the smart-ass comment. "That gives you two weeks to find somewhere else to live."

The woman's mouth dropped open before she closed it with a snap.

"I'm not going anywhere. If you don't like me being here, you need to take that up with Ice. He's the only one that decides if I stay or leave and, *baby girl,* Ice likes me here just *fine.*"

Refusing to return the woman's barbs, Grace plastered a fake smile on her face. "Two weeks, *Porsche.* Or, should I say *Colleen?* Which one do you prefer? Personally, I would stick to Colleen. You don't remind me of a Porsche at all."

The woman had turned a sickly shade of grey at being called by her given name.

Grace gave her a feline smile. "The next time you want to brag about fucking someone's husband, you should be smarter about whom you confide in. Not only is T.A. my stepmother, but she also has friends who are bounty hunters. I'd really hate to use my relationship with my new step-mother to get rid of you, but"—Grace gave a careless shrug —"she did offer. I'd really hate to go that route, but hey, if you want to be here when Ice comes back, go for it. He won't thank you when the cops come busting in here to arrest you."

Porsche gave a half-laugh that Grace didn't believe for a second.

"You wouldn't. Ice would be furious at you for drawing the cop's attention to the club."

Grace widened her eyes in pretend indignation. "Me? I'm not the one that has an ex-boyfriend that robs banks and drove the getaway car. That's all you." Grace gave a low whis-tle. "Damn, I almost feel sorry for you. You're looking at some hard time when you get caught." Then she shook her head. "Never mind. I really wouldn't care.

"By the way, your lie about fucking Ice and that he was going to leave me for you didn't work. T.A. knew you only told her because you were hoping I would play right into your hand and cause trouble between me and my husband." Causti-cally, Grace let the pain of the last three weeks roll off her back, releasing the last burden she had been carrying. "It might have worked if you had tried it with anyone else, but one thing you couldn't have anticipated was that T.A. is used to dealing with sluts like you, which fortunately, I'm not." Flipping the burner back on, she moved away from the stove. "You should make Max another grilled cheese. That one's too burnt."

Coming out of the kitchen, Grace came to a full stop at seeing Jackal, Penni, Stump, Griffin, and Max standing just outside the door while the other men were practically leaning over the bar to eavesdrop on the conversation she had just been having in the kitchen.

Grace waited for one of the men to say something about her telling Porsche to leave, but it was Penni who broke the silence.

"Can we go to lunch now? What are you in the mood for?" Penni hooked an arm through hers, leading them from behind the counter.

Grace's eyes shied away from Jackal's and the other men, knowing that they would be getting in touch with Ice before she and Penni were in the car.

Penni waited until they were outside before saying anything else.

"Why didn't you tell me you thought Ice was having an affair?"

Grace looked at her friend from over the roof of the car. "Because if you found out he was, you would have told me the truth."

Looking sympathetic, Penni rested her hands on the roof. "I would have told you that he wasn't. Jackal says that Ice doesn't even look at any of the women in the club. Not only that, he had already ordered her to get out before he gets back, Lizard has been trying to find her a place to stay, regardless she has to be out before he walks in that door again."

"Well, hell."

"That's why you should tell your BFF these things." Penni cracked up, trying to keep a straight face.

"Besides it wasn't his looking that I was worried about." Relieved that the altercation with Porsche was over, and she had been lying about Ice wanting her to stay.

"There will always be Porsches at the club," Penni stated frankly.

The small victory she just achieved seemed hollow at Penni's realistic observation.

"You could have at least given me five minutes before bringing me down to earth," she snapped.

Penni's joyful laughter brought a smile to her lips, despite her irritation with her friend.

"Don't worry; our husbands prefer to ride their motorcycles."

Joining in with her laughter, they got in the car.

Grace snapped her seatbelt in place, then started the engine. "You're right; she would have had a better chance if she had called herself Ducati." Grace was laughing so hard she had to wipe a tear away.

"Hell no! Ice wouldn't be seen on a Ducati. She should have passed off as a Harley." Penni stopped cracking jokes long enough to ask, "Where are we eating lunch?"

Grace pulled into traffic. "You know… you're right."

"I am? About what?"

"About our husbands. And I've come up with a plan."

Penni was usually the one with harebrained ideas, but Grace wasn't going to let some other big boobed witch in the future try to get one over on her.

"Do I want to know what it is?"

Penni was her one friend that was game for anything, and she had no intention of embarrassing herself without someone doing it right along with her.

"How do you feel about pole dancing?"

HALO FOR THREE

CHAPTER 1

The whirling sound of an empty soda dispenser had Mika looking at the button on the vending machine. There was no red light on the old machine to show that the brand she wanted was empty.

Aggravated at herself for not stopping at a convenience store before checking in to her motel room, Mika pushed the button for her second choice. The whirling sound came again, but this time it was followed by a loud *thump* as the bottle dropped.

Bending over, she reached for soda, but it wasn't in the tray.

"Dammit!"

"Need some help?"

The deep, masculine voice had her jumping and turning around, then wishing she hadn't. The blue-green eyes staring back at her had her mouth dropping open.

"Ah… no thanks."

Turning back to the machine, she bent over to open the metal door flap, hoping the bottle would suddenly appear. It didn't.

Squatting down, she shoved her arm inside, trying to reach farther up the mechanism. She had heard the thump of the stubborn soda, so it should've been just within her reach. Extending out her fingers, she came up empty again.

"You sure you don't want me to try?" The dry amusement in his voice had her wanting to tell him no again, but she knew she was holding him up from getting his own drink.

"I would appreciate it. Maybe you can reach it? Your"—standing to face him again, she made a conscious effort not to swallow her tongue at the rugged man in front of her —"arms are longer."

Moving aside, she expected him to try the same method she had. However, he used his powerful arms to grab each side of the machine and easily tipped it toward him, causing her eyes to widen as the stubborn bottle easily slid down the dispenser.

"That'll work, too," she said drily as he set the machine upright again, then grabbed the soda.

"There you go."

"Thank you." Taking the bottle from him, she kept her lashes lowered as she went around him, conscious of his eyes following her.

As she was exhaling a breath of air, she found herself face-planted against a masculine chest that was coming around the corner at the same time she was.

Raising her startled gaze upward, gray eyes met hers.

"Excuse me," she muttered in embarrassment.

"I'm sorry. It was my fault. I should have been looking where I was going. Are you all right?"

The hard face staring down at her had her giving a brief nod before she stepped around him, her feet hurrying her away from the unsettling encounter.

Jesus, if all men in Kentucky look the way these two did, she should move here.

Once safely locked in her motel room, she turned on the television to break the lonely silence. Then she set the bottle down on the dresser, wanting to wait a few minutes before opening it in case it spewed. She used the time to unpack a change of clothes, taking out a pair of jeans, a white scalloped sleeveless top, and a jean jacket. Laying them out on the bed until after a shower, she went back to the dresser to open her soda.

"*Excuse me*," she mocked herself out loud. "Mika, just once, couldn't you have done something cool? Why didn't you say, *hey, handsome, what's your name?* Why couldn't you have just said *hi* to the other one?"

Though she laughed at herself for the wishful thoughts, Mika knew she was incapable of making small talk with men. Especially not two who looked like they were cover models for *Hunky Studs Weekly*. The fictitious name for a magazine that didn't exist at least showed that she did have a sense of humor, even if it was bad.

She wondered if the men knew each other or if they were friends. Then another thought occurred to her. *Maybe they are a couple.*

Not only did she consider herself low on the scale of hotness when compared to other women, but she also ranked herself competitively against men; she received a failing score. Hotness had never been a descriptive word she would use to describe herself, and as luck would have it, neither did men.

Her male friends and coworkers always put her in the "friend" category, despite how hard she tried to get herself out of that group—when friendship wasn't what she was after.

Slipping out of her flat shoes, she sank her tired feet into the carpet and wiggled them. It had been a four-hour drive from the airport, where she spent the entire flight from California squished. Arriving at Treepoint at precisely 2 p.m., she had searched and found the motel. Now the rest of the night was hers to do with as she wanted, and the plans Mika made caused nervous butterflies to swirl in her empty stomach.

Taking a drink of her soda to relieve her parched throat, she then screwed the lid back on before going to the phone beside the queen-sized bed. Picking the receiver up, she pushed the number for the front desk.

"Front desk," the irritated male desk clerk answered.

"Yes… I… Could you tell me …?" The butterflies flapped around in tighter circles, making her want to vomit up the small sip she had taken. "Are there any bars close by?"

A small pause, and then Mika heard a faint rustle in the background before he answered with, "Sure are. Take a left out of the parking lot and go straight for about three miles. You can't miss Rosie's; it's sitting on the left side of the road. Tell Mick I sent you, and he'll give you a free beer."

"Okay, I will. Thank you."

Hanging up, Mika stared at the phone as if it would reach out and bite her.

"Don't do it, Mika. Stay here and get some sleep. You need sleep." She tried to convince herself not to do the thing she convinced herself she would do just days before.

She tried to bolster her courage. "If you're going to change your life, you have to start somewhere. We can do this, Mika. Where's your backbone?"

She grimaced at herself, for not only talking to herself, but also at the business suit she was taking off.

Mika wished she had gone to get the soda in the new outfit she bought and planned to wear tonight—at least then she could have had a better chance of attracting the attention of the two men outside.

Her inner demons battled as she showered, which Mika

tried to ignore. However, the insecurities she'd dealt with since college wouldn't be silenced.

Men didn't like to fuck smart women. It had taken her a while to figure that out. In fact, it had taken a male friend to clue her into why she wasn't getting asked out. In a new university, she was not only the youngest, but also no longer having her BFFs around that she could have turned to for their support at how to fit in better.

"Mika, a guy doesn't want you to call them out on their bullshit."

She'd been hurt by Cory's observation, having just over-heard him promising to take one of the girls in their class to a concert that weekend.

"The tickets are already sold out," she'd informed him, thinking she was being helpful by letting him know. Instead, Cory had given her an angry look in addition to the "advice." The remark stung, but nothing was more truthful than a hormone-ridden boy when he didn't get what he wanted. Then, when the young woman had switched her attention to another male classmate, he'd taken his failure out on her.

She might have been gifted with a smart mind, but the drawback was that the same intelligence allowed her to see through the crap that men used to get women in bed. And it only grew worse as she got older, and their lies became more skilled and covert.

Like the boy who had asked her to go with him to home-coming their senior year, she had seen through his schemes, that he'd only wanted to make his ex-girlfriend jealous.

Her first job out of college hadn't gone any better. The men hadn't given her nerdy appearance a second glance until she moved up the ranks. If they hadn't loved gossiping loudly in the break room so often, she would have been fooled a couple of times. One day she had gone to work early and had heard her name. Outside of their line of vision, the full effect of what they felt for her was revealed.

"If Mika wasn't such an ugly cunt," Carter Long told another coworker, "I'd think she got that award by giving blowjobs."

The crude comment had her ignoring her embarrassment and humiliation, and walking into the break room with the pretense of getting a cup of coffee. Their startled eyes were unable to meet hers, the deafening silence heightening their unprofessionalism.

"Good morning, Carter."

Her scorn-fueled greeting had the man she was addressing going pale.

She shifted her eyes to their crotches, waiting for one or both of them to piss themselves after the obvious fact that she'd heard their remarks. "*Maybe* if you didn't turn in papers that were filled with so many errors a five-year-old would write, you might have actually gotten that last award. But then, what do I know? According to you, I'm a brainless cocksucker." Usually, Mika let such crass behavior slide off her back, but being called an ugly cunt had lit a fire in her that her thick skin couldn't tolerate. "I'll have to ask Nancy in HR if cocksucking is in my job description because, according to you, I've been slacking on that duty." The others in the group began to disperse at frightening speed.

That Carter looked like his leg had become ensnared in a bear's trap hadn't given her any pleasure. She'd been too hurt and disgusted at the level some men went to take the blame off their own shoulders, and instead putting it on an innocent who took her work seriously.

It wouldn't be the last time she'd had to deal with that type of behavior, but at least they'd been smart enough afterward not to do it within earshot.

After toweling herself off, she opened the bag of makeup

sitting next to the sink in the hope of doing an adequate job at applying it on her face.

Taking a step back, she admired her handiwork. "Not bad, Mika. Not great either, but it'll do."

If any of the men had a few drinks under their belts, it could get her a passing glance in a darkened bar.

She was certain that neither of the two men outside would've given her a second glance, even with the casual clothes and makeup.

Thankfully, she wasn't looking for men who reminded her of Hawkeye or a dark-haired Thor. She was searching for basic. And the more basic, the better. Someone who didn't stand out. Someone she could use to find out if she were capable of being normal during her brief stay in Treepoint.

Classified as a prodigy since she was three years old, she spent her life in classrooms, striving to learn more to satisfy the thirst of knowledge that, despite the hours of dedication she put in, was never enough.

She had few friends, and the few she'd kept throughout the years considered her boring and lifeless. They asked her how to fix a computer but never bothered to ask her opinion on the latest movie. And she loved movies, yet her "friends" never asked her to go to one. They'd used her as their listening board or shoulder to cry on, but anytime she ventured to give advice or expand the limits of the "friend-ship," it was not just ignored, it was criticized.

That was why she decided to use the opportunity being in Treepoint would provide.

A one-night stand. A way to get her feet wet with no repercussions, no guilt.

Nothing but a brief encounter, one that would spring-board a more confident and assured Mika. Then, when it was over, she would go back home to California. And the next time one of her friends talked about sex, she would have the experience and knowledge to contribute.

She believed you learned by doing, but so far the only experience she had with sex was a goodnight kiss after her one and only date. That had been two years ago when she had agreed to meet someone on a dating app.

Picking up the tube of red lipstick, she glided the vivid red color on her pursed lips. She had done her preliminary research, discovering that men found the color red sexually arousing.

Preening in the mirror, she smacked her lips, then winced at her reflection.

"This is going to be a disaster."

Yes, it is, the little voice at the back of her mind spoke up.

CHAPTER 2

W hile sliding a bill into the money slot, Jonas was unable to take his eyes off the auburn-haired woman as she turned the corner. If she hadn't been giving him a death glare, he would have tried to make small talk.

A finger was hovering over his selection when his partner and the redhead bumped into each other. His mouth twitched in a small smile when he saw that Hammer was just as disconcerted as he had been. But when the redhead moved aside, continuing on her way without giving Hammer the time of day, he was just as disappointed as when she had done it to him.

"Damn." Hammer had a heavy frown as he approached him.

"I know, right?" he grumbled. "She say anything to you?" Making his selection, he then bent down to grab his soda.

"She said, 'excuse me.'" Taking his wallet out, Hammer grabbed a bill to get himself a drink as well.

"What'd you say?" Jonas asked, unscrewing the bottle, then hastily holding it out so the bubbling liquid wouldn't spill on him.

"What do you think I said? I said, 'I'm sorry.'"

"That's it?"

"The rest is kind of a blur. Man, did you get a look at her?"

"Yeah. Damn, I wonder how long she's in town for. Or if she's married."

"She didn't seem like she wanted to stop and chat." Hammer got his drink, not bothering to open his after seeing the mess Jonas was dealing with from the overly shaken bottle.

"It doesn't matter. She doesn't seem the type to take us on anyway."

"No shit. Can't imagine her taking on either one of us, much less both."

"Damn. You think she was here for the wedding?" Jonas knew that wasn't possible, but he wanted to make sure. It had been hard to let the compelling woman walk away.

"No." Hammer strode next to him as they made their way back to their room. Opening the door, he went inside first, letting Hammer follow and close the door. "T.A. and Dalton invited close friends and relatives to the wedding and reception, and since we're the ones who checked them all out, you know damn good and well she wasn't there."

Jonas set the soda on the nightstand before sprawling out on one of the two double beds. "This is getting ridiculous. There has to be a woman somewhere that we can agree on, and who won't run away when we tell them that we want to have a triad relationship."

Hammer sprawled out on the other bed. "If you come up with any ideas, let me know. I'm out of them. The last woman you wanted me to consider gave me the heebie-jeebies."

"Don't blame me for that one. You're the one who picked her out from her profile. I was just willing to take more of a chance and actually meet her, instead of wasting time sharing texts. At least we knew after five minutes it wasn't going to work out."

"It would have been a dumpster fire."

Jonas agreed.

Grabbing the remote, he turned the television on, settling on a murder drama. They watched in silence until the alarm on his watch went off.

"You ready?" Hammer asked, already getting off the bed.

Jonas switched the television off, then each of them grabbed their jackets before going outside to their Escalade.

Letting Hammer take the driver's seat while he climbed into the passenger's seat, he scoured the front of the motel building, hoping to catch another glimpse of the redhead.

"Give it up," Hammer advised.

Jonas buckled his seat belt, gloomily looking outside at the bleak landscape. He hated winter months with the trees bare.

"You should start seeing Debra again."

Jonas looked at his lifelong friend. "It's useless. She already said no to us."

"She said no to a relationship with me, not you. You liked her. It could work out."

"It won't work without you. We've talked this over a million times. A polyamorous is the only hope we have of making a relationship work. Sooner or later, we'll find someone."

He tried to be positive, but he was beginning to mirror the doubt that he saw in Hammer's face.

"We both know the problem isn't with you. It's me. Find a woman and settle down, Jonas."

He gave Hammer an unsparing glance as the man drove into the parking lot of the local bar. "I haven't exactly had a successful relationship without you taking part in it. I don't know why you think I have all these women falling at my feet." Jonas gave an angry huff. "We're both miserable sons of bitches alone. Without each other, we'd end up in divorce court before the honeymoon was over. So, cool it. We'll find her." Jonas attempted to perk his friend up by trying to joke about their predicament. "You never know, the lucky woman could be in Rosie's right now, just waiting for us to make her night."

Hammer pretended to heave at his joke. "You're full of shit."

Jonas laughed as he got out of the SUV.

The outside of the bar was nondescript, sitting nestled in the middle of the mountains, not far from The Last Riders' clubhouse.

Walking inside, Jonas was disheartened to see there weren't any women. He ignored Hammer's I-told-you-so glare as he strode toward the bar.

"Hey, Mick."

"Jonas, Hammer, what can I get you guys tonight?"

"We'll take a couple of beers."

Recognizing one of the men sitting at the bar, he gave a brief nod at Moon who sat glumly, staring into his glass of whiskey.

"Rough night?" Jonas asked, reaching for the beer that Mick set down in front of him.

"Fuck off."

Jonas wasn't offended by the man's insult. It looked like he and Hammer weren't the only single males who were unhappy at spending Valentine's Day alone.

Letting his eyes slide around the bar, he took in the other men sitting around. Outside of one guy sitting at a table by the wall, the rest of the men were all looking just as down-cast as Moon. It was dark in the bar, but Jonas was experienced enough to recognize that the man sitting alone was pretty lit.

"What are you two doing here instead of hanging out at T.A.'s wedding?"

At Mick's voice, Jonas turned his attention back to him. "It was too crowded."

"Uh-huh." Mick gave them a quizzical look before refilling Moon's glass.

Jonas was sharing a glance with Hammer when the sound of the bar door opening had him casually turning his head to see who was entering.

Hearing Hammer choking on his beer, it was hard not to look to make sure his friend was okay, but he was afraid that if he did, the woman walking toward the bar would become nothing more than a figment of his imagination.

"You okay?" Jonas finally asked from the corner of his mouth, still refusing to cast his eyes away from the approaching beauty.

"Yes. Is that …?"

"Yes."

Jonas tried to appear casual as she took a seat farther down from where Moon was sitting, but he still gave a silent groan.

He and Hammer ran a bounty-hunting business with Killyama. They had been in her life since she was a young child and both considered her more like a daughter than a business partner. When she married Train, one of The Last Riders, they'd met Moon.

Killyama had told them how Moon earned his nickname, and if that confidence she shared with them was true, then he and Hammer didn't stand a chance with the familiar redhead who was sitting closer to Moon than to them.

His gut twisted when he saw the smile spread across

Moon's face. There was no way Jonas was going to let The Last Rider steal her away from them.

Jonas's ass was about to slide off the stool when Hammer's low warning stopped him.

"Chill. She's not interested."

Jonas took another look and saw the same disinterest on her face that she had treated them to at the motel.

Remaining seated, he and Hammer watched as the woman ordered a beer.

Jonas took his eyes off her long enough to shoot a questioning glance at Hammer. "Should we make a move?"

"You go ahead. I'll hold back until you signal for me."

Jonas made a face at his friend. Hammer always preferred he make the first move.

He almost decided not to make the effort. If Hammer had a spark of interest in the woman, then he'd be the one to make the move and not always leave it up to Jonas. It was the only thing that he worried about when it came to sharing a woman with Hammer—that his friend wouldn't have the same attraction to the third as he did. That Hammer'd think his feelings weren't as important as Jonas's.

"What's the holdup?" Hammer asked.

"I'm going—"

"Too late."

Jonas swung his head around to see the redhead carrying her beer toward the solitary man sitting at the table.

"What the fuck?" Jonas couldn't believe the woman had chosen the drunk over Moon, him, or Hammer.

He snapped his mouth closed, turning back to his beer and taking a drink to ease the ache of disappointment.

"Fuck that!"

Jonas was now the one snorting beer out of his nostrils as he watched Hammer stride across the bar toward the table where the woman was now sitting.

Grinning, Jonas hastily grabbed his beer and Hammer's, moving to follow him. The way Hammer was now looming over the occupants at the table, it was clear his wish for Hammer to be more involved had been granted.

"Ask and ye shall receive," Jonas said, laughingly out loud to himself.

"Huh?" The bartender looked at him as if he was crazy as fuck.

"Nothing," Jonas replied as he watched Hammer take a seat at the table without asking.

This was what he had been waiting for. When his partner set his mind on something, he broke through it, despite the resistance he met. It was how he had earned his nickname in the Army Rangers.

The woman had no idea she was now Hammer's target.

Jonas plastered a friendly smile on his face, ensuring that, if Hammer wasn't successful, he was the perfect backup. God, how he loved being a part of a team.

CHAPTER 3

Mika found the bar easily enough. What wasn't easy was forcing herself out of the car. Her mind was in turmoil on whether she should or shouldn't.

Just go in and get a beer. If you don't like it, just leave, she reasoned with herself.

Stroking her confidence up, she shakily got out the car and walked toward the door. Feeling like an idiot for coming up with this plan in the first place, she almost ran back to her car.

"You're so fucking lame, Mika. Dillion loves me."

"When I want advice from Dear Abby, I'll email her."

"When's the last time you got laid? Have you ever even been laid?"

"Don't give me that look. You're so predictable that even your cat got bored with you and ran away."

Replaying the last conversation she had with her friend still stung. She hadn't talked to Julia in three months, and it still hurt, both the argument she had been drawn into when she tried to discuss her friend's toxic relationship, and Julia's refusal to text or call her

back regardless of the numerous messages—she Mika
—left.

The memory of the argument bolstered her to go inside.

Holding her breath all the way to the bar, she kept her
eyes forward, not paying attention to the men inside. She
then took a stool situated away from the others and ordered
a beer from the bartender who looked like he expected her to
ask for directions instead of the beer she requested.

Turning her gaze away from the bartender, Mika glanced
briefly at the man sitting closest to her to see whether or not
he was a viable option. It only took two seconds to figure
that one out.

His come-hither smile was meant to be enticing, but he
was too good-looking not to be aware that women found
him attractive. Therefore, Mika didn't buy into the illusion
that he was just the good ole boy he was trying to portray.

When her eyes shied away from his, she saw "the men"
sitting farther down the bar. She hadn't even noticed them
when she entered, too self-conscious upon realizing she was
the lone woman in the room.

Not seeing any prospects that filled her crazy plan, she
brightened when she saw the man sitting next to the wall...
alone.

"Hey, pretty lady. The name's Moon. What's yours?" the
good-looking man at the bar asked.

Ignoring him, Mika paid for her beer, then slid off the
stool to make her way across the room.

Her pulse quickened when she realized he was drunk.
With any luck, if she was successful, whoever he was
wouldn't remember what day of the week it was or that he
had bagged a stranger he met at a bar.

"May I join you?"

His blurring eyes had trouble focusing on her. "You want
to sit down with me?"

"Yes."

Mika cringed at the sexual interest he looked over her with.

"Sure, go ahead."

You have lost your freaking mind, Mika castigated herself but sat down next to him anyway.

"Are you from Treepoint?" she asked before taking a drink of her beer.

"Born and raised." The cackle of his drunken laughter had her taking another drink, wishing she ordered something stronger.

"My name is ... Mary. What's yours—"

"I hate drinking alone. Mind if I join the party?"

Mika gaped up at the man who she recognized as one of the men she bumped into at the motel. That he wasn't alone and his buddy was here too, still seated at the bar sent off alarm bells.

Men like them never gave her the time of day. This one was like a high school star quarterback, who only dated the prom queen. She hadn't even been a member of the queen's court.

She opened her mouth to refuse when her chosen prospect spoke up.

"Sure. Why not? The more, the merrier."

Feeling uncomfortable, Mika didn't look at him as he sat down, trying to keep her attention focused on the prize. Well, not really a prize. More like a booby prize, but she was more than happy with that.

When she finally had sex, she wanted a man who would make her feel confident and sure of herself for the first time, not one who already had her feeling like she would never measure up when the clothes were off. The gorgeous man was undoubtedly used to doing playboy bunnies, not Dear Abbys.

"Is there room for me?" His buddy took a seat before she could even answer. "I hate to drink by myself."

Mika narrowed her eyes on the guy who had lifted the soda machine like it was a cup of coffee. Soda guy was just as gorgeous as any of the high school quarterbacks she remembered.

Beginning to think she was on an episode of *What Would You Do?*, she felt a coil of disappointment that her plans weren't going in the direction she intended, now that both "men" had joined her.

As she attempted to figure out what she was going to do, another gorgeous man walked into the bar. When he sat down on a stool facing the door, her gaze skittered away.

Hell no. Why couldn't I walk into a bar where normal men hung out?

Mika was carefully rethinking her choice of city to spread her wings, feeling the chill of danger skating along the edge of her mind, warning her to get out while she still could. The only thing that kept her seated was that she had never been ruled by emotions, always letting cold, hard reasoning dictate her life.

Her inner demon snapped back, reminding her it was her reasoning that put her in the predicament she was now stuck in.

"Go ahead." Booby prize waved his hand airily at the last chair at the table.

Mika had to grit her teeth not to contradict the invitation. She quickly tried to re-evaluate her plan and come up with a way to get Quarterback and Soda guy out of the picture.

"We met earlier at the motel," Soda guy broke into her thoughts.

"I remember."

"We didn't get a chance to introduce ourselves. I'm Jonas, and this is my friend Hammer."

Of course they are, Mika thought snidely. Soda guy had to have a sexy name like Jonas, and Quarterback looked like he could nail anyone who got in his way on the football field.

"I'm Harvey."

It was everything she could do not to roll her eyes at Booby prize's real name.

Feeling Jonas's and Hammer's steady gaze on her, Mika repeated the same fictitious name that she gave Harvey. "I'm Mary."

"You don't look a Mary."

Mika nervously took a drink of her beer to buy herself some time, unsettled at the skepticism in the one sitting closest to her.

Deciding to go on the offensive before Hammer could get too curious about her, she said, "It's an old family name."

"You don't look old to me."

Mika wished that Harvey would stay silent.

"Me neither."

Her mouth went dry at the way Hammer was looking at her, confused at the unexpected interest he was showing.

Unable to hold his stare, Mika was turning back to Harvey when Jonas's eyes entangled with hers.

What the hell was going on? Were they planning to lure her out to the parking lot to rob her? There was no way these two men were interested in her.

Her rational mind cautioned her to be careful. She was glad she had left her purse in the trunk of her car and had a small amount of cash on her in the pocket of her jeans.

"Can I buy you another beer?" Jonas asked.

"No thanks, I'm good."

"How about you, Harvey? Or have you had enough?"

"Can't ever have enough beer."

"Looks like you've had more than enough," Hammer stated, shaking his head when the bartender approached.

"Not yet, I haven't. I might need something stronger than what I've been working on."

Her eyes flew wide when she felt a hand on her crotch, accidentally giving a shriek that had the others at the bar wincing. Booby prizes's pushy hand was trying to worm its way inside her jeans, with Hammer and Jonas watching. She was willing to give the goods up, but she hadn't intended for it to be in the bar.

Snatching his hand out from under the table, she slammed it down on the table. Embarrassed, her temper got the better of her due to the fact that the other two men had seen what Harvey did—and hadn't done a thing to stop it.

"Groping is for teenagers. I was looking for a man, not a boy. Can you be the man I need you to be tonight, Harvey? If not, I can go to Redbox and rent a movie."

The stunned silence had Mika wanting to bite her tongue. Dammit, she wanted to curl into a ball and roll her ass right out of the bar.

Jonas eased the awkward situation when he started chuckling. "The shape he's in, he'll be lucky to make it to his car."

"I think you're right." Dismally, she saw her plan disintegrating in front of her.

"Jonas and I can give you a better time than Redbox, and we've only had one beer."

Her eyes flew to Hammer's. Did Kentucky have serial killers? She should have done her research better. Technically, they were staying at a motel, so they may not be from Kentucky either.

"Where are you and Jonas from?"

"We live in Tennessee."

She wasn't any more familiar with Tennessee than

Kentucky. Redbox was the safer choice, but she hadn't given up on Harvey yet.

"Are you two trying to get in on my action?" Harvey managed to raise himself up in his chair, glowering across the table.

When Hammer and Jonas looked at him like they wanted to squash him under their shoes, Mika felt sorry for him.

"Last call!"

The bartender's shout had her wanting to cry. What bar closed this early?

"What the fuck, Mick!" The first man who had talked to her at the bar was just as unhappy as she.

"Chill, Moon. It'll only be for two hours. I'll give a free beer to anyone that comes back when I reopen. Lily wants to give Shade his Valentine's Day present without you yahoos around."

That the bar was going to reopen in a couple of hours restored her faith that her goal was still within reach. She could go grab a bite to eat and come back. Maybe then there would be more options to choose from.

"Well, it was nice meeting you gentlemen. Jonas, Hammer, enjoy your trip home. Harvey"—she gave her booby prize a pitying look—"you should call a cab."

"I thought you and me ...?"

"I decided Redbox would give me a better thrill."

Mika rose from the table, giving a polite nod, then waited for Hammer to stand so she could get out from behind the table.

Hammer didn't move, trapping her. "What's wrong with me and Jonas?"

She gaped at him and said the first thought that came to her head. "Does Tennessee have serial killers?"

CHAPTER 4

"What?" Perplexed, Quarterback stared up at her in confusion.

"Huh? Tennessee might have cereal, but so does Kentucky." Harvey reached out, snatching her wrist. "Come on, I'll buy you some on the way to the motel." Harvey drunkenly tried to rise but was met with a firm hand on his shoulder.

"You shouldn't be driving, and you certainly won't be going anywhere with her."

"I have an old lady to ride my ass. I don't need you giving me your two cents worth." Shrugging out of Jonas's hold, Harvey used the table to get to his feet, then looked at her. "You coming?"

The old lady comment doused the flame that was left of her plan.

"No. And I advise you to take my suggestion and call a cab."

"You don't know what you're missing."

No, she didn't. And that was her problem. But she didn't tell Harvey that.

With Harvey swaying back and forth on his way to the entry door, she was free to slide around the table. Walking to the door, she was conscious of the two men from the motel following on her heels. It would be her luck to get mugged out in the parking lot. She should have just found the darn Redbox and stayed in. Her plans always went to hell when it involved her personal life.

Using the palm of her hand to open the door, she went outside into the fresh air, seeing that, despite her suggestion, Harvey was getting into his car. It actually made her sick to her stomach that he was. There was just no way she could watch him endanger other drivers as well as himself.

Raising her hand up to get his attention, she yelled out to him, "Har—"

Before she could finish, she was quickly turned around and found herself face-to-face with an angry Hammer.

"You are not going with him."

Mika eyed the man with a stare that made most of her acquaintances take a step back. Unfortunately, Hammer didn't know her well enough to know he was treading on dangerous ground.

Out of the corner of her eye, she noticed that Jonas had stepped to the side and was talking to someone on his cell phone.

"Take your hand off me *now*. It's none of your business what I do or don't do. For your information, I wasn't going to get in the car with him, but I would offer him a ride. He's going to get someone hurt if he drives in that condition," she snapped.

"He won't get far. Small towns like this have their own way of controlling drunk drivers. They're called speed traps."

Mika bit her lip as she watched Harvey pull out onto the road. If he hurt someone, she would never forgive herself—

or Hammer. "What was the bartender thinking to serve that much?"

"He was thinking the same thing I am. He'll be spending the night in jail when Knox catches him."

"Knox?"

"The sheriff."

Fear knotted her stomach. "Why are you on a first name basis with the sheriff? Wait, I thought you said you were from Tennessee. And, how many times have you been in jail?"

Hammer laughed, admitting, "A few times."

Jonas ended his call and walked back over. "What are you saying to her? She looks like she's ready to call the cops on you."

"I think she thinks we're escaped serial killers."

Mika didn't deny it as she tried to edge away from them and toward her rental car. The other men had already left the bar and were pulling out of the parking lot. From over Hammer's shoulder, she saw the bartender closing the door; she wanted to be safely in her car before he left.

"I better be going. Goodbye." Turning on her heels, she started speed-walking to her car.

She had a hand on the door handle when Jonas pressed a hand against the roof of her car, leaning the side of his body against the door so she couldn't get inside.

"Whoa...We're not serial killers."

She didn't believe him, especially when she was trying to open the door but couldn't due to him blocking it with his body.

"Mick!"

Mika jumped when Jonas yelled out the bartender's name.

"What?"

"Are me and Hammer serial killers?"

"Nah, they're cool," he yelled out before waving to a car that was parking next to his truck.

"He could just be vouching for you so you'll give him a cut of the money."

"What money?"

Her head spun when she realized Hammer had moved up behind her, effectively sandwiching her between the two men.

Jesus, she didn't need to be told she was in hot water; she felt it nipping at her vagina.

"The money you're going to rob off me."

"You think we're going to rob you?"

Looking into Jonas's clear eyes, she was beginning to doubt the usual, sound judgment that she was so proud of. Then she shook herself free of his mesmerizing hold on her as she watched a raven-haired woman wearing a raincoat go inside the bar.

"Mary?"

It took her a second to realize he was addressing her and that he was still waiting for an answer.

"Yes."

It was easier to keep her eyes on Jonas. Somehow, he seemed the least threatening of the two.

"Why?" His expression gentled even more.

"That's obvious."

"Not to me. How about you, Hammer?"

"Nope."

She didn't turn her head to look back at him this time. A woman could only take too much temptation before throwing caution to the wind and taking a chance, not only with her wallet but also with her body.

The sound of a motorcycle coming from up the road had all three of them watching as a lone biker pulled into the parking lot. She couldn't help staring as the biker got off his bike and removed his helmet.

What the hell? When she got home, she needed to tell all her female friends that they should pack up and move to Kentucky. Her attention returned back to the men next to her. Tennessee's men weren't anything to sneeze at either.

"Are you going to tell us why you think we're serial killers or wanting to rob you?"

The biker about to go inside the bar stopped at hearing Jonas's raised voice.

"Do you mind?" she hissed. "This is embarrassing."

Jonas turned his head, seeing that she was embarrassed about the biker overhearing them.

"Shade." Jonas raised his hand in casual greeting.

The man gave a curt nod before continuing inside.

"You know him?"

"Vaguely."

Mika wanted to lick her lips. Getting ahold of her libido, she raised her chin toward the doorway the biker had gone through. "Why didn't you ask him if you were serial killers? You didn't have a problem asking the bartender."

Jonas's smile curled higher. "Shade likes to fuck with people. I didn't want to take the chance of him getting a kick out of scaring you off me and Hammer. We're really nice guys, aren't we?"

"I haven't decided yet."

"It was more a rhetorical question for Hammer."

Mika laughed, her nervousness easing a tiny bit.

"Why don't you tell us why you think we're serial killers?"

"Don't forget the robbing part."

Mika could feel Hammer's breath on the nape of her neck as he moved closer to her back.

Jonas tilted his head to the side as he waited for her answer.

"I'm just going to be honest here. Normally, men like you two don't give me a second glance."

"And because we're interested in you that makes us serial killers?"

"Or about to rob her?"

Mika swung around to look at Hammer, then answered, "Yes."

"We're not." Hammer had stated almost innocently as if those two words alone should convince her.

"How am I supposed to know that?"

"How do you know that Harvey wasn't?"

"I don't."

"But you were going to spend the night with him?"

She tightened her lips. She wasn't going to answer that question. It was none of his business what she was or wasn't going to do with Harvey.

"How about this?" Jonas spoke, directing her attention back to him. "We have a couple of hours before Mick opens the bar again. You drive back to the motel, and Hammer and I will go grab a movie, and we can watch it in your room. If we don't kill or rob you, then we'll save you a trip back here."

He thought he was being funny, and it was everything she had not to laugh at his sense of humor.

"I know I'm going to regret this, but okay." Deep down, she felt as if she was safe with these two men, and she hadn't been wrong yet on her assessment of men's characters. It would suck if she was wrong this time and died so far from home.

"Okay?"

"Yes."

Jonas gave her a wide smile. "What's your room number?"

"Twenty-five."

"All right, Hammer and I will get the movie and meet you there."

Hammer moved around her to go with Jonas to a dark Escalade that was parked not far from hers.

"Don't you want to know what kind of movie I like?"

Hammer turned, walking backward as he talked. "Either a comedy or a romance. I think you've been watching too many horror movies."

"I prefer action."

Hammer and Jonas both stopped walking.

"We do, too."

Mika flushed at the double meaning.

"Just get a comedy. I need a good laugh."

Shaking her head at their disappointed expressions, she got inside the car.

As she pulled out of the parking lot, she saw Hammer behind the wheel as they took the road toward town.

It was only a few feet from the bar that the road turned into a winding curve. Pressing her foot down on the brake pedal, she took it slowly, seeing the spinning blue lights of a patrol car. Inching ahead, she saw Harvey bent over the trunk of his car with a deputy handcuffing his hands behind his back. Mika had no sympathy for him.

"I bet he wishes he called the cab."

CHAPTER 5

Mika paced back and forth in her motel room, talking out loud to herself, something that had become a habit since she arrived in Treepoint.

"You have lost your mind? Not only have you invited two strangers to your room, but you also need to quit talking to yourself."

Her self-criticism came to a halt when she heard a sharp knock on her door. Frantically telling herself that she wasn't going to open the door, she felt her feet moving. Even as she was yelling at herself not to do it, she found her hand turning the doorknob. She opened her mouth to tell the men that she changed her mind and was going to have an early night. However, her good intentions bit the dust at the sight of the striking men.

It was hard to choose which one she was more attracted to. Jonas seemed the friendlier of the two, while Hammer seemed more no-nonsense. They were both tall, but Hammer had about two or three inches on his friend. They both looked to be in their late-thirties. And both had dark hair, though Jonas's had more curl in his than Hammer's.

Opening the door wider, Mika allowed them inside, coming to the conclusion that she would watch the movie with them, then send them on their way.

As she said that to herself, she knew in her heart that her plan was doomed for failure. What woman in her right mind would turn down two gorgeous males just to go to sleep?

Wiping her sweaty palms on the side of her jeans, she tried to appear as if she was used to having two men in her motel room.

"What movie did you get?"

Jonas raised two plastic cases. "We got *Avengers* and *Bohemian Rhapsody*."

"What happened to getting a comedy?"

"It's Valentine's Day. I guess the number one thing to do is watch a comedy."

Mika laughed as she took the movies. "I haven't seen *Infinity War*. I was waiting for the next one to come out in March before watching it."

"Jonas is like that. He hates waiting for something he wants."

She wasn't going to touch that comment with a ten-foot pole.

Putting the movie in, she turned around and froze, not knowing what to do.

Both men had taken off their shoes and were on opposite sides of the bed, shoving pillows behind their backs.

Jonas gave her a benign smile. "Come and sit down between us. There's room for all three of us."

She wiped her palms again. "I'm going to be upfront and honest with you. My family knows where I am, I don't have any money, and there's a camera outside my door, so you won't get away with anything if I suddenly disappear."

Hammer's expression softened. "You're safe, Mary."

"I think so, too, or I wouldn't have let you guys inside."

Hammer patted the empty part of the bed by his side. "Relax. Let's enjoy the movie."

Having already taken off her shoes when she had come back to the motel room, she placed a knee on the bottom of the bed, then crawled to the center to sit between the two men. She stiffly pressed the button on the remote to start the movie, aware of the masculine presences by her sides. It was hard to concentrate. In fact, they were a fourth of the way through the movie before she could relax and sink back onto the pillow that Hammer had thoughtfully placed behind her.

"So, why are you visiting Treepoint?"

Hammer's question had her giving him a brief glance, unable to control her reactions if she stared too long. "Business. How about you and Jonas?"

"We went to a friend's wedding today. We're staying the night here instead of driving back tonight."

"Aw. Your friend got married on Valentine's Day? That's so romantic. Convenient, too. They'll never forget their anniversary."

"Are you married?"

Jonas's question had her jerking her head sideways toward him. "No. You?"

"No, neither of us are. Hammer is divorced, but I've never found the right woman."

Sliding her gaze back to the TV, she tried to focus on the *Avengers* and not the sexy eyes trying to drill holes into her soul.

"It sucks being alone on Valentine's Day." Hammer's revelation echoed her own loneliness.

"It's different for men. If you're alone, it's easy to ask someone out. A woman asks a man out on Valentine's Day and they stop talking to you."

"It's not as easy for men as you think."

Mika made a disbelieving face at the television. "If you're

trying to get my sympathy, it won't work. I'm sure neither of you are hurting in the women department."

"What makes you say that?" Hammer asked.

"Let's drop the subject and watch the movie."

"Why?" Jonas scooted slightly closer to her.

She gave a loud sigh. Then, pressing the pause button, she laid the remote down on her thigh. "You two don't need me to tell you how attractive you are, so unless you're gay, and even if you are, women will take a chance hitting on you."

"If that's true, then why didn't you?" Hammer shifted on his hip to look at her.

"I'm different."

"How? You don't find us attractive?" He raised a questioning brow. "By the way, we're not gay."

"I didn't say that I don't find you guys attractive, only that I'm different, that I know it would be useless for me to think the attraction would go both ways."

Jonas sat up off the pillow. "Why would it be useless?"

Mika nodded toward Hammer. "I bet you only dated cheerleaders or the homecoming queen in high school."

From his Hammer's chagrined expression, she knew she was right.

Tilting her head toward Jonas, she gave him a once-over. "I bet you dated the prom queen, possibly not the prettiest girl in your school but definitely the most popular."

She could tell Jonas liked her assessment even less than Hammer had.

"Neither of you come across as lacking confidence, yet you were irritated when I didn't try to approach you at the bar like I did Harvey."

"I'm not going to deny that it didn't put a dent in my ego," Hammer acknowledged.

"I'm a very good judge of character."

"Then your judgment sucks where we're concerned.

What you didn't take into consideration is that neither Jonas nor I are in high school anymore. We're grown men, and we don't date women based on their physical appearance."

"Okay. So, what do you base it on, then?"

Mika didn't miss the silent communication between the men.

"Jonas and I are limited to the women that we date because we prefer to be in a polyamorous relationship."

His explanation didn't shock her, but it was surprising that they were discussing this with a stranger.

"How many people do you want to have in this relationship?"

"Three."

"Do you both share a woman or do want to add another man to your relationship?"

"A woman."

"That's interesting. I've never met a couple who wants to be in a committed relationship between two men and one woman."

Jonas and Hammer both stared at her in surprise.

"It doesn't bother you?" Jonas asked.

Mika frowned at him. "Why should it? I'm sure you thought this over carefully. It isn't something decided on without thinking of the drawbacks and the advantages of being in a triad. I try not to judge other people, and if that's what you both think you want in your life to make you both happy, then you should.

"I can understand your difficulty in finding your third. It can't be easy finding a woman who would be willing to…" Blushing, she tried to find the least embarrassing and most delicate way to continue what she was about to say. "… have sexual relations with two men separately… or at the same time?" She posed the last part as a question.

"The same time."

"Okay. Are there websites where you can meet those type of women?"

"Yes." Hammer scooted closer to her, placing an arm on the pillow behind her back. "The problem with that is Jonas and I haven't met one who we feel the same about. Just because the women on those sites are interested in being a third, doesn't mean we'd have anything else in common with her. We haven't met anyone who has clicked with us... yet."

Giving them both sympathetic glances, she patted each one on their thighs. "That must be discouraging."

"It is," they both agreed, looking down at her hands.

Pulling her hands away, she tried to resume watching the movie, but the image of the two men making love to a woman whom they wanted to share, kept intruding like an alert bulletin during your soap opera. Her curiosity wasn't the only thing that was aroused by the discussion.

"Most of the women that we've met seem to prefer one of us over the other."

Still imagining the two men having sex with a faceless woman, it took her a second to realize that Hammer was continuing the discussion.

"I can see that being a problem. You would want her to care for you equally, like you would care for her and Jonas."

"You're the first one who gets that."

"Gets what?"

"For the triad to be successful, all of us have to be equal."

Mika frowned. "That goes without saying."

"Actually, not to them. Most want the relationship centered around her and what would make her happy."

"Ah... I see. She would want to come first, instead of Jonas." Mika turned her head toward Jonas. "Or, she wants to come first, instead of Hammer."

"Exactly," Jonas agreed. "But you get that. The women we've met don't."

"You will. You just haven't met her yet."

"Hammer and I think we just did."

Mika tore her eyes away from the TV to find them studying her with expressions that weren't hard to decipher.

"Guys, I'm not your third. I'm not looking for a relationship with one man, much less two."

"What were you looking for tonight when you went to the bar, then?"

Mika shook her head at Hammer. "Definitely not this."

Jonas gave her a wicked smile. "Well, we were."

CHAPTER 6

She was a runner.

Hammer had been a bounty hunter since he got out of the service and was experienced in being able to tell when someone would take off rather than face the consequences of their actions.

He had felt the surge of attraction the moment she bumped into him. He could see the quick intelligence in her eyes, the discerning way she watched everything around her, yet she had the common sense of a flea. Any woman who opened her motel room to two strangers in a strange town needed her head examined. Especially two who had the skills that he and Jonas had.

If they had been serial killers, as she had been frightened they were, they could have easily raped her and stored her body in her trunk, without the worry of the camera that was mounted to the ceiling outside.

"Don't panic. Jonas always jumps the gun."

Hammer hid his own grin when he saw the glimmer of disappointment that she was unsuccessfully trying to shield from him and Jonas.

"Jump the gun?"

"His standards aren't as high as mine."

Jonas shrugged. "I'm tired of just being alone with Hammer. I want a woman to spoil."

"You shouldn't rush into a relationship just because you're lonely."

"I tell him that all the time. The real problem is the kissing."

"The kissing?"

"The kissing." Hammer nodded. "I want her to enjoy kissing me as much as Jonas. They keep saying he's the better kisser."

"Do I look like I just fell off the dump truck?" Scoffing at him, she turned back to watching the movie.

"Since you're not interested in a relationship with us, you could tell us the truth."

"No."

"Come on, Mary. At least kiss him. Tell him what he's doing wrong." Jonas nodded at him. "I know it'll be hard. Most of the women we meet don't want to kiss him either."

"No."

Hammer raised himself into a sitting position. "If I end up all alone, it'll be your fault."

She laughed at his pitiful expression. "No, it'll be yours, because you're a terrible kisser." She hit him with one of the pillows. "*If I end up all alone, it'll be your fault*," she laughingly mocked him. "*Please*. You probably forgot more about kissing than most men have learned in a lifetime. If anyone sucks at kissing, it's probably Jonas." She then howled with laughter, falling back to the bed at the sight of Jonas's expression.

Jonas had always thought of himself as the ladies' man. That "Mary" was teasing Jonas showed that they might have found their perfect third.

He and Jonas had known each other since they had joined

the Army. They'd formed a bond that had saved their asses more than once. Mission after mission deepened their trust in one another, which had been cemented when they went into business together.

So many of their days and nights had been spent together, and when they found they were usually attracted to the same women, neither became jealous of the other's relationship. Still, they knew the loneliness of being alone and were happier when they were together.

They had shared more than one woman when they were randy or drunk enough. Then, when Hammer's marriage failed, they discovered why they hadn't made any of their relationships work. They had been in so many dangerous situations that their strengths and weakness offset the others.

"I'm hurt."

"I don't think a blow torch could burn your ego," Mary sputtered, wiping a tear from her eye. "You two crack me up. Do women fall for this crap?"

"One or two may have," Jonas said sheepishly.

"Then you picked the wrong woman tonight. Jeez... I don't know how long it's been since I've laughed this hard."

Affronted, Hammer narrowed his eyes on the woman. He really didn't like being laughed at by a woman who was twisting his balls in knots. From Jonas's expression, he didn't appreciate it either.

Giving a nod, they immediately knew what the other was thinking to breach Mary's reservations about them.

Leaning forward, Jonas stretched out toward the foot of the bed, while Hammer laid his head back against the headboard.

"You have a beautiful laugh," he complimented her, giving her a serious look while noticing that Jonas had reached out and was massaging one of her feet. Sensuously, he trailed a lone finger down her arm. "I wish I had met you yesterday."

"Why?"

He saw the telltale movement of her pulse beating under the translucent flesh at her wrist.

"Jonas and I would have bought you flowers today. Every woman deserves flowers on Valentine's Day."

"No one has ever given me flowers."

From the flush that was spreading across her chest, Hammer could tell she regretted telling them that fact.

"Then that's a damn shame." He growled, "Come here, Mary," and started tugging her arm so she would lie down on the bed like he was.

"I don't think that's a good idea."

"Why?"

"I don't like the way you're looking at me."

"How am I looking at you?"

"I can't explain it." She shrugged, trying to move her hand away from his touch.

"Maybe I can. Do I look like I want to touch you?"

"Yes." She gave a small sigh, finally allowing him to pull her down until her head rested on his arm.

"That's because I do. I've wanted to touch you since you bumped into me earlier today." Hammer slid his hand across the front of her neck to her jaw, raising her face so he could stare down into her eyes. "Jonas and I both did. We still do."

"You do?"

"Yes," Jonas answered, turning on his side to run his hand under one of her jean-clad legs.

"Can I kiss you?"

He caught sight of the indecision on her face and pulled his lips back from touching hers. "We won't touch you if you don't want us to. If you feel uncomfortable, we can leave."

He was giving her an out, despite the need that he was finding harder and harder to control. He wanted to taste her.

Intuitively, he and Jonas had always felt as if their third was out there somewhere, waiting to be found. Each failed relationship had dimmed their hope, however.

Hammer was almost afraid to touch her. The attraction he was feeling for Mary was so strong, and he didn't want his burgeoning hope crushed if the passion didn't spark between them.

"The movie isn't over yet," she demurred, not saying yes or no.

It hit him then that she was waiting to see if there was going to be a fire between them, too.

Moving toward her, he brought his lips closer to hers until they brushed against each other. They stayed like that poised, waiting for the other to apply pressure so it could be called a real kiss. Lying still, their soft breaths entangled creating a heady rush that had his hand going to her triceps to haul her closer to him.

"No, it isn't," he finally responded to her before using the tip of his tongue to slide along her bottom lip. He felt her give a shudder under his hand. "Don't be afraid," he murmured.

"I'm not."

The huskiness in her voice had him pressing harder against her lips before gliding his tongue inside her mouth.

The taste of her made him believe in magic again.

His mother had been a gifted piano player. He had grown up listening to her to play, and as he grew older, he could hear the differences in the music when the piano was out of tune. The reason he and Jonas hadn't found a woman to spend their lives with was that they weren't able to find the right chord that seemed natural and not forced.

Mary was the right fit. Everything about her fit. The way

her breasts fit into the curve of his chest, the way her skin felt against his, the gentle scent of her perfume. Every fucking thing had him wanting more.

"Do you know what you taste like?"

"No. What?" she whispered as if it were just the two of them.

"Home."

"Hammer...."

"Let me taste." Jonas released her foot, then moved up the bed until he was lying beside her. When he was in position, Hammer used his hand on her jaw to turn her face toward Jonas.

As his friend kissed Mary, who was now fully facing him, Hammer slid his hand down to her breast from behind. Rubbing her tit through her top, he saw the kiss between Jonas and Mary heat up. That Jonas was enjoying it as much as he had, had Hammer shaking as much as she was.

Watching Jonas make love to her mouth had him rocking his hips against her ass as he continued to play with her breasts, being rewarded with soft murmurs from her.

Hammer brought his own mouth down to her shoulder. "The movie's over, Mary. What do you want us to do?"

"Play the other movie."

CHAPTER 7

Being in the middle of the two men didn't frighten her. What did was the budding excitement that not one but two men wanted her, and they were striving to make her lose her sanity. It wouldn't work, though. Her mind was too methodical.

She had been called numerous names: a nun, a cold fish, frigid. Convinced the accusations were true, she stopped trying to find a sexual relationship that most women her age enjoyed. Devoting her time on work, content if not happy with the way her personal life was playing out, she had settled into her life being a party of one.

Hammer's kiss had shaken something loose inside of her, though, and Jonas's was toppling her over even further. Regardless, despite the barrage of sensations storming through her body, she was still on firm ground.

Mika felt a rush of air as Hammer separated himself. At first, she thought he was switching the movies, but when he turned the movie off, music started playing in the background. She hadn't realized she had missed his heat until he came back, although Jonas was still holding her.

235

She had never wished harder to flip a switch and turn her mind off, to become a malleable, wanton woman who wanted nothing and everything that Jonas and Hammer were willing to give.

Jonas lifted his mouth slightly, catching her clear eyes with his piercing ones. "She's not into us."

Her eyes widened at his assessment.

Hammer tightened his hand on her breast. "I don't think she is either. What are we going to do about it?"

"I know what I'm going to do."

Not sure she liked the fierceness pouring off Jonas, she tried desperately to shut off her mind, not wanting to stop yet. She might not be experiencing the overwhelming desire most women were able to, but it was still good.

Hammer moved his arm behind her head and curled it upward, turning her face back to his. The expression he wore was indomitable. These men weren't used to failure.

Hammer then claimed her mouth with his demanding one. He had willpower that, for the first time, Mika didn't know if she would be able to resist or if she wanted to. It was one thing to want to experience passion, yet the logical part of her brain wanted her to hold back.

Frustrated at herself, she started to tear her mouth away. It was useless. She hated herself for not being normal.

"Hammer, take your clothes off," Jonas commanded.

Mika felt Hammer slide his arm out from under her head as he got out of the bed.

Raising herself onto her elbows, she watched the two men undress. The sight of their bodies as clothes were peeled off heightened the awareness of what was about to happen, which made it even more difficult for her.

"It's no use," she confessed numbly. "It's me, I'm frigid."

The men didn't stop taking their clothes off.

"You're not frigid," Jonas told her as he finished first, then lifted her to stand next to him. "Raise your arms."

She raised her arms, complying with Jonas's thick order.

"It's no use," she repeated as Jonas took off her shirt. Behind her, she felt Hammer unsnap her bra before letting it fall to their feet.

"I wouldn't be sexy in that bra either." Hammer rested his chin on her shoulder. "Tomorrow, we'll go somewhere to get you one that will do your tits justice."

Mika frowned. "What's wrong with it?"

"Other than it's ugly as fuck, nothing."

"Let's see if her panties are any better." Jonas reached his hand to her waist, unbuttoning her jeans. Then Hammer held her up off the floor as Jonas shimmied the jeans down her legs.

When Hammer set her back down, Jonas crossed his arms over his chest to study her.

"They're worse," he stated flatly.

Mika glared at him. "What's wrong with them? I'll have you know these are designer underwear."

Jonas gave her a saccharine smile. "That's where you fucked up. No man wants to fuck a snooty bitch. A man wants a sexy woman who isn't afraid of showing him that she wants to be fucked." Jonas took a step forward, gripping her chin in a rough hand. "Do you *want* to be fucked?"

Mika had to think about the answer. Unfortunately, Hammer wanted her to answer Jonas immediately. From behind her, he circled his hand around her waist, then descended toward the maligned panties before sliding his hand inside, searching for the truth she couldn't hide from his fingers.

"I think she's getting there, but we still have some work to do."

She grabbed his wrist to jerk his hand away from her

crotch. "Not the way you two are going." Smarting off, she was unprepared for Hammer cupping her, grinding the palm of his hand against her clit.

Shocked at the unexpected pleasure, she unconsciously went to her tippy-toes as Jonas lay down on the bed. Another jolt rocked through her vagina when she watched him stroking his cock. And the more he stroked, the thicker it became.

"She's getting wetter."

Looking over her shoulder, she blasted Hammer with a furious look.

Unconcerned, he shrugged. "Well, you are."

"Shut up," she snapped.

"What do you think, Hammer? Which one of us should fuck her first?"

Mika gaped at the fact that they were talking as if she wasn't there. "Shouldn't *I* be the one to choose?"

"No," Hammer and Jonas answered together.

"Find out how tight she is," Jonas instructed.

Hammer lifted his hand slightly, moving his fingers toward her opening as Jonas watched. Then he speared a finger deeply inside of her. It was the most erotic moment of her life, her quick mind slowing to a sluggish pace.

"Damn, we might have a problem. She's tight as fuck. Her little pussy is wet, but not enough."

"Bring her here."

Mika moaned when Hammer removed his finger to lift her off her feet, while Jonas scooted to the side of the bed to make room for her. When Hammer laid her down, Jonas spread her legs, exposing her to both their hungry gazes. Jonas moved his finger to where Hammer's had been. She twisted her butt on the mattress as Jonas started finger-fucking her.

"I don't think she's frigid, Hammer. I just think it's going to take two men to satisfy her."

She wasn't easily embarrassed about her nudity, or the men's. Nor was she uncomfortable with the sexual way they were talking about her. She had lived her adult life waiting for the sexual urges that came normally to others. The lack of connection had left her unpracticed in the interactions between men and women. Maybe that was why Hammer and Jonas's actions were like a flare highlighting what was missing. Gentle caresses designed to peak her desire, kisses to induce passion, both experienced enough to break down the barrier that she had never been able to overcome.

Maybe they were right. Had she been so closed off that no single man would have been able to get past her guards?

Looking at their faces, she could tell they were determined for her to have an orgasm. Maybe that was the real difference. This wasn't about them; they were making it all about her, forcing her to react physically, rather than clinically. Her reactions weren't what one of them would have been able to accomplish alone. It took both of them to bring her to this point like a firefall that could only be seen if certain factors were present. For her, those factors were Hammer and Jonas.

Their generosity opened her heart to them more than a thousand dates could have accomplished, showing her the character of the men who were focused solely on her pleasure.

Her quicksilver mind became even more sluggish when Hammer sat down on the bed by her hip, watching Jonas as his fingers stroked her. Leaning forward, his breath fanned her breast before he bit down on her nipple.

Her pelvis unconsciously surged upward, sending Jonas's fingers deeper. Closing her eyes, she tried to savor the new sensations that were assailing her.

"Open your eyes!"

Jonas's authoritative voice had her eyes flying open.

When she first met Jonas, she assumed he was the more laid back of the two. However, since they had started touching her, she quickly realized Jonas was the one in control of the situation while Hammer held back.

At Jonas's command, she now saw Hammer's cock was just as hard as Jonas's. His thick length slid along her side as he mouthed her breast.

She experimentally reached out to touch his cock. Hammer was thicker and longer than Jonas. Her inner muscles clenched around Jonas's fingers inside her as she tried to hold Hammer in her fist. How in the world was he even able to walk?

"It's not that big."

Hammer's remark had her registering that she's verbalized her last thought.

"Thanks, Mary. He's never going to let me forget you said that."

"Yours is big, too." Mika didn't want him to feel inferior, especially since he wasn't.

"I wasn't jealous. His is hard to miss. But I know how to use mine better."

The lighthearted laughter shared between the two men sent an unexpected pang to her chest. They had done this so many times. It showed in the easy familiarity. She wouldn't be the first or the last woman they would share. She was just a stand-in until they found the one that they were searching for to complete their triad. A triad that wouldn't include her.

Why was she becoming jealous of a woman she would never meet? Because these two men were something special, like an eclipse that you waited and waited for yet was gone too soon.

"Don't let him fool you," Hammer said, then moved her

hand away from his cock. "As good as that feels, if you keep doing that, I'm going to come."

She was just as close. The snug fit of Jonas's fingers within her were hitting places that deepened her arousal, making her lose any self-consciousness of having sex with two men.

She had been pliantly enjoying the touches and kisses they were giving her, but now her body was demanding more. Jonas and Hammer had stoked her inner match into a wildfire that was consuming everything in its path. And there was no way she was going to let them remain untouched.

Using her elbows, she propelled herself away from Jonas's hand to the head of the bed. Her naked breasts heaved, panting as she tried to keep herself from climaxing.

Jonas tilted his head to the side curiously. "Why'd you do that? You were almost there."

"I know," she gritted out, trying to subdue the tremors that were still quaking in need. "I don't want to be told who to do first. I'm the one who gets to choose."

Both men's eyes dropped to her heaving belly, giving her sensual smiles.

"Pick then," Jonas said, rising off the end of the bed.

Mika did the same, pushing herself up. "Okay, I will." Standing in the center of the bed, now taller than both men, she put her hands on her hips commandingly. "I'm going to close my eyes and spin around. You can stay where you are or move if you want. When I open my eyes, the one I pick—"

Jonas started laughing. "It's like spin the bottle."

Mika did a pretend bow. "I'll be the bottle."

Hammer's smile turned seductive. "I like a woman who likes to play games. I always win."

She arched a brow at him. "I guess we'll find that out in a couple of minutes."

"Yes, we will," he said confidently.

Making sure her feet were balanced on the mattress, Mika felt a rush of excitement at playing the naughty game. She hadn't gone to school with her own age group and had never been able to participate and do things that normal girls her age had done.

Giggling at herself for making up for lost time, she started turning, extending her arm out. She mentally counted to ten as she kept spinning, stopping when she reached her goal.

Opening her eyes, she blinked several times to right her equilibrium, and to see Hammer's satisfied smirk; she now wanted to get even. "That was fun, but let's do it again."

Hammer shook his head. "Nuh-uh. I won." Walking over to his discarded jeans, he pulled out several condoms, taking one and laying the rest on the bedside table. Then he opened it and expertly covered his penis.

Reaching out, he lifted her off the bed, holding her chest to chest as he laved his wet tongue along her lips. "Don't worry; I'll go easy on you the first time."

"The first time?" she croaked out.

He nodded. "The first time for us being together. After that, all bets are off."

Mika clutched his biceps when he lifted her higher, centering her over his cock before slowly lowering her over him. Her head fell back at the tight fit, and the discomfort. Then her eyes sprang open when her head met Jonas's shoulder behind her, feeling him circle his hands around her waist to hold her breasts.

As Hammer pushed her downward, Mika forced herself to keep breathing deeply, stifling her cry of pain by biting her lip. Using Jonas plucking at her nipples as her focal point, his front pressing against her back, she closed her eyes feeling the discomfort between her thighs ease.

Both of their touches emphasized that they were having sex with her together. One was just as invested as the other, with her getting the glorious benefit of having both.

Her excitement wavered, though, when she felt Jonas's dick glide across the crease of her bottom as Hammer raised and lowered her. In unison, Hammer moved within her while Jonas moved just as fast on the outside between her butt cheeks.

If they threatened to stop unless she answered, Mika wouldn't have been able to pick who was giving her the most pleasure at each moment. It went beyond anything she would have expected, and no matter how long she lived after she left them tomorrow, she knew it would never equal the pleasure they were giving her tonight.

Jonas's gentle plucking became rougher as Hammer fucked her harder. Her muscles started to constrict as she felt the beginning of a climax she never thought she would experience.

"Do you think you're frigid now?" Hammer asked as if he was having trouble breathing.

Mika was incapable of answering as her first-ever climax continued to rage within her.

"Do you?" Jonas prodded, lifting her breasts so that Hammer could take a nipple between his teeth.

"No! No, I don't. I'm not," she whimpered, flattening her hands against Hammer's chest, regarding the slick feel of his skin under her palms as their climaxes overtook their concern that she had found hers.

She relaxed back against Jonas as Hammer disengaged himself from her. When Jonas swung her up to cradle her in his arms, she was entranced by the gentleness on his face. Taking a step forward he caringly placed her in the middle of the bed.

"You good?" Hammer asked pulling a blanket over her.

Finding herself the center of attention, with two males riveted on her wasn't how she thought her night would go when she went to the bar. It was like going out shopping and finding that special something but never realizing you were searching for it. Then, understanding it was meant to be yours despite rationalizing it couldn't possibly be real.

Snuggling down on the bed, she sleepily closed her eyes, listening lethargically as Jonas and Hammer turned out the lights and turned off the television before getting in bed with her. She was too exhausted to open her eyes to see who was on each side of her, afraid that it would set off another round of examining emotions she hadn't foreseen at coming to Kentucky.

They had talked about finding a woman who they wanted to make theirs, while all she had wanted was something quick and easy. What kept her awake after she was sure the other two were asleep were two questions: Was she going to stick to her plan or take a chance on theirs?

CHAPTER 8

Hammer awoke with an arm over his eyes, unconsciously blocking out the sunlight streaming into the room. Lowering his arm, he saw that Mary was still sleeping between him and Jonas. She was lying on her side toward him, with a leg draped over both of his and her hands clasped under her cheek.

His eyes met with Jonas's, who was curled against her back with an arm holding her possessively around her waist.

Giving a silent nod, Hammer began maneuvering himself out from under her. When she started to stir, Jonas shifted her closer to him, while Hammer remained still until she fell back to sleep.

Rising silently from the bed, he tugged on his clothes and shoes as Jonas lay watching. Dressed, he looked toward the bed. Jonas gave the signal that she was still sleeping.

Looking around the small room, he didn't see her purse. He had noticed she hadn't carried one into the bar last night either. Finding her suitcase in the closet, he pulled it out and opened it, seeing she had few clothes, evidencing she hadn't planned to stay long in Treepoint.

Skillfully searching through the suitcase, he wasn't able to find any identification. He meticulously repacked her things, putting them back the way he found them, before closing the case and storing it back in the closet.

Going to the foot of the bed, he picked up her jeans. Sliding his hand into the back pocket, he came out with four bunched twenties, yet still no ID. Searching the rest of her pockets, he didn't find anything else with her identity. Replacing the twenties, he let the jeans fall back to the floor. The only thing left to search was her car.

Seeing the keys on the small desk by the door, he took a step forward, only to come to an abrupt halt at the small sound of Jonas clicking his tongue in his mouth, alerting him that Mary was waking.

"What time is it?"

Her sleepy voice was like a punch to his gut. There was no way he was going to let the woman slip out of their lives.

Hammer sat down on the side of the bed opposite from the one that Jonas was lying on. "It's about six. I was about to go get us some coffee and food from the diner. What can I bring you?"

"Coffee and toast would be great. Thank you."

"Just coffee for me."

Hammer bent down to kiss her, noticing the flush going to her cheeks at his action. "I'll be right back."

"Take your time. I'm going to grab a shower while you're gone." Giving both him and Jonas a quick glance, she started to climb over Jonas. Jonas, on the other hand, wasn't going to have her ignore him.

Gripping her around the waist, he pulled her down on top of him. "Where's my good morning kiss?"

"I need to brush my teeth," she mumbled.

Jonas playfully smacked her on her bottom before releasing her. "Go ahead. I'll wait."

Hammer waited until he heard the bathroom door click shut before he spoke as low as he could. "She's going to bolt. I can see it in her eyes."

"Me, too," Jonas agreed.

They had been catching runners too long not to know that Mary had no intention of seeing them again. She thought they were a one-night stand, and they needed time to prove to her that they could be a part of her life. That wasn't going to happen if she took off.

"I'll go get the coffee and food. Make fucking sure she doesn't get away while I'm gone."

"I won't."

Nodding, he went to the desk to slip her keys into his pocket, when Mary suddenly came out of the bathroom, giving him a curious look that he was still there. To cover up his actions, he went to Jonas's jeans to take their room key out of his pocket. "I thought I'd change my clothes before going to the diner."

Innocently accepting his explanation, she took her suitcase out of the closet and placed it on the bed, needing a change of clothes for herself.

Frustrated that she would be suspicious if he kept hanging around after telling her that he was going, Hammer started to leave the room without her car keys, meeting Jonas's eyes one last time before heading out the door.

Swearing to himself that he would have to change his clothes before getting the food, he hurried, not wanting to leave Jonas and Mary alone for long. He wanted it settled that they would be able to see her again before she left town.

Taking a quick shower, he was in and out of their motel room within twelve minutes. However, he ran out of luck at the diner. There were several customers waiting for their orders, and the waitress took her time finishing his order.

Irritated, he was rushing back to the Escalade when a thought occurred to him.

Instead of taking a left toward the motel, he swung a right, going to the grocery store. Hurrying inside, he found what he was looking for sitting in a metal cart by the front entry. Picking up several items, he checked out and back was outside in minutes.

Satisfied, he drove back to the motel, anticipating Mary's reaction at what he bought her. It might be a day late, but the meaning was the same, regardless of the date on the calendar.

He didn't take a deep breath of relief until he pulled back into the motel parking lot and saw that her car was still there. Grinning in expectation, he knocked on Mary's motel room door, waiting for her or Jonas to answer. When neither did, Hammer juggled the coffee and take-out in one hand as he twisted the doorknob. The door opened easily to an empty room, with the television left on to a game show.

It wasn't the sound of the game show that was filling the room, though. It was the sound of Jonas's yells and bangs from inside the bathroom.

"I fucking knew it!" Setting the coffee and food on the desk, he hurried to unwind the luggage cord from the door-knob that she had attached to the foot of the bed. The bath-room door flew open when he released it.

Jonas's face was filled with rage. "Where's—"

"She's not here, but her car is still outside."

"Fucking hell…." Jonas dropped the towel he had wound around his waist to pull on his jeans.

"Why in the fuck did you take a shower? I told you not to leave her alone!" Hammer strode over to the window, pulling the drape back to make sure the car was still there. Sure enough, it was gone. The wily woman must have made a run for it when he was getting Jonas out of the bathroom.

"The car's gone! Let's—"

Jonas was already grabbing his shoes and T-shirt as Hammer started for the door.

"When I get my hands on her, she's not going to be able to sit down for a week," he snarled.

Hammer would have laughed if he wasn't just as angry.

Heaving himself into the driver's seat, he ignored Jonas's growl when he saw what was on the passenger seat. Picking up the red roses wrapped in cellophane, a red stuffed mouse, and two large, heart-shaped boxes of candy, he tossed them into the back seat.

"I'm going to use that luggage cord to tie her to the bed."

Hammer didn't pay any attention to Jonas's threats as he barreled out of the parking lot. There were only two ways out of town. One headed toward Jamestown and the other led to Virginia. There were easier ways to get to Virginia without traveling through Treepoint, so Mary had to be heading back through the thirty-mile stretch of road toward Jamestown. The problem was, if they didn't catch her before then, their chances of finding her would become more difficult. She could turn onto a number of county roads that led to several cities in Kentucky or take another road that headed to Tennessee. If she made it to Jamestown, odds were, they would lose her.

"Calm down." Speeding up, he blew through town. "Call Knox before one of his deputies pulls us over."

Jonas was reaching for his cell phone when the blue lights and the sound of a siren came from behind them. "Keep going," he said. "Knox can radio them to let us go."

"Dammit." Hammer hit the steering wheel with his fist as he started to slow down.

"Why are you slowing?" Jonas yelled at him. "Knox—"

"Save your breath." Hammer pulled to the side of the road, reaching for his wallet. "It's Greer."

"Son of a fucking bitch!" Jonas punched the side of the door.

He and Jonas both knew that Greer wouldn't listen to Knox. In fact, if the sheriff tried to call him off, Greer would just as likely arrest them instead of giving them a ticket.

"Here. Give him this. Tell him we're in a hurry." Jonas started pulling cash out from his wallet.

Hammer was a step ahead of him, his own cash already in his hand.

In his side-view mirror, he saw Greer saunter up to the side of his vehicle. Rolling the window down, he waved at Greer to hurry. Greer Porter went slower, pretending to peer through the dark, tinted windows.

"Fuck!" Hammer grabbed Jonas's cash, then got out. "Greer, we're in a hurry." Showing him the cash, he tried to give the deputy a smile, knowing if he irritated him, Greer would take his sweet time before letting them go.

"Are you trying to bribe an officer of the law?"

"Yes."

Greer took the cash, counting the bills. Satisfied, he stuffed it into his shirt pocket. "Works for me. I'll give your ticket to Killyama. Make sure you don't miss your court date."

Hammer was so frustrated that he was about to rip Greer a new asshole, but Jonas's yell stopped him.

Getting back inside, he slammed the door. "That son of a bitch shouldn't be a deputy," he snarled, putting the Escalade back into gear. "He should be the governor."

Jonas didn't respond, his eyes on the road ahead. "Mary's going to get away. She got too big of a head start. She could turn down any of these side roads and we wouldn't know. She could have family in the area and might not even be on the road anymore."

"I know." Jonas's thoughts were echoing his own early

ones. "You want me to keep going to Jamestown or turn back?"

"Keep going to Jamestown. If we don't catch up with her, we'll stop at the gas station at the turnoff. Maybe she doesn't have much gas, and we could luck out and catch her there."

Hammer pressed harder down on the gas, knowing deep down it was useless.

"How did you get yourself locked in the bathroom?"

"She tricked me."

"No shit."

"I forgot to take a condom to the shower," he admitted.

"Let me guess; she offered to get it for you?" he said snidely.

"Yes."

"She would have gotten me that way, too."

Hammer wasn't angry anymore. Jonas wasn't ready to drop his anger, though, and Hammer couldn't blame him. It had to have hurt his pride that she had taken off when he was buck naked.

"We'll find her."

"Yes, we will," he seconded. "You can count on that. And when we do, I'm going to give her two choices."

Hammer knew how Jonas's mind worked too well not to know their future plans.

"Stay tied to our bed or marry us."

"Exactly."

"When she does, can I tell Killyama how Mary got away from you?"

"Only if you want to die."

Mika kept hidden against the side of the vending machine as she watched for Hammer's vehicle to pull into the parking lot. Gripping the handle of her suitcase, she wanted to go back inside her room and pretend she was just playing a game with Jonas.

She wanted to go back to the day before and do a re-do. She would never have gone to the bar. Hell, she wouldn't even have gone for the soda. Because her plan had backfired. Her heart was breaking in two, and each part had a name: Jonas and Hammer.

She had wanted a simple one-night stand, yet it was anything but. That's what her friend Julia had been trying to make her understand, yet she hadn't seen the full picture because her heart hadn't been involved.

There was no such thing as a one-night stand. You might only have one night in someone's bed, but the memory of it lasts a lifetime. The casual encounter she planned had become so much more than she could have anticipated.

She deserved a broken heart. Jonas and Hammer had made it plain that they wanted an open and honest relationship, yet she wasn't able to give them that. She would have only made it worse for them all if she stayed. It would have been like building a house of hay and not expecting a hard wind to blow it away.

Besides, Mika had no intention of leaving her job and moving to another state. She had worked too hard to get where she was at now. She couldn't throw all her plans away because of the two men she just met.

What if they only wanted a one-night stand and all their talk was just a ploy to get laid? Instead of being angry that she had taken off, would they be relieved that she was gone?

"This is why one-night stands don't work."

Beginning to feel ridiculous that she was blowing the night out of proportion, Mika started to step out of her hiding place when she saw Hammer's Escalade turn into the parking lot. She would have been able to face an angry Jonas for locking him in, but confronting two angry men in a motel room wouldn't be a wise choice.

Holding her car keys ready, she held her breath as Hammer got out and walked toward her room. Giving him a few seconds to get inside, she then took off at a run.

Unlocking the car, she jerked the back door open and tossed the suitcase inside before getting in the driver seat. She didn't start breathing again until she was on the main road heading out of town. When she did, hiccupping cries filled the car as she imagined Jonas and Hammer hurt.

What if they were as upset as she was? But what if they weren't? It would have put them on the spot when they explained to her that they weren't interested in a relationship with her. So, had she really done them a benefit by leaving first?

The drive back to Lexington and the flight home seemed to last for an eternity. Returning to her lonely apartment made it even worse. How could two men that she had only spent a few hours with change her life so drastically?

After unpacking, she went to her spare bedroom that she had used as an office. Turning on the computer, she buried herself in work. Normally work held her full attention, but now her thoughts were centered on Hammer and Jonas.

Looking at the time on the computer screen, she wearily turned it off, then went to her bedroom. She had to be at work in a few hours, and unless she got a few hours' sleep, she would be useless.

Crawling into the empty bed, she told herself that she would get over the men. It was just that she had enjoyed their encounter. She reminded herself that after a couple of days in their company, they probably would have hit the door anyway. This way, she saved them all the heartache by skipping out on them.

Whacking her pillow with a pounding fist, Mika couldn't believe she was making such a big deal out of a casual encounter. Thousands of women did it all the time. Was it because that night had been her first time?

Unable to answer her own question, Mika forced herself to close her eyes, promising herself that within a few short days she would get over meeting Hammer and Jonas. If not, well, she had wanted more experience, and she did what she'd set out to do. The problem was she realized she'd gotten more than she had bargained for, and the cost was much higher. It was a cost that she was afraid came at too high of a price.

Her heart.

Mika waited impatiently outside the restaurant. It was freezing.

When she texted Julia that morning, she hadn't expected an answer. Surprisingly this time, Julia texted back, asking if she wanted to have lunch. Hopefully, their friendship would be on the mend.

She counted Julia as the only close friend she had in town. They had met freshman year in college, and while she was older, they had shared the same interests. Julia loved biking and hiking like she did, and they had gone on several camping trips together. She missed riding with her in the mornings.

Seeing Julia approach, Mika waved and smiled as she started to walk toward her to meet her halfway. Her smile then slipped when she saw the dark circle under Julia's eye that her makeup had no hope of concealing.

Hiding her concern, she hugged Julia when she came within reach. "Hi!"

"Hi!" Julia's self-conscious smile wavered. "I'm sorry I was such a bitch—"

"Don't," Mika cut her off. "You don't have anything to be sorry about." Hooking her arm through hers, she pulled her in the direction of the restaurant. "You know I hate this restaurant. Only you can get me to brave the traffic to get here. Next time, I get to choose."

"Okay. I can live with that."

Mika bit her lip at Julia's choice of words.

It didn't take long for them to get a table and order their food and drinks. While Julia was placing her order, Mika tried to come up with a way to ask her about the black eye. Before she could ask, though, Julia brought it up herself when the waitress walked away.

"Go ahead and ask. I know you're dying to."

"What happened?" she asked gently.

"Another argument with Dillion, of course."

"It's not of course this time. He hit you!"

"Yes."

"Are there other places he hit you?"

"Nothing that won't heal," she admitted.

Mika reached across the table to take her friend's hand. "Did you report it?"

"Yes. He's in jail. He gets out tomorrow. I have a restraining order, so he has to stay away from me."

"That's going to make it difficult with you living in his house," she ventured.

Several times she had tried to talk her friend into leaving the toxic relationship. Dillion was overly possessive, monitoring every move Julia made.

"Yes, it does. I have to find a new place to live before he gets out of jail."

"You can come and stay with me." It wasn't the first time she made the offer, but Julia always refused.

Her friend gripped her hand back. "I wanted to ask, but I've been such a bi—" Julia hastily cut herself off before continuing. "I would appreciate it. I won't stay long, just until I can find myself my own place."

"You can stay as long as you want. You can have my spare bedroom. I'll move my computer and desk to mine, so you'll have plenty of space for your things."

Julia looked out the window, evading her gaze. "You warned me, and I didn't listen."

"You love Dillion. You wanted to give him a chance."

Julia swung her gaze back to Mika, giving her a strange look. "You never said that before."

Mika moved the napkin so the waitress could set her plate down. When they were alone again, Julia didn't make a move to touch her food.

"You always asked how I can keep loving someone that I fight with so much."

"Oh, I see. I'm sorry. I shouldn't have said that to you. Whatever you want to do, I promise I'll support your decision."

Julia smiled and picked up her fork, but Mika didn't move to pick up her own.

"Unless you decide to go back to him," she told her honestly.

Julia laughed. "You won't have to. I learned my lesson. No more Dillion."

"I'm going to hold you to that," she warned her friend.

"Go ahead." Julia shuddered. "He hit me, Mika. He's never done that before."

Mika grabbed her free hand that wasn't holding the fork. "I'm glad you're moving out and in with me. I'll have someone to watch movies with. Have you seen the new *Avengers*?"

"No, but I've seen *Death Day 2*."

Mika zoned out as Julia started describing the movie. It didn't sound like her kind of movie.

Trying not to stare at the bruise on her friend's face as she pretended to listen, she worried that Julia wouldn't be strong enough to stay away from Dillion for long. They'd had several fights before, and she didn't know if she believed that Dillion hadn't hit her before. But she was willing to let it go since Julia said she wasn't going to be with him anymore. Hoping she would stick with her decision when he was released, Mika would stick by her friend regardless. That was what friends were for.

CHAPTER 10

"Any luck?" Hammer asked as Jonas got back in the Escalade.

"No."

"Why not?"

"He wasn't exactly in a cooperative mood after you threatened to rip his windpipe out." Jonas sent him an admonishing look as he buckled his seat belt.

Frustrated, Hammer leaned his head back on the headrest. "I know. I should have let you handle it. I just lost it when he kept shutting me down. He was being a dick. So, what were you able to get out of him?"

"Nothing," he told him as he started texting on his phone. "Let's go."

Hammer started the vehicle. "Where are we going?"

"To The Last Riders. We need Killyama's help."

"Fuck. Do we have to?"

"Do you want to find Mary?"

"Dammit."

"It could be worse."

"How?"

"At least it isn't Greer."

~

"Why aren't we meeting Killy at her house?" Hammer asked as they walked up the back walkway behind the clubhouse.

"Killy said it was her turn to do lunch, and that if it was that important to talk to her now, we'd have to meet here."

"This day is just getting better and better," Hammer complained, reaching for the back door of the kitchen. Before he touched the handle, the door suddenly burst open, and two men came flying out, their fists pounding each other so hard grunts of pain filled the space.

"Whoa." Jonas started to try to break the two apart, but then stopped, recognizing the one with the fucked haircut. He couldn't see who the other one was since Gavin had him in a headlock, his head buried under Gavin's armpit as Gavin battered his back with his free hand.

Hammer, also recognizing Gavin, stepped out of the way so he wouldn't become a casualty.

"I'm not going!" Gavin snarled, pounding his large fist on the man's back again.

"Yes, you fucking are!"

Jonas finally realized who Gavin was fighting when Rider reached out for Gavin's chest. He winced when he saw what Rider was doing.

"I taught him that move," Hammer said proudly.

"You always get a kick out of teaching that technique. I prefer using other, less cruel ways."

Hammer shrugged. "I prefer to win."

"Me, too."

A feminine snicker had them both taking their eyes off

the fight to see Killyama watching enthusiastically with a bloodthirsty look.

"Should we try to break them up?"

While Hammer gave him an are-you-fucking-crazy glare, Killyama thankfully didn't take him up on the offer.

"No. I'll wait until Rider gets tired. Train and Cash are working out in the basement; they can break it up."

"Why don't they just do it now?"

She rolled her eyes. "Because that wouldn't be any fun, now would it?"

"I guess not," Jonas said, moving her out of the way as the men barreled back in their direction.

"So, what did you need to ask me?"

"I need you to ask Shade if he can find out who rented a motel room in town."

It hit both Hammer and Jonas's pride that they had to ask Shade for information, but it was the quickest way they could find Mary.

Killyama gave him a puzzled look. "Why don't you ask him yourself?"

"I've tried to call him twice. We were hoping he would be here or at the factory, but his bike isn't here. Pretty pissed off at him for him not answering, Hammer and I did a favor for him last night. Today? He can't take five seconds to answer a text?"

Jonas was becoming so aggravated that Shade hadn't texted or called he thought about becoming involved in the fight just to blow some steam off. It only took him a minute to think it over; he didn't want to spend the rest of his life being pushed in a wheelchair by Hammer.

It was everything he could do not to intervene in the fight. Gavin had Rider by the throat and was shoving him up against the side of the clubhouse as if he were a paint-brush. It was hard for Hammer to take just standing there, too, since they both knew what Gavin had been through. Then again, they'd fought missions so they knew full-well what Gavin was capable of. The only reason Rider was still breathing was because the Reaper was holding himself back.

"Let up, Gavin." Hammer moved closer to the two men. Jonas could tell his friend was getting ready to step in now that Rider's face was turning blue.

"You should get Train and Cash," Jonas told Killyama grimly, bracing himself for when Hammer stepped in.

"I'm not going, got it?" Gavin yelled up at Rider's purple face.

"Fuck." Hammer couldn't take it anymore. He reached out to touch Gavin when Rider struck out, smashing his hands on each side of Gavin's head.

Gavin doubled over, holding his ears and allowing Rider to slide to the ground. Before Gavin could recover, Rider flashed out a foot, kicking Gavin in the stomach.

"Someone is watching Jo and Crux, so either you convince Shade to go," Rider choked out hoarsely, "or you go. I don't care which you choose, but it won't be me. I'll give up being a Last Rider if it comes to that. And if you think I fucking won't, *fucking try me!*" Turning his back on Gavin, he stormed back into the house, leaving Gavin lying there, watching him leave with a haggard expression on his face.

Hammer and Jonas both turned their gazes away when Gavin followed him back inside.

"Well, that was intense."

Killyama watched them both go inside before turning back to Jonas and Hammer. "So, why do you want to know who rented a room?"

This was the tricky part that neither he nor Hammer wanted to go into.

"It's for a job we're thinking of taking on."

"Bullshit. Moon said he saw you with a woman last night. Who was she?"

"We don't know," he admitted.

"Ah. Well, I guess I can use my magic on Shade and find out for you."

"What's the catch?" Jonas knew better than to take Killyama's offer at face value.

"No catch. Just curious to see who the woman is that got you two interested enough to chase after her."

"We could be working a case."

"No, Moon said you didn't let any grass grow under your ass when you saw her at the bar."

Hammer scowled. "Moon has a big mouth."

"No shit." Killy took out her phone. "Let me see what I can find out." She went to sit on the picnic table as they waited.

"He didn't answer for me either," she said from the table. "You said she stayed at the motel?"

"Yes. We tried to get the information from the clerk there, but when Hammer threatened to tear out his windpipe, his cooperation stopped."

"Did you offer him cash?"

"We didn't have any on us. We'd already given everything in our wallets to Greer, and Hammer didn't want to go to the ATM."

"You two are hopeless without me. You're going to tell me why you had to give Greer all your cash?"

"No," both Jonas and Hammer said curtly and at the same time.

Killyama tried to call Shade again. When he didn't answer, she stood, putting her phone in her back pocket. "Let's go."

"Where are we going?" Jonas asked.

"To the motel."

"You have any cash or should we stop by the ATM?"

"Neither."

"He won't give you the information either. And if he starts reading off those privacy laws again, I'll rip out his windpipe myself."

"He'll tell me," she assured them, giving them a confident grin. "Besides, you should have called me before you talked to him. Never send a man when a woman can do it better."

Jesus, she was never going to let this down. Hammer's expression showed he was feeling the burn as badly as him.

"What makes you so sure?"

"Because I'll have his windpipe in my hand."

CHAPTER 11

Mika plopped down on her couch, tucking her legs underneath her. Pointing the remote at the television, she shouted out to Julia, "You ready for me to start the movie?"

Her friend came out of the bedroom that she was still settling into. "I was thinking of taking a nap."

"At three in the afternoon? You'll be up all night. Come on." Mika patted the couch cushion next to her. "Keep me company." She knew that Julia was going to call or text Dillion in privacy.

Mika could tell Julia's anger and determination of the day before was switching trajectory. She was going to do everything within her power to stop that from happening. It was a sad way for her to ignore and dampen the heartbreak she'd been feeling since being back. Leaving "the men" was not something she was going to recover from soon, but dealing with Julia's drama was at least a way to keep her mind off her own problems.

"You win. But if I watch *Avengers* with you, then you have to watch *Happy Death Day* with me."

Mika shuddered. "I'm squeamish at the sight of blood." She pressed the button to start the movie and said, "You're going to love it. There's enough man candy to quench both of our sweet tooths."

"You're so lame. You're excited about a movie hunk? You should go out more. Guys like these don't exist in real life."

Mika shrugged. "I don't think the actors would agree with that sentiment."

"Well, you sure won't be meeting Renner or Hemsworth."

"Don't worry; next month *Aquaman* comes out. He might steal the spotlight. By the way, when it comes out, will you go to the theater with me?"

"No."

Mika picked up her cell phone, showing her the actor that portrayed *Aquaman*.

Julia took a long look at the picture, bringing Mika's phone closer to her face before giving it back. "I'll buy the tickets. It'll be my treat."

"Thought so," Mika said smugly, taking another glance at the picture herself before setting her phone aside.

She was raising the volume on the television when she heard a knock on her door.

"Are you expecting anyone?"

"No." Pressing pause, Mika jumped up from the couch, then walked to the door to look through the peephole. She had to plant her face harder against the door, sure she was mistaken about seeing the two men standing on the other side.

"Who is it?"

Mika spun around, pressing her back against the door as if Jonas and Hammer were about to knock it down. "No one," she shrieked, biting her lip when she heard another loud knock.

Mika started trembling. She was so fucked. She had no

idea how they had managed to find her, but they had. What was she supposed to do now?

She quickly calculated how much food and water she had in the apartment, because there was no way could she face them.

Julia got off the couch to come to the door. "Mika, someone's at the door. I hear them knocking."

"It's your imagination. Mine, too. Let's go back to watching the movie."

"I knew it was only a matter time before writing all those papers would fry your brain. Let me see! Is it Dillion?"

"No! It's not Dillion!" Mika dug her socks into the carpet, trying to keep Julia from opening the door. "Julia, do not open the do—"

From Julia's excited expression, Mika knew it was only going to be a matter of time before Julia went back to Dillion.

"Don't! It's not Dillion!"

Mika found herself wedged away from the door as Julia parted it open a crack. Hammer and Jonas did the rest, shouldering inside and sending her in her socks sliding along the carpet without any traction.

She had never been so embarrassed in her life, and she'd had some doozies. It was right up there with the time she was absently working on a math problem in her head as she strode into the men's bathroom. It was only when as she was closing the bathroom door and saw the urinals that she realized what she had done. Hearing the sounds of male voices, she closed a stall door, shutting herself inside. She ended up being stuck in there for two hours before she was brave enough to make her escape, only to open the stall door to find one of her coworkers taking a wiz. Because of the incident, she received a delicately written email questioning if she knew there was a gender-neutral bathroom on each floor. It had taken her a year to live that down.

This was worse—the embarrassment at seeing Jonas's and Hammer's accusing gazes.

"Hi, guys."

Julia's stunned eyes turned to her at the greeting. "You know them?" Astonished, she switched back to the men, daring her to deny it.

Mika licked her dry lips. "Vaguely."

She knew as soon as she said it that it was a big mistake.

"Vaguely?" Hammer straightened to his full height as he walked closer to her while Jonas shut the door.

"Okay, a little better than vaguely. I met them when I was out of town."

"Where in the fuck did you go? I want to buy a ticket—"

"Not now, Julia."

Feeling uncomfortable, Mika didn't know what to do. She was thrilled to see them again but was awkwardly aware of how she had sneaked out, and with Julia there, she was weirded out at how to react.

"How did you find me?" She could tell from their expressions that she shouldn't have started that ball rolling. Clearing her throat, she decided to ask the question that was most on her mind. "What are you two doing here?"

"We decided to come for a visit," Jonas coldly informed her. How had she ever thought he was the nice one?

She started to tell Hammer that Jonas was being a jerk and realized she had it right the first time.

"Julia"—Jonas gave her friend a teeth-baring smile that sent a jealous twinge in her breast—"I'm Jonas, and this my friend and business partner, Hammer."

"What business are you in?" Julia asked with interest.

"We're bounty hunters."

Mika wanted to slap herself silly for not asking that question herself. She hadn't a chance in hell of them not finding her. *Why didn't you ask them?* she wailed at herself. *Because you thought it was a one-night stand.* She mentally smacked herself again.

"Is there a private place we can talk?" Hammer asked politely, though his eyes told her that, if she didn't, they would have no problem discussing it in front of Julia.

"We can go to my bedroom, I guess." *Dig the grave a little deeper, why don't you?* Mika blasted herself quickly while motioning toward her bedroom.

Julia gave her an envious look. "I'll go ahead and start the movie. Who needs imitations when you can have the real thing?"

She saw Hammer and Jonas understand her meaning when they saw the paused Thor on the TV.

Going into the bedroom, she waited until both men were inside before nervously shutting the door.

"I'm sorry...," she started, when her world began spinning as she was tossed onto her bed.

Shoving her hair out of her face, she stared up at two furious visions of masculine fury. Then her mouth dropped open when they started taking their clothes off.

"Have you lost your minds?" she whispered loudly. "Julia is right outside."

Hammer threw his shirt down on the bed before going over to the door to lock it. "Problem solved."

"Okay... I can understand why you're both so upset. I acted like a five-year-old, running off without any explanation."

"I think it's pretty plain that you fucked us and ran," Jonas said snidely, sitting down on the side of the bed to remove his shoes. "You used us."

"I wouldn't exactly say used," Mika tried to start again, then had to reach for the comforter under her to keep herself from being pulled off the bed as Hammer, his clothes now off, started tugging her sweatpants down her legs.

"You see that, Jonas?"

Mika fell back to stare up at the ceiling in embarrassment, aware of what they were staring at.

"I see you took my advice."

Mika didn't like Jonas's dull response to her new panties.

Hammer climbed onto the bed next to her. "We were supposed to go shopping together to pick them out for you," he reprimanded her. "How many new pairs did you get?"

"A few," she lied.

"How many is a few?" Jonas asked, laying down on her other side.

"Eight," she reluctantly admitted, not putting it past them to go to her drawers and see for themselves. It wouldn't take a rocket scientist to figure out which ones were new. The stark white ones had been pushed to the side, while the new ones were neatly folded in her drawer.

"You didn't do a half-bad job," Hammer complimented, sliding a finger under the lace at her belly. "I could have done better."

"You weren't here." She turned her head on the mattress to stare at him.

"No, we weren't, and whose fault is that?"

Mika pursed her lips, rubbing them together. Should she just own up to her regret at leaving them behind?

She looked beyond the anger in his eyes to see what was lurking underneath. The same was in Jonas's. It was easy to answer her own question.

"Mine. I shouldn't have left like that." She turned her head in Jonas's direction. "Especially the way I left you in the shower. I regretted it as soon as I did it."

"Then, why didn't you come back?" Jonas wasn't exactly ready to forgive her yet.

JAMIE BEGLEY

"I knew you would be furious. And truthfully, I didn't think you would want me to. I thought it was an easy out for guys, too."

"Just so, you get it—" He stared her down. "—and so there are no more misunderstandings… there isn't going to be an easy out for us, or for you."

She shifted closer to him. "I'm getting that." She kissed him gravely. "I missed you." Turning toward Hammer, she kissed him just as passionately. "I missed you."

"Dammit. I'm not ready to get over being mad at you," Hammer groused. "Not only did you sneak out on us, but you also could have told us it was your first time."

"How did you—"

"When I was fucking you. We were going to talk about it the next morning, but you left before we could," Jonas grumbled. He might want to pretend to be angry at her for not telling them, but she could see the emotion just wasn't there. No, Jonas just wanted another turn to be pacified.

She moved closer to him until her breasts snuggled against the curly hair on his chest.

"Don't be mad." She placed a kiss to the hollow of his throat. "Get even."

Hammer gave a low groan. "Jonas?" he snapped.

"I can deal with that."

"Me, too."

"Me, too." Mika laughed against Hammer's throat.

"What do you have to get even for?" Jonas asked, curving his body against her back.

"That it took you two days to find me. For bounty hunters, you kind of suck."

"We do," Jonas conceded, trailing his mouth down her spine, pausing at her bottom to place a kiss on each of her cheeks as he grabbed her hips to lay her on her back. Raising

270

up on his knees, he slid her silken, ice-blue panties off, throwing them over his shoulder.

She gave a low moan when Jonas's mouth found her heated core, spreading the lips of her pussy to delicately lick the already damp flesh. Then, lurching upward at the sensations attacking her, she traveled her mouth down Hammer's chest, poised above her from her side, exploring every ridge and angle until she reached the hard cock that was begging for her attention. Rubbing her thumb over the bulbous head, she felt Hammer jerk above her as Jonas nudged her thighs farther apart so he could circle his tongue around her clit before sucking it into his mouth to tease it with his teeth.

She tried to keep stroking Hammer's cock while Jonas played her body like a magician, making it hard for her to concentrate on Hammer. It was like being a kaleidoscope, and every movement of their bodies created different shards of pleasure to form a picture of such beauty that she couldn't believe it existed. Deep down, she knew that was why she had run.

It couldn't exist.

And if they really did it, it wouldn't last.

So many things could tarnish their perfect picture, like others who wouldn't condone a polyamorous relationship. Or they could implode it themselves. Would jealousy rear its head and break them apart? The relationship had so many potential barriers that she couldn't foresee.

"Mika, it'll work." Hammer's voice settled over her like a comforting mantle.

"I was talking out loud again, wasn't I?"

"Yes. And it's the truth. Jonas and I are strong enough to protect you."

Her brow furrowed. "I don't need you to protect me. I really don't care what people say about us. I'm worried about you and Jonas. I don't want either of you hurt."

"Babe, no one is stupid enough to say anything in front of us." Jonas brought his mouth to the tender skin of her thigh, giving her a small love bite. The exquisite pleasure had her wanting him to do that to her clit.

Lifting her thigh, she used her leg to put his mouth back where she wanted it. Jonas's shoulders shook with laughter.

Hammer showed her what he wanted her to do by using her hair to place her mouth over his cock.

Looking up, she saw his face twisted in agony and desire. Out of the corner of her eye, she saw the same expression on Jonas's face. Suddenly, she got it.

They cared about her. They might have only known each other for a few days, but they had been searching for her for what felt like an eternity. During the lonely years of studying for her degrees, through long hours at work, that she knew would only end in going home to an empty bed, through bouts of sickness when she fervently wished someone cared enough to bring her a bowl of soup….

The bone-deep loneliness that only could be filled by someone loving you.

For her, it wasn't just one person who would break that loneliness; it was two. They might be a couple consisting of three individuals, but there was only one heart between them all. And it was a heart that was filled with enough love for all three of them. It was a precious gift, and she would be damned if she refused something so special.

She tightened her hand around Hammer's cock, taking him deeper into her mouth until Jonas turned her around and raised her up on her knees. Continuing back to teasing Hammer's cock in her new position, she saw him hand Jonas a condom that he had taken out of his shirt pocket.

Hammer grinned at her. "We came prepared."

Mika held on to Hammer's cock as Jonas entered her from behind, his moan echoing hers as he surged then retreated, slowly stretching her until he could smoothly move faster and faster.

Jonas made love to her, she made love to Hammer. Each of them shared the pleasure of the other, dragging it on, not wanting it to end, absorbing the sensations and joy until they couldn't take it anymore. Then the kaleidoscope turned one last time, bringing a burst of colors that were so beautiful that all three of them would remember and celebrate for the days and years to come. It was the day they fell in love.

CHAPTER 12

"It's just not fair," Julia complained.

"What isn't?" Mika asked, stirring a small amount sugar into the pitcher of iced tea she was making.

"Hammer and Jonas."

"Let me tell you a small secret I learned when I was sixteen years old. Life isn't fair."

"No shit. Dillion won't stop calling, so I blocked him."

"I'm proud of you. I thought you'd break."

Looking sheepish, Julia sat down at one the high-back counter chairs as she watched her fill the pitcher with ice cubes. "I probably would have if Hammer and Jonas hadn't shown up."

"How did *that* keep you from taking him back?"

"I figured, if you can find two men like them, then maybe I can at least find one who will treat me better than Dillion."

"Did you just compliment or insult me?"

"Don't ask. I'm not in a great mood right now."

Mika poured her a glass of iced tea, then gave it to her before going to the cabinet to take out four plates.

"You need some help?" Julia offered.

"Nothing else to do. The guys should be back any minute with the pizza."

Placing the plates down on the counter, she was filling the three remaining glasses when she heard them knocking on the door.

"I'll grab it. It's the least I can do," Julia joked as she made her way to the door.

Mika was taking a sip of her drink when she heard the loud sound of the door being banged open. Dropping the glass, she took off running to the door at the unexpected sound, Julia's terrified screams spurring her on.

"Stop, Dillion! You're hurting me!" Julia yelled out, trying to get her ex-boyfriend's hand out of her hair.

"You fucking slut, you should have answered my calls."

Mika rushed forward, grabbing Dillion's shirt and trying to tear him off Julia. "Let her go!" she raged, frightened that, because it was the middle of the day, most of her neighbors would be at work and they'd be hurt long before Jonas and Hammer got home.

A split-second later, she felt Dillion smack her across the face.

Her hand went to the burning pain, but instead of backing off, she started for him again as he hit Julia. Before she could try to tear him of her again, though, he pulled Julia closer to him holding her with one hand around her neck while taking a long knife out of his back pocket with the other.

"Back off, Mika. This is between me and Julia," he shouted as he pulled Julia farther back into the living room.

Mika started walking backward, not wanting to incite him even more. "Dillion, this isn't the way you should treat a woman you love," she said, taking another step in hopes of lessening the energy surging through the room.

"What does it matter what I feel? She doesn't love me! I'm

not stupid, Mika. You take another step toward that cell phone and I'll hurt her," he warned, clearly seeing her intent.

Mika nodded, taking a step away from the phone.

"Don't do this. Just leave while you can. One of the neighbors will have called the police by now."

Julia's terror-stricken face tore at her, but Mika remained calm. She just had to keep him distracted until Jonas and Hammer returned.

Moving to the back of the couch, her thigh touched the side table.

Julia's cries were starting to get to Dillion, and he started shaking her, his face filled with fury that Julia was still trying to get away.

Mika watched in slow motion as Dillion raised the knife, preparing to strike Julia with it, his eyes focused entirely on her. She used the opportunity she had been waiting for and reached for the gun her father had insisted on for her protection. "Look up!" Mika yelled as loudly as she could.

Distracted by Mika's sudden shout, Dillion looked up. It was his fatal mistake.

A bullet hit right through his throat and out the back of his neck.

Julia's hysterical screams didn't abate, even after she lowered the gun. Mika would have run to hold her, but she didn't think her friend wanted to be touched by her after she just killed her ex-boyfriend.

"Julia, shut up! It's over. Jonas, call the police," Hammer shouted over Julia's screams.

Mika wasn't aware they had come into the apartment.

"Is he dead?" Julia asked shrilly.

Exasperated, Hammer looked down at the man sprawled on her carpet. "His brain's all over the place; what do you think?" he snapped.

"Be nice. She's hysterical," Mika—ever the pragmatic

thinker—scolded him as she sat down on the side table, waiting calmly for the police to arrive.

"The cops are on their way," Jonas said, grimacing at the mess before turning to look at her. "You keep a gun in a candleholder?"

"It's not a candleholder." She bought it an antique store, just for the exact purpose she used it for.

"Why did you keep a loaded firearm in a candleholder?" Hammer asked as he strode to the metal canister to look down inside it.

"There's not another one inside."

Hammer cracked a smile at her sarcasm. "How'd you learn to shoot like that?"

"My father taught me."

"He did a hell of a job."

"I always thought so."

"Take it from me, he did." Jonas took Julia's arm, guiding her to sit on the couch. "Please tell me that gun is licensed."

"Of course. Why would I have an unlicensed gun in my home?"

"I don't fucking know. I never expected you to have one in the first place," he said, placing his arm around her shoulder.

"I don't know why. I told you I can protect myself."

"Believe me; we see that now."

"Mika, is he really dead?"

"Yes, Julia, he's dead."

"I should be sorry he's dead, shouldn't I?" Anguished, Julia pressed a hand to her mouth.

Jonas left the living room to go into the bedroom, coming back to place a blanket over Julia's shoulder.

"He was going to stab you when I shot him. So, no, you don't have to have any sympathy for him."

"Thank you, Mika." Julia wiped her tears away. "You saved my life."

"No, you saved your own life when you decided to leave him. He would have found another reason to go after you that way."

∾

The rest of the day was spent in a blur. Julia had called another friend to stay with, apologizing that she couldn't stay with her. Mika understood. Fortunately, Jonas and Hammer had stayed with her throughout the day and the ensuing drama. After all the police questioning and returning back to the apartment, Hammer helped her pack a suitcase for the night, while Jonas found them a hotel room.

"Ready?" Jonas asked as they came out of her bedroom.

"Yes," Mika answered.

The landlord was still repairing the door for her. As she talked to him, Hammer and Jonas stood to the side, talking. When she finished her conversation, they took the elevator downstairs, leaving the apartment building and scene of the crime.

At the SUV, Hammer held the back door. Climbing inside, she was surprised when both men got in the back, too.

"Is there a problem with the hotel room or something?" she asked.

"I couldn't find a room. Every room in this city is already booked."

"So, what are we going to do?"

Hammer reached up and pulled down a DVD screen as Jonas motioned for her to raise up.

"What are you doing?"

A click had the overly large and comfortable seat laying

back down into a bed. Both men patted the leather bed. Pulling her shoes off, she crawled in between them.

"This isn't bad."

Jonas and Hammer snuggled closer to her as Jonas reached for the remote.

"What're we watching?" she asked, rubbing her cheek against Jonas's chest, while Hammer fit his hips snuggly against her bottom.

"Guess."

When the screen came to life, Mika reached out to take the controller away from him.

"You don't want to watch it?" he asked.

"Who needs imitations when I can have the real thing?"

Hammer rose up on an elbow to stare down at them. "I think we need to discuss how far California is away Tennessee."

"I've already thought about that." She slid her hand under Jonas's shirt. "I emailed my resignation when I came back from Kentucky. I told them I'd be searching for a new job and gave them a month's notice.

He grinned, laying his hand on hers to hold it still, but it was Hammer who asked the question she could see in Jonas's eyes.

"Where are you going to be searching for a job?"

"I've always wanted to see Tennessee."

BEFORE

DANGEROUS LOVE

"You really won't come out with us?"

Mika finally sat up in the hotel bed, wrapping the expensive duvet cover around her so tightly that only her eyes were exposed, making her look like an Eskimo who was about to brave a winter storm. However, the goose down comforter did nothing to combat the chills rippling through her body from the inside out. "If you're willing to push me and this bed along with you all day, then sure, I'll come, Adrienne."

Adrienne came over to her, placing a hand on her forehead, immediately feeling the warmth. "You're burning up."

"I told you." She sniffled.

"Maybe we should stay and watch her?"

Avril came over then, barely placing a hand on her forehead before pulling it away and rolling her eyes. "Oh, please. She'll be fine."

Simone, who was posing her model face in the mirror,

looked back at them. "We did not lie to our parents and spend hours getting dressed to not leave this hotel room."

Mika rolled her own eyes now. She really hated being not only the ugly one in the group, considering her friends were successful models, but also being the young one at only sixteen. For some reason, being a whole year older made any teenager believe they were a know-it-all over anyone who was even a day younger.

"I really don't think we should leave h—"

"I said she'll be fine, Adrienne," Avril insisted as she grabbed her purse as she headed toward the door.

"Thanks." Mika smiled at Adrienne, not wanting to ruin her friend's day. "But I'll be okay. I'm just going to sleep it off."

She had spent too many vacations with her group of friends not to be familiar with how the hierarchy worked. Avril was the leader, Simone was next, then Adrienne; she came in last. It had never bothered her, too thrilled at being given the opportunity to be friends with the other girls.

If her father and Adrienne's father weren't best friends, she wouldn't be lying in their hotel room, feeling like she was at death's door. She was closest to Adrienne, but she had been spending more time with the other two since her father started allowing her to travel to France with Dalton and his family. The three girls gave her a sense of normalcy that had been missing from her life.

Her childhood was unconventional, with her father being the president of the Road Slayers, and her parents finding out they had a child prodigy on their hands. Her father and Adrienne's met when they had belonged to another motor-cycle club. Even when her father had split and formed his own motorcycle club, he remained close friends with Dalton.

She had grown up nonchalant that her "Uncle Dalton" was famous, and then the friends who showed her how to put on her makeup were becoming famous in their own right, each with a career in modeling. To her, they were just another branch of her family, not related by blood but just as loved.

"Come on; let's go. The cab is waiting," Simone said.

"Call if you get worse."

She nodded. "I will."

Watching Adrienne gracefully walk away, it was everything she could do not to tell them to stay with her. Something in her gut nagged at her to open her mouth and try to talk them into doing just that. In reality, it wouldn't have been that hard, considering Adrienne could be swayed to stay in an instant. But then the fun would have been knocked out for the other two since, unlike Mika, Adrienne was an integral part of the group. Therefore, she didn't say anything, always afraid of being the party pooper, considering she was the youngest in the group.

Out of the four of them, it was her dumb luck to be the one to get sick.

"Bye." Avril blew her a kiss, staying well away from her.

"Bye," Mika said, blowing her a kiss back, then giggling as she sent another one in Simone's direction.

Her friends gave her horrified looks, rushing out the door as if afraid her airborne kisses were contagious.

Adrienne was the last one to say it before the door closed. "Bye."

"Bye... Love you," Mika whispered, regret slowly seeping in that she didn't at least try to get them to stay even five minutes longer....

AFTER

DANGEROUS LOVE

As she approached the nurses' station, Julia placed a sheath of daily reports in the basket that would have to be copied and placed in patients' files.

"I'm glad you listened to my suggestion and came in today. How are you doing?" Mika asked in concern.

"Fine. Thank you. You were right. All day yesterday, I just kept replaying what happened in my mind. Here, I'm too busy to fix myself a cup of coffee, much less wonder about the what ifs."

"There shouldn't be any what ifs, unless you're trying to blame yourself for Dillion's actions. He brought a knife and broke down a door to get to you, not out of love, but because the only thing on his mind was hurting you. You survived. That's all that counts, and certainly nothing to feel guilty about." Mika repeated the last sentence her father and Uncle Dalton had tried to convince her of for years, but it took her repeating the same words to Julia to truly appreciate their truth.

She shrewdly took in her friend's harried movements as she answered calls from wanting patients. "The patients seem restless this evening."

"Of course, it's a full moon. Plus, half the staff is off and at the motorcycle rally. It'll calm down when it's bedtime." Julia laid two charts in front of her. "Your new patient is causing a ruckus. He's been setting off some of the other patients in the ward. I can see why they contacted you for help. Have you decided which medications you want to start him on?"

"Not yet. I want to observe him for a few more days. If he gives you too much trouble, have Linc deal with him. He seems to be able to keep him calm," Mika said as she opened the folder on top, seeing an addressed envelope inside.

Julia saw her staring at the letter. "Winston had a new volunteer today. He wrote another letter."

"So I see." Mika neatly spread the letter out, with *Adrienne Graciene Brown* printed on the front with the address. I don't know how he convinces them to write them for him. They know they'll be searched by the guard at the main entrance.

"He just won't give it up." Julia shuddered at the sight of the letter. "Thank God I'm not her. I've lost three nurses because he freaks them out so badly. He watches every move they make, and you can just see how scary as hell he was before his neck was broken. He still is.

"I have to take valium when I am on duty at his end of the hall. I hope he does get moved to a prison hospital ward. It'll be nice when I don't have to listen to the nurses beg me not to have them take their turn."

"His hearing is next week; you might get your wish." Mika closed the folder, laying it back down.

"Does Dr. Butler think Winston will be successful?"

"I haven't asked. Dr. Butler and I haven't conferred on his case. Like you, I'll have to wait and see."

"If he is, I'll have to plan a party to celebrate." Julia twirled an ink pen in her hand. "I can always invite Linc. I haven't dated any of the male aides before, but with him, I'm willing to make an exception. Have you heard if he's married?" she asked, lowering her voice when the new aide came out of room down the opposite end of the hall from the nurses' station.

"Yes, he's married," Mika answered as the new aide went behind the nurses' station to take a chair, waiting for the next call.

With brown hair that was neatly cut and a body that looked well-built, despite the ugly scrubs he was required to wear, he had garnered the interest of several female staff members.

To disguise the fact that they had been talking about him, Julia told Linc apologetically, "I was just mentioning to Dr. Foster that the nurses and aides complain when they have to go to Winston's room. I gave you a couple of days becoming more familiar with the other patients before making you take a turn. Tomorrow night, though, you get his end of the hall."

"I don't mind." He shrugged. "Are Liz and Patty still on break? And where's Corbin?"

"Yes, and Corbin is in room twelve. He's giving a shower. If you need him to show you anything, he should be finishing up any minute."

"It's nothing important. I was just going to ask him if he wanted to take his dinner break with me when Liz and Patty get back."

"If he doesn't, I can ask Molly, the floating nurse, to switch with me. We switch dinner times all the time."

Mika gave her friend an admonishing glance for flirting with a married coworker.

"I can wait for Corbin."

Mika felt bad that Julia was unsuccessful in her pursuit. Then again, she really wasn't.

Opening the other file that Julia gave her, she was reading it over when Corbin exited a patient's room from across the nurses' station.

"You want to—

A buzzer went off, interrupting Linc.

"Dammit… that's Harvey." Corbin turned, walking down the long hallway.

"I guess that's going to be a no." Linc pulled a clipboard from off the desk and started making notations.

Julia frowned. "It's time for Winston's catheter and colostomy bag to be emptied."

"I can do it," Linc said, setting the clipboard down, then getting up to head toward the opposite end of the hall.

"Corbin can when he come—" Julia frowned, reaching for a lighted button on the intercom.

"I got it. See what Corbin needs," Linc said.

"Julia, Harvey said he's having chest pains. I'm trying to take his blood pressure, but he's fighting me." Corbin's raised voice had Julia immediately standing up, but then she jerked to a stop when the red alert light came on the board for Winston's room.

"What happened?" Julia asked calmly after pressing the intercom button.

"I don't know. I just walked in the door," Linc answered back on the intercom.

"I'll check on Winston," Mika answered, picking up the folders. "Go help Corbin."

"Yes, Doctor."

Mika quickly walked down the hall, watching Julia's reflection in the large circle mirror as she ran down the hall and entered Harvey's room. Then she brought her hand up to the keycard that hung around her neck on a long ribbon.

Instead of opening Winston's door, she swiped her identification card into the card reader. Seeing the red light turn green, she pushed down on the metal lever and opened the emergency exit door, allowing two men from the stairway to enter. Without words, they followed her into Leon Winston's room.

She looked at the man on the bed dispassionately as his eyes widened in fear when he saw the men coming in behind her. Her sympathy wasn't for the man on the bed; it was for the man who strode into the room to stand by the bedside, while Mika stayed by the closed door in case Harvey wasn't able to pull off his fake heart attack and Julia came to check on Winston.

"Hello, Winston. You look like you've gone to shit since I last saw you at the courthouse. Time hasn't treated you well, has it?"

Mika shivered at the cold, emotionless voice that came from her Uncle Dalton. His features spoke for the hatred he felt for the man who had kidnapped his daughter.

Winston's beady eyes went from Uncle Dalton, to Ice, then to hers, going back to the nursing aide that remained by the myriad of machines that kept him alive, before returning to hers. "Get a guard. They want to hurt me!"

"They don't want to hurt you. They're here to kill you," Mika told him matter-of-factly.

"You're a doctor. How can you stand there and do nothing!" he yelled.

Mika gave an uncaring shrug. "You're not my patient. It's not my fault you destroyed other people's lives and feel like you have the right to keep tormenting them over and over." She opened the folder and took out the letter. Raising it, she showed it to him before crushing the threatening letter in her hand like she wished she could him.

Ice moved closer to the bed to stand next to Uncle

Dalton. "Just so you know"—fires of hate shone down on Winston from Ice's eyes—"the only letter she received from you was the first one. I made sure she never got another."

The revelation angered Winston more than anything else since they entered the room. Mika had to literally swallow down the bile that threatened to come up her throat at the loathing she felt for her friend's kidnapper.

"As much as I want to kill you with my own hands, this will have to do." Uncle Dalton went to the machine that was breathing for Leon.

"I told you that one day this was going to happen. I think you deserve a bottle of Drano poured down your throat, but watching Dalton be the one to turn off that machine is almost as good. Enjoy Hell, motherfucker." With his final words to Winston, Ice stepped away from the bed as if he didn't trust himself to save Dalton the trouble of flipping the switch.

"Dr. Foster, help me!" Winston cried.

"I'm not going to save you. You were lost long ago. You're not even human. You're a cancerous growth." The memory of Adrienne, Simone, and Avril's youthful images from that tragic day when she was sixteen numbed her to the compassion that she would normally feel for a patient's plea to save their life.

"Adrienne survived. She was able to be with her mother before she died, get married, and will be starting a family. Simone and Avril weren't given that chance. Simone's mother died alone after she committed suicide last year. Avril's parents won't be given a chance to have grandchildren, since she was their only child.

"I can tell from your eyes that you couldn't care less, and that pretty much sums up my feelings about you. Consider yourself lucky that Oceane passed away before we were ready to pull your plug. She would have voted for the Drano.

I would have, too, but you've ruined enough lives, and I couldn't figure out how to accomplish that without me and Uncle Dalton going to jail for the pleasure. I'll have to settle for the happiness I'll feel when I sign your death certificate and the satisfaction that your power to hurt anyone again will cease to exist, just like you."

Mika glanced at her watch, then nodded at the man who had been waiting for this day to come. "I'll get Ice in position and be right back."

Cracking the door open, she saw a still clear hallway. She slipped out the door with Ice following her, and then swiped her card again, letting Ice go through the door. He would hold the door open for Dalton once he came out of Winston's room.

Hurrying back inside, she watched as her uncle ended the life of the man she had invested years of her own life in destroying, just to give him the justice he deserved.

The alarm sounded as soon as he turned the light off. Dalton didn't even look at Winston as he went out the door.

"Mika...." It was the first time she had seen any softness on his face since they entered the room.

She had to blink back tears at the expression on his face. She knew what he wanted to say.

"I did it for me, too. Go!" she urgently hurried him to leave through a tear-clogged throat.

As soon as he cleared the door, she moved closer to the bed, watching as the life drained out of Avril's and Simone's killer's face. Then she waited for several minutes to pass before she turned toward the man who was standing behind her.

"He's gone."

Nodding, he opened the compartment that housed the memory card. Taking it out, he then took another one out of another pocket and slid it inside before closing the compartment.

Unable to prevent herself from critiquing his appearance as her eyes traveled over his hair to his feet, she told him, "Black hair suits you better."

"I prefer it myself."

"How did Jonas and Hammer find me so fast?"

"Killyama."

Skeptical, she crossed her arms over her chest. "My room was registered under my mother's half-sister's maiden name."

"They're bounty hunters. They're used to tracking people down despite the odds."

"The only ones in Treepoint who knew my home address were Uncle Dalton and Ice."

"Then that shows how good they are," he said noncommittally.

Her mouth quirked at his refusal to admit to his culpability. She wasn't buying it.

"Maybe so. I'm just interested in which one broke and gave me up?"

"Maybe," he mocked, "I'm just that good."

"Could be, but I don't think so." Her mind went through the possibilities with rapid-fire probabilities. "It had to be Dalton. How did you convince him?" Mika feigned certainty at her guess. Either way, she had a fifty-fifty chance of being right.

"I explained the principle of the 'rule of three' to him." His clever gaze showed he knew she was bluffing her certainty. He was only giving her the explanation because he wanted to.

"Most people consider relationships with three partners one too many," she unintentionally voiced her thoughts to a man that she had never spoken to before today, too distracted in thinking about how the obstacles ahead of Jonas, Hammer, and her actually making a relationship work in the long-range future ahead of them loomed dauntingly.

He gave her an understanding smile that didn't reach his detached gaze. "Don't worry. Lily tells me all the time that a halo is strong enough to hold more than one."

"I gave up my right to a halo the day Adrienne, Simone, and Avril were taken," she said, turning back to the dead body on the bed. "You should go. Tell Harvey that I'll sign the paperwork to get him released in two days." The memory of seeing Hammer's Escalade pulled over by a police officer as she was pulling out of the sheriff's office still made her feel guilty that she had turned toward Virginia so they wouldn't see her car pass by them. It had been useless. They had found her anyway.

Moving around the bed, he didn't spare a glance at the prone body as he told her, "I've known Hammer and Jonas for a long time. If anyone can make a halo for three fit, they can. They're Rangers"—Mika heard the conviction in his voice as he walked toward the door—"they lead the way."

Ice walked down the flight of steps, side by side with his father-in-law. As they made it to the end of the stairway where the emergency exit was located, they found a brother waiting for them.

Seeing them, the brother slid the visitor's pass through the card scanner. "I was starting to get worried."

As they went out the door, Ice came to a dead stop at seeing the enormous group of brothers waiting solemnly outside, all wearing leather jackets. The difference was the patches proclaiming their loyalties. "I thought we're supposed to be inconspicuous."

"They are," Whip spoke before Dalton could. "There're over two hundred thousand brothers attending this rally. We're just taking a rest stop before heading home."

Ice looked at the massive fence that barred the entrance of the hospital where they had to pass through to the private parking lot. As he studied beyond the gate, he saw bikes lined up on both sides of the road, stretching as far as the eye could see.

Whip saw where he was staring. "Hollywood has a lot of friends who wanted to say goodbye."

"More than a few." Throwing a leg over the saddle of his bike, Ice watched the two friends say their own goodbyes.

Dalton raised his hand to grasp Whip's firmly in his. "Thanks, brother."

There wasn't much that touched Ice in life, but the friend-ship between those two men did. It was a bond that had stood the test of time and spoke of the character of both men.

Dalton swung onto his bike, then gave the hospital a last look. "God help me, but I often wondered if Mika had gone with them that day, if it would have turned out any differently."

Ice's cold heart twinged at the remorseful expression on his father-in-law's face.

"You warned me to teach Adrienne how to protect herself better. I failed," Dalton continued, looking at his long-time friend.

"You didn't fail. You just protected Adrienne in a different way than I did. With four of them together, they might have been forced to take another cab. Maybe four would have been too many for Winston to have tried to kidnap. Or the ways I taught Mika to protect herself could have made a difference. We'll never know. We aren't meant to. If you had raised her differently, maybe she might not have been in the place where she met Ice, or Mika wouldn't have been in the place where she met the two men that she wants to introduce me to tonight. It is what it is." Whip waved his gloved hand toward the brothers waiting for them. "We learned that the hard way when we were just snot-nosed kids and joined the Angels. Regrets are for the weak—"

"—and victory is for the strong," Dalton finished for him.

Whip's formidable face broke into a grin. "Amen, brother."

Dalton's head fell back in laughter before he gave Whip another clasp of his hand.

Ice sat back and watched the two shoulder-hug each other before the Road Slayer smacked Dalton on the back of his leather jacket before getting onto his bike.

He was waiting for Whip to start his bike when his cell phone rang. Taking it out of his jacket, he saw it was Grace.

Sliding the answer button, he put the phone to his ear, then wished he hadn't when he heard Grace wail, "Where are you?"

"I told you that I won't be home until later tonight," he reminded her.

"But I'm ovulating *now*!" she cried.

"Well, there isn't a lot I can do about it right this minute, unless you can figure out a way to transport my dick there."

"Don't be gross. Call and see if you can get an earlier flight."

"Do you know how expensive a ticket like that would cost?"

Her voice went dangerously low. "I'll buy it."

"I'll drive to the airport now."

"*Dépêchez-vous, mon amour.*"

His dick went as hard as a stick. Grace hadn't spoken in French since her mother had died.

"I love you, too."

Dalton looked at him quizzingly when he disconnected the call. "Was that Grace?"

"Yes, she told me to hurry home," he told him the partial truth while starting his motorcycle. "You know how you said you regretted not teaching Grace how to protect herself better?"

"Yes. So?"

"Don't," he said, gripping his handlebars.

"She giving you hell?" Dalton gave him a sympathetic glance.

"Always. But it isn't anything I can't handle."

"I'm sure you can. You're not a man who runs from danger."

"No, I'm not, especially when she talks to me in French."

Dalton's gaze became even more empathetic. "Brother," he said, shaking his head in agreement. "I know what you mean. That's how Oceane caught me, too."

Ice cast his father-in-law a covetous stare at his leather jacket. "So you know, when you do bite the dust for good, I want that jacket."

"Sorry." Dalton grinned unapologetically. "You have to earn a jacket like this. But if you want to chase that rainbow, go ahead."

"Already earned it the day I married Grace." He grinned back. "But if you want me to keep going at it, I'm game."

Dalton's expression turned grave. "No, you earned it when you finally told me what was going on between you and Grace. I just wanted to wait until we could be sure there wasn't any fallout for Mika."

"Like Whip said, there's no need to cry over spilled milk." Ice motioned with his hand for Dalton to go first. "Take your victory lap. You deserve it. It was a long time coming."

Ice saw Dalton's eyes grow moist as he reached into his jacket to pull out three different colored hair ribbons. Ice knew who they had belonged to. Mika had given them to Oceane the day Adrienne, Simone, and Avril had been kidnapped. And Oceane had kept them until her death. Then Dalton had taken possession of them, promising on her grave that Winston would see the true justice he deserved.

Raising the ribbons high, Dalton rode toward the gates as the mass of riders grew louder and the gates parted, allowing them to leave.

Riding behind Dalton was the proudest moment of his life, one that he would never be able to tell Grace about, or any of the children they would have. It was only a memory that he and Dalton would be able to share.

It was Dalton who had shown him that the shithead responsible for his birth wasn't a true father. Dalton had stepped into those shoes, and not only did he wear them like a man should, but he also wore them as an example that Ice himself could only hope he could follow as an example for his own children.

The wind ripped his own tears away as the line of bikers cheered for Dalton as he passed.

Damn, chasing a rainbow had never felt so good.

"So, we good now?"

Shade turned his head to the side as Harvey prepared to get out of the borrowed truck.

"You're safe from me. I promised I wouldn't lay a hand on you, and I meant it."

"I swear I won't say anything about being in that mental hospital."

Shade wouldn't believe anything promised if Harvey swore it on a stack of Bibles, but he kept that doubt to himself.

"That's good to know," he stated, unmoved at the fear he could practically smell in the cab of the truck.

"Just making sure," Harvey said nervously, getting out at the police station parking lot where his car had been towed when Greer pulled him over for drunk driving. "Go to Drake Hall's office after you get your car keys back. He's lined up an apartment for you to live in until you can get on your feet."

"Thanks. I'm going job hunting tomorrow."

Shade didn't believe that any more than him not telling anyone where he had been.

"Good luck with that, then. Mind shutting the door? I'm going to go grab a bite to eat."

"Sure, sorry. Thanks again, Shade." Shutting the door, Harvey moved away from the truck.

Minutes later, he was walking into King's restaurant, where his father-in-law was seating customers as he got in line at the hostess station.

The hostess was writing his name down when King took a menu from the side of the podium. "I got this. Take the next one."

"Yes, sir."

"I'm expecting a guest," Shade informed him.

King took another menu, then led him through the restaurant to a booth. Sliding inside, he took the menu from him.

"When'd you get back from your trip?"

"Just now," Shade answered, opening the menu.

"Lily said you told her that it'll be the last one you'd have to take for a while."

"That's true," he replied, not looking up.

"She also said I'm expecting another grandchild."

"We are," he confirmed.

"Congratulations."

"Thanks. I'll take a whiskey," he said, cutting off any

further conversation when he saw the man coming up from behind King.

"I'll take one of those myself."

King's face grew dark. "How many times do I have to tell you not to come here—"

"I invited him."

"So did Rider the last time he came. He did nothing but complain the whole time that his steak was overcooked."

Greer gave King a one-shoulder shrug. "It was."

"It was still mooing when I put it on your plate." King took the menu away from him, not giving Greer time to look at it.

"See? That shows you it wasn't done. Unless it's crying, it ain't done."

Shade took the menu away from King before he shoved it down Greer's throat. "I'll take the prime rib and baked potato," he ordered, trying to hurry King away from the table.

"I'll take the appetizer and—"

"I know your order. You order the same thing every time you come."

"Then you shouldn't have any problem getting it right this time, should you?" Greer snidely opened his eyes as wide as buttons, rocking his head back and forth on his shoulder.

Shade hastily grabbed for King's hand before he could wrench Greer from the booth. "Go put orders in and send a waiter to take care of us. You won't even notice we're here. I need to talk to him."

King dislodged Shade's hand from his arm. "I better not."

Shade didn't miss the devilment in Greer's eyes at getting on King's nerves as he left. Then, when Greer returned his attention to him, he saw the smile of satisfaction that he made no effort to hide. Shade made no effort to warn Greer that he was poking a tiger with only a tennis shoe for protection. Besides, he had his own bone to pick with the provoking hillbilly.

He waited until he had his drink in hand to steady his nerves before discussing the reason he had invited Greer to dinner.

"I'm not hiring Bubba permanently. He wasn't part of our deal."

Greer drank his drink in one swallow, then motioned the waiter for another one.

"Aren't you on duty?"

"Yeah. So? What's your point?"

Shade swallowed, lifting two fingers when the waiter looked his way.

"Okay, let's start over. I'm not hiring Bubba. He's not part of our deal."

"That's true." Greer nodded. "But it was my deal with Rider."

"We… agreed," Shade slowly pronounced each word to drive them home that he wasn't going to be saddled with Bubba.

Greer leaned into the table, unfazed. "Bubba won't tell his pa that he was fired. I don't like waking up every morning to share my breakfast with Jessie's cousin. He eats my biscuits before I can get my ass out of the shower. I ain't having it. So, unless you want me to tell Rider about that mysterious car sitting out in front of Jo's house, you're just going to have to suck it up," he hissed in a low voice.

Shade seriously thought of driving to his house and getting his gun to get rid of him forever.

Greer narrowed his mean eyes at him. "Don't think I don't know what you're thinking. The only thing I can say is, *try it.*"

Taking just a swallow of his drink was useless. He needed the whole fucking bottle for it to do any good.

"Now." Greer's voice switched to a friendlier tone. "I don't give a fuck why you want to raise Rider's protective instincts for his woman. Personally, I think you wanted to get Gavin off his ass, but I'm just saying that's what I would do. You may be smarter than me, and you may have a totally different reason. I really can't say I give a rat's dong anyway, as long as, when I come down to breakfast tomorrow morning, I don't have Bubba sitting there. *Capisce?*"

"*Capisce,*" Shade ground out as the waiter set Greer's appetizer tray down on the table.

"Good. Glad we talked this out." Taking the whole plate and sliding it in front of him, Greer picked up his fork and started eating. And when he was almost finished, he magnanimously held out the lone stick that was left over when the waiter brought their steaks. "You want a mozzarella stick?"

"No," Shade replied shortly.

Greer transferred his fork to his steak, cutting a small bite to taste. He gave King a thumbs-up as he escorted a couple to their booth.

King looked like he had the perfect place to tell Greer to shove his thumb. Shade was sure King was infuriated by Greer enough that he would be told never to come back himself for inviting him to dinner.

Greer hungrily ate as if he hadn't just eaten an appetizer meant for four people. Cutting a large bite of his steak, Greer slathered it with A1 sauce before putting it in his mouth. Shade was cutting his own steak when Greer started cutting another piece, the food on his plate rapidly dwindling before he was a quarter near done with his.

"Nothing tastes better than an expensive cut of beef and A1, except...," he qualified his statement, "another piece cut of beef."

"I'm not buying you another steak," Shade informed him.

"That's rude." Greer heaved of a sigh of contentment as he

leaned back and patted his belly. "Here I do you a big-ass favor and what thanks do I get in return?"

Shade cut another piece of his steak, aware that Greer was eyeing it greedily. "You got quite a bit in return. Not only did I pay you to feed Rider that information, but you turned around and stuck it to Rider. Which is the only thing I'm not actually complaining about, except for Bubba."

"Seems to me you've done nothing but complain since I sat down. Hell, you're making me lose my appetite for dessert. I'm getting kind of insulted...."

If he ripped his fingernails off one by one, it would be less painful than dealing with Greer. He fucking knew better than to piss him off.

Cutting into another piece of his steak, he wished it was a piece of Greer's liver. He kept his mouth shut as chewed the meat that was tasting like sawdust.

"Here I was doing you a favor, and you're turning it around like I'm being a bad guy asking for a job for an in-law. After all, we aren't talking about giving Bubba a high paying job, but one any Tom, Dick, and Jane could do with their hands tied behind their back."

Shade forced another bite into his mouth.

"Furthermore..." Greer paused, taking a deep breath before resuming his tirade. "I ran that plate for you, since you never bothered to go by the car rental."

Shade forced the bite down. "What plate?"

Peeved, Greer frowned. "What do you mean, what plate? The one I told you, Viper, and Rider about."

Confused, Shade laid his fork and knife down on his plate before he started carving Greer into tiny pieces. "You and I made up the story about a rental car in front of Jo's house, so how was there a plate to run?"

"Oh... I must have forgotten to tell you the part about the license plate being real."

"You must have." Shade said through clenched teeth. "Tell me now."

"I was kind of listening in to that little chat you were having with Harvey. So, when he said how that money was in his truck one morning, I drove over to the apartment building he and Nicole lived in. It's the same one Jessie lived in."

"May I get you gentlemen another drink? Dessert?"

"No." Shade gave the waiter a frustrated glare, wanting him to disappear.

Greer had other plans.

"I seem to have gotten my appetite back for dessert."

At Greer's smug expression, Shade knew he was going to have to pay for not properly kissing ass enough to him.

It was painful, but he managed to force a smile to his lips. "Order whatever you want. It's"—he practically had to pry the last two words from his lips—"my treat."

"Well, ain't that nice of you."

"Matter d', I'll take a couple of those appetizer platters and four of those dinners I just ate to go." Greer leaned across the table as if he was confiding to him. "Holly and Jessie have to work tonight. They wanted me to cook dinner for them. This works out better, don't ya think?"

"For you," he agreed.

Greer gave him a jaunty wink before turning back to the waiter. "I'll take the hot fudge cake with extra ice cream and cherries on top. I'll polish it off while the other food is cooking."

"Yes, sir." The waiter started moving away.

"Hold up a sec. My wife don't like her steak as rare as mine. Burn that son of a bitch."

"Bring me another drink first." Shade stopped him before he could escape. "Make it a double again."

"Hitting that sauce a little hard, ain't you?"

Shade pressed his lips together, chanting to himself not to say anything.

Greer gave him another jaunty wink. "Don't worry; I have connections with law enforcements if you get pulled over."

He gave a murmur of appreciative as the waiter brought the cake and gave Shade the drink he ordered.

"Anyway," Greer returned to what they had been discussing. "If you remember, Jessie was kidnapped from the building—"

"I remember." Shade took a drink. He wasn't a praying a man, but he was going to be praying over Greer's grave if he didn't get to the point.

"Management decided their best interest was to install working surveillance cameras. Management is also one of my customers… Not that I'm still selling," he added quickly. "He *used* to be one of my customers, and he let me have a gander at those videos of his."

Shade clutched his glass at the information.

"Couldn't see his face. All I could see was a black rental car, and someone get out in a big, gray raincoat. That's the plate I ran down for you. It's not a rental from town, but I called around when you never went by and found out where it was rented from."

"Here you go, sir."

Greer raked a spoonful of cake into his mouth as the waiter set the two bags of food onto the table.

"Thank you kindly. I'm very appreciative of the service you have given me," he complimented him. "Shade, make sure you show him my appreciation."

"Of course." Shade started to take another drink of his whiskey when he realized it was empty.

Greer waited until the waiter left to offer his advice. "I'd drink a couple of coffees before I hit the road if I were you."

Patting his belly, he rose up from the table. At the same

time, he reached inside his uniform pocket, coming out with a slip of paper that he laid down on the table.

Shade reached for it, but Greer didn't remove his hand from the paper. Expecting him to ask for an outrageous sum of money for the information, he looked up to see Greer staring shrewdly down at him.

"Don't feel bad about making Gavin get off his ass. I would have done it a year ago."

"How'd you know...?"

"Shade, there isn't much I don't know." Winking, he removed his hand. Then, taking the bag of food, he left him staring after him.

He was taking his credit card out of his wallet when King stopped at the booth.

"Next time you want to take Greer out to dinner, take him to the diner or the Pink Slipper."

"It'll definitely be cheaper. Grab some coffee and have a seat with me."

"Dinner crowd is starting to come in—"

"King, *have coffee with me.*"

"I'll be back."

Shade put the slip of paper in his wallet as the waiter took his credit card. He was scrawling his signature on the receipt when King came back with the coffee.

His father-in-law sat down across from him. "What did you want to talk about?"

"How would you feel if someone in town tried to black-mail me by pretending to have pictures of Lily nude and spreading them around town?"

King's gaze went glacial. The sophisticated host and owner of the most expensive restaurant was gone, and in his place was the cut-throat businessman who used to rule Queen City. "I'd ask you two questions."

"What are they?"

"Why don't you take care of him yourself?"

"I promised Lily I wouldn't lay a hand on him."

"Then I only need the answer to my next question."

"Which is?"

"What's his name?"

~

Shade entered his home to see Lily sitting on the floor by the couch with Clint, John, and Logan, playing Monopoly.

"Daddy, you're home!"

He smiled as the boys jumped up and ran to him, throwing themselves into his arms.

"Don't get up," he said when he saw Lily starting to stand. "I'll come down there."

Sitting down behind her, he kissed her as the boys resumed playing the game.

"Are you going to play with us?" Greer's nephew Logan asked.

"No thanks. I'll just watch." He placed his arm on the couch cushion as Logan took his turn.

Lily leaned against his chest as they watched. "Logan came home with Chance and Noah until Jessie can pick him up. She's running late, and the boys have football practice, so I offered for him to visit with us. Have you eaten?"

Shade looked up from winding a tendril of her hair around his finger. "I ate," he told her, then asked the children, "What have you boys been up to?"

"I finished my homework before starting to play with Logan," John said, rolling the dice on the gameboard.

Logan stood up. "You can take my turn, Mrs. Lily. I need to go to the restroom."

Lily rolled the dice, moving her piece the required number of spaces.

"How about you, Clint?" he asked his younger son.

"Logan and I colored while John did his homework. You want to see my picture?"

"Yes."

Clint hopped up from the floor to run into the dining room, coming back with two pieces of construction paper. It was easy to see whose was Clint's and whose was Logan's.

Seeing his expectant face, Shade looked at Clint's first. It was a big cupcake with a candle on top.

"It's Mrs. Bliss's birthday tomorrow. I made her a cupcake."

"I see. You did a good job. She'll love it."

Shade looked at the other picture in his hand as Clint sat back down on the floor. Greer's nephew's drawing wasn't what he was expecting. John and Clint had both loved to draw since the first moment Lily put crayons in their hands. He had also gone to their school enough times and had seen the pictures the students had drawn, hanging up in the hallways. Logan's was on another level. He was already showing signs of being a gifted artist.

As soon as the word gifted appeared in his mind, Shade studied the picture closer, his throat tightening.

He was still counting the twinkling stars in the dark sky in the picture when Logan came out of the bathroom. He was about to sit back down when he noticed what was in Shade's hand.

"That's my picture!"

Shade immediately noticed the fear in the little boy's face as he snatched the picture out of his hand. "Sorry. I should have asked if I could look at it," Shade apologized thickly.

Logan stuffed the picture into his jeans pocket. "I'm not allowed to let anyone see my pictures," he explained.

"Why not?" Lily asked curiously.

"Uh… I'm not supposed to be coloring when I haven't done my homework."

"I see." Lily gave him a sweet smile. "We won't tell. Will we, boys?"

Shade didn't pay attention to their assurances as he tried to commit the details of the artwork before Logan had snatched the drawing away.

"Boys, Jessie will be here any minute. Let's get the game picked up. Logan, make sure you put everything back in your backpack."

Shade rose from the floor as the children followed Lily's directions. "I need to see Viper for a few minutes. I'll be right back," he said huskily, going outside before Lily could say anything.

His throat worked in fear as he stared out at the same mountains that were in Logan's picture. Reaching out, he braced his hand on the banister to steady himself. His thoughts were so scattered that he didn't notice Logan had come outside until he spoke.

"I told Ms. Lily that I would wait out here with you, if that's okay?"

Shade could only nod, still staring out at the mountains.

When a childlike hand took his, Shade tore his eyes away from the mountains to stare down into his eyes.

"Don't be afraid."

He swallowed hard. "I'm not afraid."

"Good. I was afraid the first time I went by myself," Logan childishly confided. "The second time I went, Uncle Greer took me. I wasn't afraid then. Well, only a little, but it's not scary when you're with someone."

Shade couldn't speak at the earnest expression looking up at him.

"Logan!"

Their attention distracted by Jessie's voice calling for him.

His stepmother was waving as she walked up the path to his house.

"You ready?" Jessie asked when she was within talking distance.

"Yes, ma'am."

"Let's go. Greer's got something special for dinner."

"Yay!" Logan jumped off the porch to start running down the path.

"Thanks. Will you thank Lily for me also?"

Shade nodded. "I will. Have a good night."

"You, too."

After they were gone, he stayed on the porch, gathering himself before he went back inside.

"I thought you were going to see Viper?" Lily said, coming up behind him to wrap her arms around his waist.

"I changed my mind."

She loosened her arms around his waist so she could move around him to see his face. "Is there something wrong?"

"No."

She moved her hand to his cheek to tilt his face down toward hers. "It's just a picture," she said softly.

"He showed you?"

She mischievously shook her head. "I sneaked a peek."

"I wished you hadn't."

"Why? It was a beautiful picture. He's very talented."

He didn't agree or disagree with her.

She leaned against him, tightening her arms around him. He moved his arms around her, too, holding her as close as he could, as if he could hold them still in this moment in time forever.

"I heard Logan ask if you were afraid. You said you weren't. I'm not either, Shade."

"Lily…." Shade choked up at the unwavering faith coming

from her. It was hard for him to admit there would come a time that he wouldn't be able to prevent the inevitable from happening. That he didn't have the power to shield her from the aspect of life that sooner or later no one could escape from.

"I'm not. It's the truth. I'm not afraid. How could I be afraid of Heaven when Heaven sent you to me?"

"Lily..." He pressed his lips to hers, giving her the kiss he would have given her when he got home if the children hadn't been the room. "I've never been afraid of dying," he told her honestly, sliding his mouth along her jawline to her ear to nibble, feeling her give a little shudder. "But I have to be brutally honest about one thing. And to be fair to you, it's non-negotiable. If Greer Porter is there, we're not going."